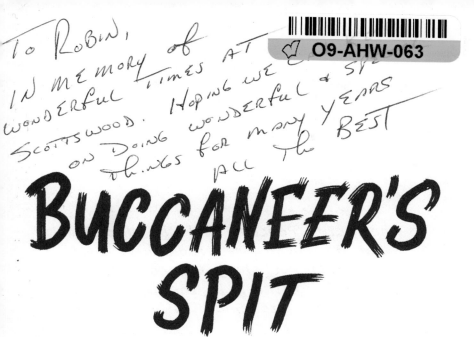

To Robin, In memory of wonderful times at Scottswood. Hoping we [...] on doing wonderful & spe[...] things for many years all the BEST

O9-AHW-063

BUCCANEER'S SPIT

A Race for the Treasure

J. E. THOMPSON

PELICAN PUBLISHING
New Orleans 2021

ISBN: 9781455626076
Ebook ISBN: 9781455626083

Printed in the United States of America
Published by Pelican Publishing
New Orleans, LA
www.pelicanpub.com

BUCCANEER'S SPIT

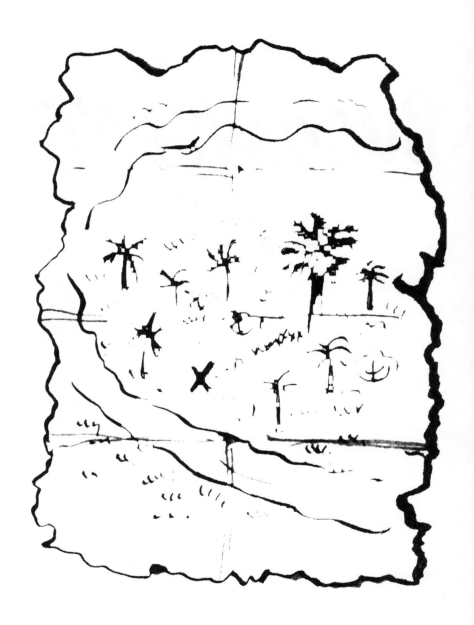

To the fine people at The Coastal Conservation League, Charleston, South Carolina, who work so tirelessly to protect the land, water, air, and biological diversity (and places just like Buccaneer's Spit), and to the staff of the South Carolina Aquarium, where there really is a turtle hospital

1.

Ever heard of a slithy tove? In his poem, "Jabberwocky," Lewis Carroll never explains what slithy toves are, but I've always thought they must be pretty gross, like New York City in March when it's gray, cold, maybe snowy and icy but definitely muddy and wet. What sixth-grade kid in their right mind wouldn't jump at the chance to get out of the city in March and visit their grandfather and the beach in South Carolina?

Me.

Why, you might ask. Well, I adored spending spring vacations with Poppy—that's what we call my grandfather—and his dog, Plankton, and I loved the South Carolina beaches, so those weren't the reasons. The problem was my parents were keeping some kind of big secret and they *definitely* wanted me out of the house. Parents may think they're smart, and they may think they're being all subtle and super-secret, but they're not as clever as they think they are.

I'd caught them whispering too many times. I'd seen my dad staring out the window, looking like a kid who had just lost his favorite puppy, but then he'd fake a happy smile the moment he realized I was watching. I'd heard my mom cry when she thought I wasn't near enough to hear. Something big was going on. I knew exactly what it was, and it filled me with dread.

The few times I gathered the courage to ask one of them what the big secret was, they would plaster on one of their fake smiles and say, "Nothing!" in a too-happy voice. I would have pushed harder, but there was part of me—a really big part—that didn't want to hear the truth. I was still feeling that way when Mom took me to LaGuardia to catch my flight to Charleston, South Carolina.

My baggage was checked, I had my boarding pass, and me and Mom were standing near the entrance to the line for the TSA security check. It was one of those awkward moments parents always create when they have to say goodbye to their kids, but it was also my last chance to demand knowing about the big secret. I could tell Mom didn't want to walk away, and I didn't want her to leave. Maybe that was the moment I could have forced it, but we both kept sliding around the truth like it was coated with grease and too slippery to grasp.

"Well, I hope you have a wonderful time with your grandfather," Mom said for about the fiftieth time.

"I still don't understand why you and Dad aren't coming. We've always gone down together before." I knew I sounded like a baby, but it was as close as I could bring myself to pushing.

"I've already told you, your dad and I have some things we have to do."

I rolled my eyes when she said that because *"some things"* were adult code words. They were getting a divorce. I knew it sure as anything because they were no different from Sophie and Janet and Adrianna's parents, who had all gotten divorced over the past couple years. Like I hadn't known what was going on right from the start. Spoiler alert, when parents are getting divorced, they *never* tell the truth. And they don't necessarily act like they hate each other. My parents acted like they really loved each other, but I knew it had to be fake.

Mom must have caught my eye roll because she hurried to say, "I've also talked to your grandfather. He knows you don't want to go on nature walks every day."

Changing the subject was Mom's way of making sure we stayed away from the truth. I went along. "You mean bug bite expeditions," I said.

In case you don't know anything about South Carolina, I'll tell you. It is really beautiful and warm, but it has clouds and clouds of mosquitoes. It also has these bugs called no-see-ums that are so tiny you can barely see them, which is kind of obvious from the name, but they bite like tiny pit bulls. And these things called banana spiders that are about as big as Godzilla's baby. Poppy says they're harmless, but *nothing* that looks that scary can be harmless. And in addition to bugs, Poppy's nature walks also involve seeing tons of slithery snakes and huge scary alligators.

"I still don't see why I couldn't have gone to Palm Beach with Nancy," I said in my best whiny voice. "Florida's hot enough to go to the beach and swim every day. South Carolina's not. And Nancy's grandmother promised to take us shopping every single day, and in Palm Beach we wouldn't have to go stare at little brown birds and tour some turtle hospital."

Mom took a deep breath, which told me she was trying to remain patient. Good, I thought. Truth was, I didn't want to go to Palm Beach with Nancy. I would much rather have spent vacation with Poppy, but this was payback. If you're getting divorced, you deserved a little torture from your kid.

"Your grandfather is very excited about the new turtle hospital," she said. "You know he volunteers every year when the turtles are laying eggs."

"Maybe he could volunteer to take me shopping instead. There aren't any bugs or snakes in stores."

"You're lucky to be going to South Carolina. The weather will be a lot nicer than Brooklyn, and I'm sure your grandfather will have some fun things for you to do."

"Yeah, memorize the Latin names of plants

and bugs, and go to hunting and fishing stores so I can buy camo gear for our nature walks." I knew I sounded like a brat, but I didn't care. "Face it, Mom, Poppy wishes he had a granola-eating grandson who likes to dig in the dirt, shoot guns, and doesn't mind having fish slime all over his hands."

"*Callie,*" Mom said in her best warning voice, letting me know I'd pushed things about as far as I could. Leaving it at that, we kissed goodbye and I got into the TSA line, then headed to my gate.

To be completely honest, spending two weeks with Poppy in South Carolina really did have some drawbacks. I loved him as much as any kid could love their grandfather, but I was a city girl, and he really was seriously bonkers about birds and nature and hunting and fishing. Poppy loved anything that was outdoors, any time of year. It didn't matter whether the weather was a hundred and fifty degrees or freezing, or whether it was raining, or whether mosquitoes were sucking all your blood. Poppy just loved to be outside. While I didn't love the boiling and freezing and mosquito parts, there were other things that I really did love about nature, especially walking the unspoiled beach on the land Poppy and Grandma had bought before Grandma died. If I hadn't been all sad and mixed up about my parent's divorce, I would have been kicking up my heels at the thought of going to South Carolina.

2.

When my plane landed in Charleston the beauty improved my mood right away. The sky was a cloudless blue and the sun was bright and warm. When I'd left New York, crusts of dirty ice and snow still littered the curbs, and none of the trees showed a single leaf. A day earlier, I'd caught sight of what I thought was the first glint of crocus pushing up in Prospect Park, but it had turned out to be a piece of green gum.

In addition to spending two weeks with Poppy, I was excited about being able to spend time with Plankton, Poppy's rough coat Jack Russell terrier. His name had come from Poppy watching *SpongeBob SquarePants* with me when I was little. Plankton the dog was a lot like the tiny green creature in the show, both of them small creatures who acted like big shots. While Plankton in the show wanted to take over the world, Poppy's dog was willing to fight even the biggest dogs. Since both my parents were teachers and nobody had time to walk dogs, we had never had one in Brooklyn. It was a huge treat for me to spend time with Plankton.

Plankton went almost everywhere with Poppy, so the two of them were waiting right there in baggage claim when I came off my flight. I spotted Poppy right away because he was taller than most of the people in the crowd, with a full head of long white hair that swept back over his ears. Daddy said Poppy looked like "a senior statesman," because unlike a lot of older people, Poppy's face wasn't a bit flabby. Instead of having bags of wrinkles around his eyes and turkey wattles under his chin, Poppy had a tight neck, a nose you could use for a ruler, and a jaw that looked strong enough to crack pecan shells.

"Callie," he called out in his deep voice as soon as he caught sight of me. While Poppy hurried over and gave me a big hug, Plankton barked and jumped and rolled on his back and kicked his legs in the air, furious that I would pay attention to anyone or anything but him. As soon as Poppy let me go, I bent over to pick up Plankton and got my face licked about a hundred times.

My bag came off the carousel, and minutes later we were in the car heading out to the country. Poppy lived about forty-five minutes outside of Charleston in a small coastal village that mainly had shrimp fishermen and retired people.

The sun was already getting low in the sky, and as we went farther from the city, Poppy began to point. "Look over there at the egrets and herons flying toward their evening roosts."

"I see them," I said as I watched the birds settle gracefully onto the branches of the big live oaks that grew along the marsh edge.

As we drove farther, Poppy pointed again. "There are some redbuds in bloom, and our first azaleas. Oh, and there's a flock of ibises," he said, sounding as excited as if he'd never seen them before. Even I had to admit that the ibises looked cool as they glided over the car, their white wings catching the late sun and their curved orange beaks pointed before them like swords.

"I just love seeing wild creatures," Poppy said with a happy smile. "Almost as much as I love seeing you and having you to myself for two whole weeks."'

"Thanks," I said. "I love being here with you, too." I really meant it.

Poppy smiled, and then he shot me a sideways glance. "Your mom warned me that you like to sleep in these days and that you might not want to do our early morning walks."

"I think the silence of sleep is just as nice as the silence of nature," I said, answering with a small smile of my own.

When I was little and my parents were trying to sleep, Poppy would get me out of bed and take me out to where the only sounds were the cries of all the different birds and the occasional plop of a mullet jumping in the marsh grass at high tide. Even though I didn't want to get up that early anymore, I had to admit that it was beautiful watching the

sunrise come through the Spanish moss that
hung like smoke from the huge live oaks in
Poppy's yard. His house was old and wooden,
and those trees spread their massive limbs
over it, holding the house and all of us inside
in a gentle embrace.

I could feel the peace of Poppy's home
seeping into me almost as soon as he turned
off the main road and his tires crunched over
the oyster shell surface of the narrow lane
that would take us through the village. He
put the windows down, and cool spring air
that smelled of pluff mud, tea olive, and salt
water flowed into the car.

"Too cold for you?" he asked.

I was shivering a little, but I shook my head
as I looked out at Poppy's little village with
its post office, hardware store, small grocery,
gas station, and single restaurant. In such a
picturesque place, it was hard to think about
the bad things going on between my parents
back in New York. Hard, but not impossible.

As we left the village behind, it struck me
that Poppy had sunk into a strange silence.
Normally, when we drove through town, he
would tell me the news about this person
having a baby, or that person getting married,
or how the shrimp fishing season was this
year, but he hadn't said a word. I shot him
a sideways look, noting that he was driving
with both hands on the wheel, his eyes locked
straight ahead, even though the road was
deserted. Also, Poppy's lips were moving, as if

he was having some kind of deep conversation with himself.

"How come Mom and Dad sent me down here alone?" I asked. "Is there a problem no one's telling me about?"

Poppy jerked the wheel and slammed on the brakes as if a raccoon had just run out in the road, but there wasn't a thing there. He looked at me, his eyes wide like I'd just snuck up behind him and said, "Boo!"

"No!" he said in kind of a too-loud voice, the kind of tone adults use when you've got them dead to rights about something, and they don't want to admit the truth.

"They're getting a divorce, aren't they? You can tell me. I know all about these things," I said. "Three of my friends' parents got divorced in the past year. Plus, I googled it. Back in the 1980s about eighty percent of American marriages ended in divorce. The number has gone down a lot since then. If things stay the way they are today, two-thirds of marriages will last. I think it's wrong for my parents to get divorced when so many other people are finding ways to stay married. Don't you?"

Poppy started to cough as if he'd been drinking soda and some went down the wrong pipe. For a few seconds that was all he did. He was driving about twenty miles an hour now, but both hands were still choking the wheel as if we were on black ice. Finally, he managed to say, "Your parents aren't getting a divorce. Wh-why would you think that?"

"Well, why else have they been acting all weird? Why else wouldn't we all come down to visit you together the way we always have?"

"You're sorry you're here?"

"You know I'm not. I'm very glad to be here, but every other year we've come as a family."

"Well, some years are different."

That was a typical adult thing to say, the kind of statement that pretended to be an answer but wasn't. I was about to tell him that, but then Poppy snapped his fingers as if he'd just remembered something.

"You remember Jimmy Finnigan, don't you?"

I had a flash of memory from a spring vacation about three years earlier. "Yeah," I said, responding as if he'd asked me if I liked getting shots at the doctor's.

"Well, he's down here for the next two weeks, just like you. His grandfather thought it might be fun for you two to get together."

I hadn't seen Jimmy Finnigan for a couple years, but I remembered him perfectly—a tubby, short little boy who was obsessed with baseball. Every time I'd seen him he'd been wearing a Detroit Tigers tee shirt and had a baseball glove on his left hand. It's fine for a person to wear a baseball glove when they're actually playing baseball and totally ridiculous to wear one into a restaurant, but that was Jimmy Finnigan. He told me he was a pitcher and wanted to be a professional baseball player someday. One time when his grandfather brought him over to Poppy's house,

Jimmy even brought an extra glove that he called a catcher's mitt, a hunk of leather as big as a serving plate.

We went out into the yard, and he'd asked if I would catch while he practiced pitching. His first pitch went about twenty feet to my right, the second way off to my left, and his third pitch bounced in the grass and slammed my ankle. I threw Jimmy his ridiculous catcher's mitt and told him I was done with baseball.

Now, on top of being upset about my parents, the idea of spending time with Jimmy Finnigan was about the worst thing I could think of. "I'm going to be doing a lot of reading and walking," I told Poppy. "I don't think I'll have time for Jimmy Finnigan."

"Oh, I'm sure you'll have a few hours to get away from your other activities."

I was about to tell Poppy that the things I had to do were very serious and they would *definitely* not allow me to spend *any* time with Jimmy Finnigan, however right at that moment we were driving past the path that led to Buccaneer's Spit, and the familiar sight pulled my attention because it was my absolute favorite place in all of South Carolina. Buccaneer's Spit was a skinny slice of land that Poppy and my grandmother had bought and made into their own private nature preserve a few years before she died.

Spit means one thing when you're talking about chewing tobacco, but it means something totally different when you're talking about land. A spit is a narrow piece of land between two bodies of water, in this case the Raccoon River on one side and the Atlantic Ocean on the other. Poppy and Grandma didn't have a lot of money because they'd both been teachers like Mom and Dad. Even so, they had scraped together what they needed and bought Buccaneer's Spit because it had been offered cheap and had a perfect white beach where sea turtles came to lay their eggs, and a maritime forest on the backside where many different species of seabirds roosted. I know all this by heart because Poppy has repeated it only about a thousand times.

It was totally understandable why Poppy and Grandma loved the spit so much. They spent hours and hours studying all of its bugs and plants and watching the wild creatures and doing whatever they could to protect them. But the truly amazing thing about the spit is that despite being very quiet and at first glance looking like there isn't much to do, it's absolutely magical if you open your eyes and just take the time to look around.

That was why, as we drove past, my eyes went right to the narrow path that led from the road to the spit. It had always been overgrown, nearly hidden from anyone who didn't know it was there, and the maritime forest was so thick that strangers didn't even guess there was beach access. Neighbors, bird watchers, and nature lovers were always welcome, but Poppy didn't want bunches of people who brought loud music and left their litter.

For that reason, when I saw what was happening there my jaw dropped. "Poppy, there's a truck parked in the path," I said, "and there are men with chainsaws who look like they're cutting things."

3.

To say the men were cutting was an understatement. It was obvious they had been working for a while already because they had widened the narrow path enough so they'd be able to back their truck a fair way down. I could see lots of cut branches stacked where the men had piled them.

Poppy must have had his mind on something totally different because he hadn't seemed to notice until I said something. However, when he looked where I was pointing, he slammed on his brakes and swerved to a stop on the side of the road. A pickup truck that had been behind us honked, and the driver made an angry gesture as he shot past.

"Stay here," Poppy growled. He turned off the car, jumped out, and stomped back toward the path.

"You stay with me," I said to Plankton, who was growling and barking like he wanted to get out of the car and start biting the men.

In spite of Plankton, I could hear Poppy yelling, "Hey!" to get the men's attention and then waving his arms when he got closer.

At first the workers didn't hear Poppy over the roar of their chainsaws, but then one of them looked up, turned off his saw, and went over to see what Poppy was yelling about. He stood patiently as Poppy lowered his voice but continued to order the men to stop what they were doing.

Instead of obeying, the man pulled a piece of paper from his pocket, unfolded it, and handed it to Poppy. I couldn't hear what the man said, and I couldn't hear Poppy anymore either. He had fallen silent and just stared at the paper. When he finished reading, he didn't start shouting again like I had expected. Instead, he balled up the paper, threw it on the ground, then turned and stomped back toward the car.

He climbed in without a word, closed the door, and started driving but didn't look at me.

"Are you okay?" I asked.

He nodded.

"What's going on?"

Poppy shook his head, keeping his eyes locked on the road. "I just forgot about some work I'd agreed to have done," he said in a choked whisper.

Right away, I knew he was lying. He had to be. No kid would *ever* tell such a lousy lie, but I had no idea *why* he was lying. It gave me a terrible feeling in the pit of my stomach.

"What kind of work?" I asked. "I thought you *never* let anybody take machines on the spit. It looked like they were trying to cut the road wide enough so they could drive all the way down. You wouldn't let them do that, would you?"

Poppy mumbled more words, but they were too soft or jumbled to understand. I would have asked him to say it louder, but he looked too upset. Nothing about this was making sense. My mom always liked to say that Poppy was just like his dog, that both of them were "irascible," and I guess it was true. Plankton could snarl at almost any stranger, human or animal, and sometimes Poppy was the same. When Grandma was still alive, she had always been able to make him soften, but now, since she was gone, he had gotten grumpier with people who weren't family or friends. Poppy could be especially tough when he thought he was right about something, and he hated to back down. That's why it struck me as even weirder that he was just giving up the fight and driving away from those men who were cutting into his special place. What made it even worse, he couldn't seem to get the words out to tell me why he was doing it.

We rode the rest of the way in silence. Seeing him act so strangely made me think about Mom and Dad and how all the adults in my life seemed to be acting sketchy. Adults were supposed to be steady, the kind of people a kid could depend on, but clearly that wasn't the case in my family.

As soon as we got to Poppy's old house

with its long front porch and big living room with creaky floors and lots of wicker furniture, I took my suitcase to my bedroom, unpacked, and then went looking for somebody who was at least normal. That meant I headed straight into the kitchen to say hello to Martha. She was the widow of a shrimp fisherman who had died a couple years earlier, and now she cooked for Poppy and generally took care of things around the house. I hoped having Martha there meant at least one person in Poppy's house hadn't gone nuts.

Martha had come to work for Poppy after Grandma died. Poppy said he couldn't afford her, but Mom insisted that he couldn't afford *not* to have her. Mom said Poppy couldn't find the kitchen without a map and couldn't boil water without directions. She said having Martha around was the only way we could know for sure that Poppy wouldn't starve.

As soon as I pushed through the swinging door, Martha turned away from where she'd been cleaning a bunch of fresh shrimp. She quickly rinsed her hands then swept me up in a huge hug.

"What's for dinner?" I asked as soon as she stopped squeezing and let me breathe.

"Shrimp and grits," she said. "You still like them?"

I clapped my hands. "You know it's just about my absolute favorite."

"Nice to see that nothing's changed." She held me out at arm's length and looked me up and down. "Well, a few things have. You've grown at least a couple inches since I saw you last."

I just smiled and rolled my eyes because that's the kind of thing adults always say to kids. They would tell you something like that even if you'd shrunk.

"I'm glad you're here," Martha went on. "It'll do your grandfather a world of good to have you around for a couple weeks."

That sounded odd, another indication that something weird was going on. "Is he okay?" I asked, thinking again about his reaction to the men cutting bushes on the spit.

She gave a shrug. "He's fine. Things have just been a little mixed up around here recently."

"Mixed up how?"

She shook her head like it was no big deal. "Just mixed up."

I shook my own head. Adults always wonder why kids don't want to sit around and talk to them, but why bother talking when all they do is hide stuff. Any kid would have recognized Martha's smile for just what it was—a trick to change the subject. The next words out of her mouth confirmed it. "So, are you hungry?"

She wasn't going to give me any more information, and I was starving, so I said, "Yes."

"Here," she said, handing me a freshly baked chocolate chip cookie. "This should tide you over, and I'll hurry dinner along. I still have to make the grits."

That was her signal that she needed to go to work and I needed to stop interrupting. "Okay," I said with a mouth half-full of cookie.

I walked out of the kitchen with my head full of questions. What was going on with Poppy? Martha had said things were "mixed up." What did that mean? Why was Poppy letting people cut down part of Buccaneer's Spit? Was Poppy acting strange because of my parents splitting up? One way or the other I needed some answers. That would tell me if I could do anything to change this.

4.

The next morning, I woke up early with a wet nose poking into my neck. I rolled over, at which point so did Plankton, and I scratched his belly. "Why don't you go back to sleep?" I mumbled.

Plankton answered with a growl that said it was time to get up because it was light outside, his belly needed rubbing, and he wanted to go run around.

I could easily have gone back to sleep for another couple of hours, but Plankton wasn't going to let that happen. I pulled on my clothes, washed my face, and brushed my teeth, then walked out of my bedroom, surprised to see Poppy's door still closed at the other end of the hallway.

In previous years, Poppy had always gotten up the minute the sun started rising over the ocean, but today he seemed to be sleeping late. Remembering what Martha had said the day before, seeing that Poppy needed more sleep was one more sign that things were changing. I picked up Plankton, tiptoed past his door, and headed to the kitchen. After a quick bowl of cereal and some food in Plankton's bowl, I loaded a bottle of water, a towel, and some sunscreen in a daypack, grabbed Plankton's leash, and headed out for a walk.

Plankton was only six years old, and like any Jack Russell Terrier, he had more energy than a souped-up race car. His usual game was to run around at the speed of light and bark at every single creature he saw, whether squirrels, cats, other dogs, birds, frogs, or whatever. Sometimes, Plankton also decided that he should fight, usually with other dogs, especially really big ones like Labs or Rottweilers.

To my amazement, a lot of the biggest dogs actually put their tails between their legs despite weighing nearly a hundred pounds more than a Jack Russell. Those big dogs seemed to suspect that Plankton knew something they didn't. Otherwise, how could such a little creature be so certain that he could beat them up? Poppy liked to say that when Plankton looked in the mirror, instead of a little fifteen-pound terrier, he saw something more like a giant timber wolf.

Plankton strained against his leash, whined and made other sounds of great misery as we walked past houses that I thought might have dogs. "Stop complaining," I told him. "If you didn't act crazy, I'd let you run free, but I can't trust you." Plankton growled to let me know how wrong I was, but I didn't care.

Poppy's house was a couple blocks from the

water, set along a street of low bungalows mostly built in the early twentieth century. The closer we got to the water, the bigger and newer the houses became, until we were walking past the really large and fancy places of the people who could afford to build right on the beach. The houses ended when we came to the parking lot for the town beach. In the summer there would have been lots of kids my age here during the day, but this time of year was still too cold for swimming, so there was nobody around other than a couple of early fishermen who were surfcasting.

Plankton and I stayed on the road, walking to where the beach ended and what Poppy called "maritime forest" began. The trees weren't tall, but the forest was thick with vines, thorns, and wild, scraggly bushes, which made it as hard to get through as a metal fence, so that stopped most people from going any farther in that direction.

After another quarter mile, just before the narrow bridge that ran across the Raccoon River, I came to the path that led through the maritime forest to Buccaneer's Spit. No thanks to the truck and men with chain saws, what had been an almost secret path was now an ugly gouge through the solid wall of vegetation that screened off the spit. The truck was gone, but the damage was done. Piles of uprooted bushes and cut branches lay in the deeply churned sand and dirt, and the once narrow cut now gaped like an open wound.

Plankton continued to pull at his leash and made the worst moaning sounds yet as we started down the path. To anyone overhearing, it would have sounded like I was tearing out his toenails. "You're not getting loose until we get away from cars," I told him, as we picked our way through the deep ruts down to where the horrible new slash opened onto the beach.

The spit had never been private. People had always been able to get there by boat, by swimming around the point from the public beach, or finding the narrow path through the maritime forest that ran along the entire landward side. However, no matter how a person arrived, there were signs that said, "No Picnicking, No Plastic Containers, No Fires, No Smoking, No Alcoholic Beverages, No Plastic Bags, No Off-Leash Dogs. Big Fines for Failure to Obey."

Because of Poppy's warning signs even people who knew where the spit was tended to stay away, unless they were quiet beach walkers or bird-watchers. Just to make his point even stronger and make sure his rules were obeyed, Poppy patrolled the spit and even hired another guard to do the same during the busiest times of the year. The other person wasn't any more of a real guard than Poppy, just a retired shrimper whose tee shirt said, "Buccaneer's Spit Security," just like Poppy's. Poppy's rules couldn't really be enforced because they weren't actual laws and because of that, no "Big Fines" could be given out, but people didn't know. Having guards walk around with official looking shirts made those rules seem even more important.

Only now, with the path to the spit no longer secret but more like a big, hacked up driveway, the world couldn't help but see the way in. What was going to happen to the spit, I wondered, now that its cover had been ripped wide open? Poppy and Grandma had always wanted it to be a nature preserve, but how could it stay that way if it became just another public beach? The signs were still there telling people all the things they couldn't do, but how long before people just kicked them over and did what they wanted?

"'No off-leash dogs' means you, too," I said to Plankton, just to torture him as he yipped and pulled at the leash. "Oh, well, Poppy does own the place, and you're his dog," I said when I thought we were far enough down the path.

As soon as I unclipped him, Plankton streaked toward the water and went racing down the shallows barking at all the little brown shore birds that ran in flocks along the tide line, making them take wing and fly farther down the beach. He went about a hundred yards, then circled away from the water and loped back to me, only to dart away again.

When he got bored with the birds he turned and shot into the wall of thick undergrowth that bordered the shoreward side of the beach. I watched a rabbit burst from cover, run across a few yards of open sand, then dive back into the bushes and disappear. Plankton chased another rabbit, then put a squirrel up a palmetto tree. Once at a safe height, the squirrel turned upside down and chattered insults just a foot or so out of the range of Plankton's frantic jumps.

About halfway down the spit, the maritime forest crept closer to the sea, the land narrowing as the river that ran along the landward side of the spit drew nearer to the ocean. At that point I leashed Plankton up again. He growled to let me know he didn't like it one bit.

"I don't care if you don't want to be leashed," I told him. "But you don't want to get eaten by an alligator, either."

I couldn't see the river yet because of the thick tangle of bushes, vines, and palmetto trees that grew between the beach and river, but even so, I knew there might be alligators sunning on the riverbank. Poppy had shown me some huge ones on our nature walks, and he told me that they could run much faster on land than anyone would have guessed.

Plankton growled again, then he turned around and gave me a pleading look. "Poppy says alligators eat dogs like popcorn," I told him. "You might be crazy enough to think you could beat an alligator in a fight, but I'm going to make sure you don't even try."

When I looked toward the wall of bushes, I spotted the narrow path Poppy had cut through the thick jungle of salt myrtle, buttonbush, and other shrubs to make it easier to get to the river for fishing. Other than this path and the other one that was now torn up and widened, the spit was totally wild. Unlike most beaches, there were no houses, and Poppy had always said there never would be any because he wanted to keep it wild forever.

When Plankton and I finally reached the end of the spit I stopped and let out a sigh. Walking here and watching Plankton had been fun, also smelling the salt air that felt so soft against my skin and watching the early sun sparkle on the ocean, but now the silence really hit me. "It really is quiet here," I told Plankton, realizing just how different this was from Brooklyn. There, I heard sirens and car horns at all hours. Here, there was nothing to do but watch the pelicans dive bomb for fish or look down the beach where little brown and gray birds ran down to the water each time a wave retreated to peck at the sand for food.

The spit was beautiful, and it made me feel happy and calm to look out at all the emptiness of sky and ocean. But how long could I sit around and just feel calm? In addition to all this beauty, there was part of me that also wanted noise, music, other kids my age, exciting shops and things to do. There was none of that here.

Plankton was whining again and straining against his leash. I looked down at him. "You're looking for a little excitement, too, aren't you?" I asked.

He growled to let me know he had better things to do than have me hold him back, so I went down the path through the maritime forest and checked the riverbank for alligators. Seeing none, I took Plankton back to the beach and let him loose again. Right away he took off barking and headed toward a bunch of those little gray birds that were always running around in the tide.

Each time he chased them, they would rise into the air, flying farther down the beach, then land and start doing their exact same routine—running down to the water when the waves went out and running away when they came in again. Plankton kept chasing birds for the next few minutes, charging and making them fly farther and farther away. Finally, panting hard, he trotted back to me.

He rested for a few seconds, then started yapping again and racing in circles, spooking some gulls that were hunting the shallows for food and generally making a very big racket.

"Plankton!" I called, as I reached into the daypack and brought out his favorite toy, a slimy, chewed-up tennis ball that I threw as far as I could and watched him race in pursuit as if his life depended on getting it. He caught the ball as it rolled over the hard sand, then turned and sped back to me, dropping the ball and turning in insane circles while he barked for me to throw it again.

I threw the ball another six or seven times until Plankton's tongue was hanging out of his mouth, at which point I took the water bottle from my bag and poured some into my cupped hand to let him drink. Afterward, he trotted beside me as we walked toward the very end of the spit where the river met the ocean.

The morning was cloudless, the temperature already getting up into the 70s, and a nice sea breeze keeping the gnats away. I sat on a palmetto log a few yards above the tide line that had been washed in by a storm. Unlike most beaches where the water gets deep slowly, the river had scoured out the ocean bottom here, so it dropped sharply just a few yards offshore. Also, because of the river, the current was often powerful and unpredictable, and could easily sweep a person out to sea.

I knew never to swim here, and Plankton didn't want any more to do with water than get his feet wet, so I didn't worry as I watched him trot down by the ocean's edge and sniff the shells. Out past Plankton on the horizon, a distant freighter looking as small as a toy boat angled its way toward Charleston Harbor. Closer in, a sailboat with all of its canvas up was heeling down the coast, its white sails looking like the wings of a seabird.

"Everything sure is peaceful and quiet," I said to Plankton. "But some people might also call it boring." I was thinking that a lot of kids I knew would roll their eyes and ask what there was to do, but if Mom and Dad had been there, they would have sighed and said how perfect it all was.

That started me thinking about my parents again. I was angry that they had shipped me off while they plotted their divorce. If they'd let me stay home, I could have convinced them that they were being ridiculous, and that there was more to think of than just themselves. There was me. I could have shown them what we all meant to each other, but without me, I was afraid that they would end up doing what a bunch of my classmates' parents had done and just go their separate ways. Then there would be weeks with Mom and weekends with Dad and separate vacations with just one of them.

I was hunched over, lost in my own dark thoughts when it happened. For a few seconds, nothing was different. Plankton was right in front of me sniffing near the water's edge, but then he came to sudden stop, laying his ears back as he looked out at the quiet sea. After a second, he started to growl, but not the kind that said he wanted attention or was getting bored; it was a really deep one, the kind he made when he was getting set to fight.

One thing about Jack Russell terriers, they don't back down. Not ever. They might be little, but they have the courage of lions. They're also smart, but here Plankton was acting totally wild with his hackles sticking up, growling at absolutely nothing but empty ocean.

At least I thought it was nothing until the

first mullet jumped right out of the water onto the shore. Then about two seconds later, another mullet jumped onto the sand, and then a couple more and then a whole bunch of them started erupting right offshore in a huge flopping tangle that reminded me of popcorn popping. Some of the mullet landed back in the water, but a lot of them came clear out of the water onto the sand. With the fish frantically slapping their tails into the sand on either side, Plankton whipped his head one way then another and let out an even angrier growl.

Even though I had to admit it was very weird, I almost started laughing at the idea of Plankton being scared by a bunch of silly fish. There's nothing unusual about mullet jumping—they're probably the most jumpiest fish there are. Nobody knows for sure what makes them do it, but while they jump a lot, they tend to do it one at a time, not all together in big groups. And I had never, ever seen them jump out of the water onto land.

I stood up, thinking I would throw the crazy beached mullet back into the ocean when the shoreline *really* exploded. Four huge gray torpedoes shot out of the water partway onto the sand. Each of them had a pointy mouth full of big teeth, and they started eating the mullet that had jumped ahead of them and were now flopping helpless.

I froze, shocked by what I was seeing, even fearing for a second that the big gray shapes were going to keep coming right up the shore to grab me. Even as scared as I was, I could already see that they weren't sharks. These were porpoises, creatures I had always thought of as cute and friendly. Part of my brain was telling me that porpoises couldn't come onto shore to eat people. But the other part of my brain saw that mass of big, squirming, snapping gray bodies and flopping mullet, with Plankton right between them, and I was suddenly terrified.

5.

"Plankton!" I shouted at the top of my lungs. "Get away!"

Unfortunately, just like any Jack Russell, even though his tail was tucked between his legs and he was probably as frightened as I was, Plankton wasn't going to retreat, not even from huge porpoises who were chewing mullet as fast as they could grab them. He just stood there with the hair on his back sticking straight up and his lips curled back over his teeth in the ugliest snarl he could manage. I knew he was halfway ready to jump on one of the porpoises and fight it, but Plankton was a whole lot more mullet-sized than most dogs. It would be too easy for one of the porpoises to grab him and drag him back into the sea.

I had to do something, but my body seemed stuck in place. I tried to shout again, wanting to call Plankton to me, but I couldn't even get more words out of my throat.

Everything seemed hopeless, when out of the corner of my eye I saw another streak of motion. A person ran past me. There had been no sign of anyone here on the spit, and

I had no idea where this one had come from. He raced toward the water at top speed, then bent down and scooped up Plankton without slowing, leaping over a porpoise just as it chomped down on another mullet.

A second later Plankton's rescuer was standing by the palmetto trunk where I'd been sitting. He was about my age, with sandy hair worn a little bit long, blue eyes, and a friendly smile. With his chest heaving somewhat from his sprint, he continued holding Plankton while the porpoises finished up the last of the beached mullet then squirmed their way backward into the ocean and disappeared.

"You're staying right up here until the danger passes," the boy said as he looked down at Plankton.

The Jack Russell wasn't even growling, which was amazing because Plankton didn't take well to strangers. Normally, a person he didn't know could never pick him up without risking a serious nip. I suspected Plankton was in shock, but it was also possible he was showing gratitude that someone had whisked him away from the gray monsters that could have devoured him. In any case, Plankton rested quietly until the boy put him down at my feet.

"Your dog almost got stranded," he said.

"Stranded?" I said. "He almost got eaten."

"That's what I meant. When porpoises drive fish onto the beach it's called stranding. It's one of the ways they feed, and this is one of their favorite places to do it."

As if Plankton understood what we were saying, he turned toward the water and stared out at the ocean. The porpoises were gone now, and maybe that was why he darted back down to the water's edge and began running back and forth sending outraged barks out over the water. He seemed to be warning the porpoises that if they knew what was good for them, they would never again come onto this beach when he was there.

The boy laughed. "You'd think he would have had enough."

I tried to call Plankton away, but his pride was apparently too injured. He just kept barking. "He's actually a very smart dog," I said.

"I'd say he's got more guts than brains," the boy said.

I glanced back at him. He had broad shoulders and strong looking arms. He was probably two inches taller than I was, and I was tall for my age. "That's easy for you to say when you're big."

"Doesn't matter how big or small I am. You don't fight something five times your size. That's called bad math."

I took a breath, ready to tell the boy what I thought of him. Then I remembered what the boy had done to save the dog. "You've seen them do that before?" I asked instead.

"Porpoises feeding like that?" He shrugged. "A couple times."

"It scared me half to death."

"Of course, if you didn't expect it."

I pointed toward Plankton. "You really think they could have eaten him?"

"Probably. They're hungry and he's meat."

"He's not meat, he's my grandfather's dog."

"To a porpoise that's the same thing."

"Yes, well . . . thank you very much for saving him."

The boy looked at me, and his eyes tightened as if he had something else to say.

"Yes?" I asked.

"If you're gonna bring the dog onto this beach, you might want to learn a little more about what happens out here before you let him off the leash."

"I doubt Plankton's going to get attacked by porpoises again in the next couple days."

"Well, you still may want to keep him on a leash."

"Why is that?"

"Those little birds he was chasing?"

"I suppose you're going to tell me those little brown birds are going to eat him, too."

"No, he's liable to kill them."

"By chasing them? Yeah, right."

"I'm serious."

"Sure you are."

"You even know what kind of birds they are?"

I shrugged. "They're little brown birds."

"They're called Red Knots."

"I thought they were Sandpipers."

He made a face. "People who don't know anything about them call all the little shore birds Sandpipers."

"Well, whatever they are, Plankton wasn't about to kill anything. He was just playing."

"That's what you think."

"He was!"

"You know how far those birds have flown to get here?"

I just stared at him. I had no idea what he was getting at. He might have saved the dog, but it didn't mean I had to put up with his nonsense. "What are you talking about?"

"Thousands of miles," he went on. "They fly up here over open ocean all the way from the southern parts of South America, and they eventually have to make it all the way to northern Canada. When they reach a beach like ours, they're super exhausted and absolutely have to rest and eat. A running dog can have fun by making the birds keep getting up and flying out of its reach. It might be funny to watch them do it, but it can actually kill the birds.

I rolled my eyes. "Pullleeeeaaaase. You don't know what you're talking about."

"Really? Call the Audubon Society and see what they tell you."

I looked at him for a long moment. "What are you some kind of nature guy?"

He shrugged. "I like nature. What's not to like? Why? You don't like it?"

It was my turn to shrug. "Yeah, I like it," I said, sounding less certain than I'd intended.

"You like it, but you think it's kind of boring.

You'd rather go to a mall."

"I didn't say that." I felt my cheeks grow red. I loved nature, but I wasn't going to admit that to him. Everything the boy said made me feel confused or defensive.

"Your dog almost got eaten by porpoises. That's boring?"

That was actually funny. I had to smile. "Well, when that's not happening."

"Where do you live?"

"New York City."

He snorted. "No wonder you don't like nature."

"I didn't say I didn't like it. I'm just not some . . . granola person like you."

"*Granola person?*"

"You know, the kind of kid who wears Salvation Army clothes even though they don't need to, eats vegan and demands that everyone else does too, and always comes out with obnoxious advice about saving the earth." I felt my cheeks grow red again. I was saying things I didn't really mean, but I felt like I was trapped in a hole and couldn't stop digging.

He looked down at his cutoff jeans and tee shirt that had a picture of earth and said, "Keep It Green." Shaking his head like he couldn't believe what planet I'd come from, he asked, "What's wrong with saving the earth?"

"I don't know," I snapped, my frustration starting to boil over. "I'm just saying."

"You don't believe in climate change?"

"Yeah, sure. The climate's changing. Sea levels

are rising. Don't buy beach property." I knew I sounded like a total jerk, but my mouth was on autopilot.

He looked at me, and his expression darkened as if I had suddenly let him down. To my surprise, I actually felt bad, and then I felt a flash of anger that I did. Was I angry at myself or at him? Why should I even care what some strange boy thought?

"Yeah," he said, like he should have expected something like that from me. "Well, take it easy." He turned and started walking away, tossing a wave over his shoulder.

Plankton watched him leave. He tilted his head the way dogs sometimes do when they seem to be questioning something. Then he let out a sound that wasn't exactly a growl or a bark but might have been his way of letting me know that he didn't like the way I had behaved.

"Keep your opinions to yourself," I said to him. "It was your fault for trying to bite a porpoise and not having the brains to run away."

6

Back home, I rinsed Plankton's fur and hosed my feet to get the sand off, then went straight into the kitchen to see what was for lunch. I was still angry at myself for having been such an idiot back on the spit with that boy, and I hoped some good food would make me feel better. I perked up right away when I smelled bacon and saw that Martha had already sliced tomatoes. It meant we were having BLTs, another of my favorites.

"Where's Poppy?" I asked.

"He's in his office with the door closed," Martha answered, nodding her head in toward the room. "He's getting ready for a meeting in town this afternoon."

"What kind of meeting?"

Martha shrugged. "He doesn't tell me."

When he had his office door closed, it meant Poppy was supposed to be left alone, so I wandered toward my bedroom to get a book. As I went past the dining room, I happened to glance in at the big table, a place we hardly ever ate. To my surprise the table was covered with a tablecloth and set with plates, napkins, fancy glassware, and Grandama's good silver. I turned and headed right back to the kitchen and pushed open the swinging door.

"Is Poppy having a dinner party?" I asked.

Martha glanced around from her bacon. "Didn't he tell you? He invited Mr. Finnigan and his grandson."

I rolled my eyes. "Tonight?"

"Yes."

"Why?" I asked.

"He wanted you to have someone your own age to spend time with."

"Great," I said, backing out of the kitchen and heading toward my bedroom. *Jimmy Finnigan.* I collapsed on the bed and threw an arm over my eyes, remembering him droning on and on about the Detroit Tigers while he sat at the dinner table wearing his baseball glove. I didn't think I was going to be able to stand it.

As I lay there, I felt a small body plop onto the mattress beside me, and a second later a tongue started licking my cheek and ventured too close to my lips.

"Gross, Plankton," I said, as I rolled onto my side to get away.

He simply jumped over me and kept up his licking until I got both hands on him and held him at arm's length. "Even though you're disgusting," I said to him, "I'd rather have you licking my face than have dinner with Jimmy Finnigan."

Poppy came to my room a short time later, telling me that he had to go into Charleston.

He apologized that he was leaving me alone and not taking me because he had to have a long, boring meeting with his lawyer. He said the good news was that we were going to have dinner with friends that night.

"Great," I said, knowing exactly who the "friends" were.

I read books and took Plankton for a couple more walks, staying in the neighborhood each time and not going near the spit again because I didn't want to take the chance of running into Mr. Know It All from earlier and have him tell me all the other things I was probably doing wrong, and have the risk of saying even worse things back to him. Finally, I went into the kitchen to see if Martha needed any help. She told me to go relax because everything was done, so I read some more, then washed my hair and got dressed for my horrible dinner.

At six thirty Poppy knocked on my door, "Come on out. Our guests are here."

I rolled my eyes and looked at Plankton. "I hope you pee on the rug or barf or do something that makes them leave early." Plankton wagged his tail, maybe thinking he would give it a try. There was always hope.

I put a mark in my book, walked out of my bedroom and down the hall, grinding my teeth as I looked for the short kid in the baseball glove. Instead, I only saw Poppy's friend, Mr. Finnigan, and we shook hands and said hello.

"Well, well, you've changed a great deal since the last time I saw you," Mr. Finnigan said.

It was such a random adult thing to say, but I smiled. "I guess we all change as we get older." What else *can* you say to such a comment?

I was starting to hope that Mr. Finnigan had come by himself, and that maybe his grandson Jimmy might have been too busy practicing his pitching to eat, but then Mr. Finnigan said, "Jimmy's coming right in. He just had to get something from the car."

His baseball mitt, I said to myself. But that thought lasted only a second because right then the front door opened and in walked Jimmy. Only, he wasn't the tubby little kid I remembered, but the tall boy from the beach earlier that morning, the one who had saved Plankton from the porpoises and told me that letting the dog run was killing the Red Knots.

Mr. Know It All stopped dead in his tracks, apparently as shocked to see me there as I was to see him. He also looked about as happy to see me as I felt about seeing him.

"Callie, you remember Mr. Finnigan's grandson, Jimmy?" Poppy said, stepping in to make the introduction. "I think you two met three or four years ago."

I stuck a smile on my face and nodded. "Yes," I said, trying to sound happy to see him. "I remember."

"Finn," Mr. Finnigan said to his grandson, "you remember Callie. The last time you saw her she had pigtails and that Ninja Turtles tee shirt that you wanted us to get for you."

I felt my face go red at the mention of my old pigtails and the geeky Teenage Mutant Ninja Turtles tee shirt that I had been obsessed with back then.

Finn—I guessed that was what Jimmy called himself now—nodded uneasily. "Yes," he said. "How're you, Callie?"

"Fine, thank you." I paused, still stinging from his condescending attitude on the spit. "Are you still playing baseball?"

It was his turn to have his cheeks turn red. "I can actually hit what I throw at these days."

His grandfather laughed and clapped Finn on the shoulder. "Starting pitcher on his school team, and he's also on a travel team. He'll have college scouts looking in another year or two."

Finn held up a hand and laughed. "Okay, Gramps, that's enough. I'm sure Callie doesn't care a bit about my baseball stuff."

I shrugged, but to be honest I was a little bit impressed. At least he hadn't totally wasted the time he'd spent carrying around that goofy mitt. And, I thought, practice *must* make perfect if a kid who just a couple years ago couldn't get within twenty feet of what he was throwing at was now a hotshot.

"What about you, Callie?" Mr. Finnigan asked. "Are you an athlete like Finn?"

Poppy came to my rescue. "Callie sure could be an athlete if that's what she wanted, but she's a dancer."

"Oh," Mr. Finnigan said, not sounding very impressed.

I was already starting to think Poppy's friend was a jerk, but I kept a nice smile plastered on my face.

"What kind of dancing?"

I swung my head toward Finn, who had asked the question. He looked like he actually wanted to know the answer. "Ballet and modern," I said.

"You live in New York City, right?" he asked.

"Yeah, Brooklyn," I said in surprise. "You actually remember that?"

"From that first time we met when we were kids? Yeah," Finn said, ignoring my sarcasm and answering the question as if we hadn't seen each other on the beach that morning and I hadn't already told him where I lived. I didn't know whether he was trying to be nice or whether he was trying to save himself as well as me from having to explain our earlier meeting to our grandfathers.

"And you still live in . . . ?" I didn't remember.

"Michigan."

We sat in the living room while Poppy and Mr. Finnigan had martinis. Finn and I talked a little bit about the places we lived, our schools, and what we did when we weren't in school, which meant I talked about dancing and he talked about baseball. When our grandfathers finished their drinks, we went into the dining room to eat.

Poppy and Mr. Finnigan did most of the talking during dinner. Mr. Finnigan kept bragging about Finn all through salad, the main course, and dessert, talking about his fastball and his curve, how he was working on a slider, and how he was also a good batter. Every time his grandfather started in again, I glanced over at Finn and could see him squirming in his chair with his eyes cast down at his plate, clearly uncomfortable. Mr. Finnigan didn't seem to have a clue, and that made me feel a little bit sorry for Finn and actually like him a little, or at least think he wasn't a total jerk.

Also, I was grateful he hadn't mentioned what happened on the spit that morning. I didn't want to admit in front of Poppy and Mr. Finnigan that I'd almost let Plankton get eaten by porpoises. Probably that was why, as we were eating our dessert, I turned to him.

"If you're not doing anything tomorrow, maybe you'd like to meet down on the spit."

Finn's head shot up, and I saw something almost like relief in his eyes. "Sure," he said quickly. "What time?"

"Same time as today?"

Smiling, he nodded.

As he did, Poppy's eyes swung toward me. "You two already met today?"

I shrugged. "We ran into each other down on the spit."

"But we didn't know, you know, who we were," Finn added.

"We just said 'hi,'" I said.

7.

The next morning, instead of sleeping late in this place where I thought nothing happened, I surprised myself by waking up even before I started getting licked. Throwing on my clothes, I tiptoed past Poppy's bedroom, ate a quick breakfast, leashed Plankton, wrote a note telling Poppy where I'd gone, then headed toward the spit. I still wasn't convinced Finn wasn't a jerk, but even hanging around with a jerk my own age was better than doing nothing or being around adults all day.

As Plankton and I turned into the gouged-up track that led into the spit, I spotted Finn already waiting for me up ahead where the track opened on to the beach. Plankton and I walked toward him, and when he saw us he smiled.

"What's the dog's name? I never asked you yesterday."

"Plankton."

He smiled. "Plankton, like the little green guy from *SpongeBob?* The one who wants to take over the world?"

"The exact same one."

Finn's eyebrows shot up. "Your grandfather watches cartoons?"

"No, well, he watched them with me when I was little, which was around the time he got Plankton. Even when Plankton was a tiny puppy, he wasn't afraid of anything, so I told my grandfather that's what he should name him, and he did."

"I like your grandfather," Finn said. "For an old guy, I think he's pretty cool."

I nodded. "Yeah, I guess he is."

"At least he doesn't talk about you all the time like you're his pet rooster."

"Your grandfather's just really proud of you," I said.

Finn shook his head. "I wish he'd keep it to himself a bit more. It gets pretty old, but," he paused, and his lips turned down, "he's got his reasons."

I noticed the sudden sadness and thought about asking what those reasons could be. Before I could shape the question in a way that wouldn't be too nosy, Finn took one more frowning look around at the deeply rutted sand under our feet and the bare roots of bushes that had been torn out and tossed aside. "Where do you want to go?"

"I thought it would be fun to walk down to the end where we were yesterday."

"Let's do it."

We swung into step walking side by side, with Plankton groaning and straining at the leash, not understanding why one day he'd been allowed to run and chase every creature on the beach, while today he was being held back. When we'd gone a short way, Finn stopped and took a long look up and down the spit.

"I think you can let him run today, if you want. I don't see any *migratory* birds."

"You mean the birds from yesterday are gone?"

"The Red Knots?" Finn shrugged. "Probably. I think they need to balance how much time it takes to get where they need to go against their strength, their food sources, and distance. When they're able to fly again, they go. They have to get all the way up to the artic."

"Seriously? You weren't joking about how far they have to go yesterday?"

He shook his head. "They have to travel something like nine thousand miles from their wintering grounds in South America to their nesting sites. So, yeah, pretty much as soon as they're rested up and fed, they take off again. Pretty amazing little birds."

"How do you know so much about them?"

He shrugged. "I've gone to some bird lectures back home, done some birding. It's pretty cool to learn about birds, and to learn to watch them."

As he spoke, a noise that sounded like a prehistoric "gronk" came from the direction of the river. "Heron," Finn said, hooking a thumb in that direction. As if on cue, a huge bird with a long neck, stick legs, and a skinny body appeared overhead, set its wings and disappeared again behind the wall of jungle as it dropped toward the riverbank.

"You knew what it was just from the sound?" I asked.

He nodded. "Herons are fascinating. They spend ninety percent of their waking time hunting because they eat their weight every day."

I started to ask another question about herons, but Finn had already moved on and was now gazing out at the water.

"Take a look out there," he said, pointing. I followed his finger and saw something big and blunt rise a foot or so above the surface.

"What is it?"

"Sea turtle. It's almost egg laying season."

"I've never actually seen a sea turtle, but Poppy talks about them. He says they're endangered. During the breeding season he's one of the volunteers who patrol the beaches to spot turtle nests and mark them off for protection. Turtles lay their eggs right on this beach. It's one of the reasons he loves this spit so much."

Finn gave me a funny look.

"What?" I asked.

He shook his head as if he hadn't heard my question. "I guess it doesn't matter here 'cause there are no houses right here, but they try to get the people who live on the beach to turn down their lights at night for the turtles."

"What's wrong with lights?"

"Lights can confuse the hatching baby turtles

and make them move toward the house lights and away from the water. Predators try to eat the little turtles, so once they're hatched they need to get to the water as fast as possible."

I liked listening to him because I could tell he wasn't trying to sound cool or sophisticated, like so many of the kids at my school. It was nice that he was just talking about stuff that he cared about.

"I think turtles are totally cool," he went on. "They're these big, peaceful creatures that wander the oceans and eat stuff like jellyfish. I got stung by a jellyfish one time, and I hate the things. I'm just glad something eats them."

I cut a glance at him, surprised at how the fat little kid I had met a few years ago had gotten so much leaner and taller and learned so many interesting things. I was starting to think he was somebody I could have some fun hanging out with for my two weeks in South Carolina.

As we kept watching for the turtle to come up for air again, we wandered down near the tide line. Plankton ran ahead barking at some gulls that had been feeding on a dead fish. They took off as he came near, calling out angrily to him to get away from their food, which of course he didn't.

When he came to the dead fish, Plankton stopped and started to sniff. I saw what was about to happen and broke into a run. "Plankton!" I shouted.

"What's the matter?" Finn called to me as

he started running, too.

"He's gonna roll in that dead fish," I yelled back.

Realizing I was closing in, Plankton shot me a glance, then before I could grab him, he dove down and rolled onto his back so that he wiped the dead fish against his neck and behind his ears. I picked him up after only a second, but the damage was done.

"Uggghhhh!" I exclaimed as the stink hit me.

Behind me Finn was laughing his head off.

"It's not funny," I snapped.

"Sorry, but it is," he said, still laughing. "The way he looked back at you, knowing you were gonna pick him up, then dove into the fish before you could stop him."

Finn's laughter was getting to me. I had to bite down a smile because I was trying to stay mad. I scolded Plankton as I carried him down to the water, intending to take a couple handfuls of wet sand and rub it against his fur to get the stink off.

I forgot about the smell when I heard a loud engine behind us. I looked back and saw a flatbed truck trying to back down the path the men had cut a couple days earlier.

"What are they doing here?" I asked.

Finn looked back and scowled. "It's really a shame," he said in quiet voice.

"What are you talking about?"-

"Your grandfather."

"What about him?"

"He's selling this place."

8.

For half a second it felt like my heart stopped. "What?" I asked when I could finally speak. I let Plankton jump to the sand and run away, no longer caring how bad he smelled. "There's no way."

"It's true." Finn was looking at me like he wasn't sure if I was kidding. "You really didn't know?"

My face reddened, partly with anger at what he was suggesting but partly with embarrassment that he might know something terrible about my family that I didn't. "Poppy would never sell this. It's . . . too special. He and my grandmother bought it before she died." However, even as I said it I had a sick feeling, because I remembered the men who had cut the wide swath where the spit's foot path used to be, and I thought about the odd way Poppy had been acting when he drove me from the airport, how he hadn't stopped the men who were cutting the bushes to widen the way into the spit, how he'd spent a good part of yesterday shut in his office and then headed into town for a meeting, how he'd been sleeping later than I ever remembered. I also thought about that strange comment Martha had made about my visit being good for Poppy.

Finn stood there looking uncomfortable, like he wished right then that he could be someplace far away from me. "I wish I was wrong," he said in a near whisper. "But then what are those guys doing?"

He pointed at the truck that by now had backed down about as far as it dared into the loose beach sand. As we watched, a couple men came around and shoved a contraption onto a platform at the very back of the truck bed. Once they had it in place, one of them hit a button and lowered the platform to the ground, then the other man pulled the thing off, fiddled with it for a few moments, then started pushing it along the sand.

"What is that thing?" I asked.

"It almost looks like a lawnmower." Finn said. It was obvious he was making a joke, but at the same time he was right. The thing the man was pushing had four big wheels and a handle just like a lawnmower, but a high-tech looking black box sat right where the motor should have been. Also, it was obvious there weren't blades to cut anything, because we could see empty space beneath the black box. Also, there was no lawnmower sound. In fact, there seemed to be no sound coming from the machine at all.

While one man pushed the machine over the bumpy sand, the other man pulled some stakes off the back of the truck, then walked off a section of beach and pounded a stake into the sand. The man with the machine then walked up and back, covering every inch of the space inside the stakes, moving just like somebody would if they were mowing a lawn. But of course, he wasn't mowing anything because there was nothing but sand under his machine.

"What could they possibly be doing?" I asked after a few moments.

"No idea," Finn said. He glanced at me, then said, "Maybe we should ask."

He started walking toward the two men. I followed a few steps behind, thinking he clearly wasn't from the city, where we never talk to strangers on the street. At the same time, I was really curious what he was going to learn.

"Excuse me," Finn called out.

The man who had been pounding stakes turned toward us, his face unsmiling. "Yes?"

"Can I ask what you're doing?"

"We're working for a client."

"Who's your client?" Finn went on.

The man's eyes went from Finn to me, then back to Finn. "Who are you, and why do you want to know?"

Finn stepped to one side and pointed to me. "Her grandfather owns this land."

"Then he knows we have permission to be here," the man said. "You kids need to move away from here. We're very busy."

I started to turn away, but Finn stayed right where he was. "What kind of machine is that?" he asked.

The man had already turned away, but now he looked back in annoyance. "It's a ground x-ray," he said, his tone becoming hard. "Now, please give us room to do our job."

As if to make his point, he walked away and went on with pounding his stakes.

My heart sank, and I suddenly felt as if I might burst into tears as we watched the men go on with their work. Why did I feel so emotional? Yes, the spit was beautiful, but so were lots of places around here. If Poppy had changed his mind and decided to sell it, why should it bother me? Only, I knew that Poppy hadn't changed his mind about wanting to keep the spit. Poppy had always cared about the spit so much that I had been certain he would never sell it. He and my grandmother had bought it so they could keep it wild forever, and I'd seen how upset he'd been when he'd seen the men cutting a wider path through the maritime forest. So, why was he selling it, and why hadn't he said anything?

"What's going to happen to the spit?" I asked after a long silence.

"My grandfather says they're gonna build houses," Finn said.

I shook my head. It should have been obvious to me, because almost all of the other beach property up and down the coast was filled with expensive houses.

"Who's going to build them?"

"A developer named Desmond Granger. Grandfather says he's a greedy jerk, and he'll stick as many houses as he can on this beach."

Once again, I felt the burn of hot tears at the corners of my eyes. Suddenly, I realized my sadness wasn't just for Poppy. It was for everything, like those little birds—the Red Knots—and for all the other creatures that had been able to live here undisturbed. Poppy and Grandma had kept this place for them, but no longer. Now men would come and cut down all the trees and bushes in the maritime forest and pour concrete all over the place and put up houses.

I glanced up and down the beach and then back at the solid wall of green jungle that ran along the river. Knowing that it was going to be ruined, it struck me, as if I was truly seeing it for the first time, that the spit was even lovelier than I had realized. It was more than pretty, it was beautiful. I felt like I really understood why Poppy and Grandma had felt so strongly about this place and why they had bought it and tried to keep it wild. It seemed wrong and terrible that Poppy was going to sell it to a developer.

"Why is Poppy selling?" I asked.

Finn shook his head. "My grandfather says nobody around here knows, but they all wish he wouldn't. People have tried to talk him out of it, but he won't discuss it."

"Well, I know Poppy wouldn't do anything bad," I said with a flash of anger, suddenly feeling like I had to defend him.

"I didn't say he would," Finn replied. "I just said people wish he wouldn't sell."

"Well, he must have his reasons."

"I'm sure he does. It's just that nobody knows what they are."

"Well, it's a free country. They don't need to know, and Poppy doesn't need to tell them if he doesn't want to," I said.

"Whatever," Finn mumbled.

"Well, I have to go," I said, feeling angry and confused and embarrassed all at the same time, and like I was digging myself in deeper and deeper with everything I said without knowing how to stop.

As I walked back toward the house, all the strange things that had happened in the past two days, plus what Finn had just told me were all rolling around in my head. I thought about how the porpoises had shot up onto the sand and almost eaten Plankton, about the turtle and the heron and the Red Knots we had seen, about how the turtles were about to start breeding, and how Poppy loved these things more than almost anything except his family, and how he wouldn't tell anybody why he was selling the spit.

The only conclusion could be that Poppy was having serious troubles that were forcing him to sell. And then I wondered what those troubles could be. Was something wrong with Poppy, or did those troubles have something to do with my parents? The more I thought, the more upset I became. I needed to find out what was going on and why, and I needed to do it soon.

9.

As I got closer to the house, I made myself feel better by telling myself that Finn might have been mistaken, at least about Poppy selling the spit. He *had* to be wrong about that. Yes, Finn might have saved Plankton, and yes, he might have been right about the Red Knots and all the things he said about herons and turtles, but he had to be wrong about the other thing. Poppy would not sell the spit. He simply would never do that.

I was halfway to actually believing it when I came in sight of the house and spotted a big black Mercedes parked in front and a huge man in a dark suit standing beside the car. He looked out of place in a little town where nobody even wore ties much less suits. Because he was buffing the car's shiny paint with a rag, I thought he must be somebody's chauffeur, which was odd because I was pretty sure we didn't know anybody who had one of those. The man stopped his buffing and watched me as I turned into the drive.

"Hello," I said.

"Can I help you?" he said back.

"No."

"Do you live here?"

I thought it was a nosey question, but my parents always made a big deal out of being polite to adults, even nosey ones. Besides that, the man was huge, with arms that seemed stuffed inside his suit coat and a neck nearly as wide as his shoulders. Also, his eyes were small and hard, and his head was totally bald and as shiny as the car. "This is my grandfather's house," I said.

"Okay," the man said, as if I now had his permission to walk up the drive. Right away I didn't like him or his attitude. He didn't say anything else, but I could feel his eyes on my back as I made my way to the front door and walked inside.

I wasn't sure why I did it, but once I got into the house I closed the door quietly behind me. Normally, I pushed it hard enough to make a loud *thunk,* and usually also called out, "Hello," just to let Poppy and Martha know I was home, but today my instinct told me not to make much noise. Even Plankton seemed to sense that something was weird, because he didn't bark or run through the house to find my grandfather the way he almost always did.

For several long moments, I stood just inside the door, listening to the silence of the house until I was able to make out voices coming from the direction of my grandfather's library. Thinking again about what Finn had said about Poppy selling the spit, and now having this strange car with its weird driver sitting in our driveway, my curiosity spiked. Needing to keep Plankton quiet if I was going to hear anything, I picked him up, scratched him behind the ears, and then tiptoed toward the voices. Plankton still smelled like a dead fish, and up close he was pretty rank, but I would deal with that later.

Opening off the far end of the living room, Poppy's library was paneled with cypress, and its walls were floor to ceiling bookcases filled with books. It was a quiet room with no TV, a room Poppy said was reserved for reading, thinking, and quiet talk.

Right now, however, it wasn't quiet at all. The door was closed tight, but the voices leaking through the thick wood and the small crack at the bottom were loud and angry. I heard Poppy's voice, along with a man's voice that I didn't recognize.

Poppy had been a school principal, and he had that silent way of letting people know that he wasn't someone to be trifled with. Even though he always tried to teach me that it was generally easier and almost always better to get what you want through logic and politeness than through anger and emotion, he didn't seem to be following his own advice today.

When Poppy got really mad, which wasn't very often, he would take a deep breath, then let it out in a slow, loud hiss. I had never been around an actual stick of dynamite with a burning fuse, but I bet the sound Poppy made reminded whoever was making him angry of exactly that. I hadn't seen Poppy do it many times, but whenever he did, it had always been enough. The other person stopped arguing before the dynamite blew. Until today, I'd never heard the dynamite explode.

To my shock, Poppy suddenly roared, his voice deep and angry. To my even greater shock, the other man actually yelled back, so that even though their words were very loud, they came too fast and rolled over each other in a way that made it impossible for me to understand most of them. At least that was true until the other man suddenly fell silent and Poppy thundered, "I told you I need the money *now,* not in a few months."

And then the other man said in a steely voice, "I said I'd give you the money when we've finished our due diligence, not a day before."

"But we had a deal! You were supposed to finish your due diligence weeks ago. If you're going to play games, I'm going to bring in other bidders."

"You go right ahead. You know how hard this land will be to build on. Other people will be hung up for months, maybe years, getting environmental approvals. You'll get your money faster by working with me, and you know it."

More harsh words followed, but in a lower tone so I couldn't make them out. What shocked me was that Poppy seemed to be giving in, which really bothered me because

Poppy was someone who almost always got his way. Suddenly, the sounds changed again. I realized that the other man had started moving around inside the office, which probably meant he was getting ready to walk out. I still had Plankton in my arms, and not wanting us to get caught spying, I stepped back from the door deeper into the living room where I ducked behind a couch that sat along one wall. I scratched Plankton behind the ears to hopefully keep him from growling.

No sooner had I hidden than the library door opened, and the man strode out. He went past the couch with fast, angry steps, then opened and shut the front door with a loud bang that seemed to shake the whole house.

I hadn't been able to see the man from my hiding place, and I was curious to know what he looked like. Poppy didn't seem to have moved from his desk in his library, so I hurried on tiptoes to the front windows and looked out in time to see a tall man in a dark suit, white shirt, and no tie climb into the backseat of the Mercedes. As he turned, I caught sight of pale skin and a long, narrow face. His hair was dark and combed straight back. He was handsome in sort of an upper-class way, which surprised me because he didn't look like the kind of person who would yell.

He was almost all the way in the car when he stopped and turned his head to look back at the house. Strangely, he didn't look angry. Instead, he had what looked like a self-satisfied smirk on his lips, like he'd been pretending to be angry and now he wondered how his act had affected Poppy. Then, as if he'd sensed me, his gaze moved and locked onto where I stood in the living room window. His expression suddenly went cold, and his black eyes glared at me from where they were set deep in that narrow head. He kept staring at me as if I'd done something wrong, and even though I wanted to duck out of sight, I just stared back. This had to be Granger, the developer guy that Finn had talked about, but even though he was handsome and very well dressed, his eyes gave me the creeps.

His expression never changed, but finally, he unfroze and slipped into the backseat of the car. The huge man in the dark suit closed the door, then got behind the wheel and drove off.

10.

As the Mercedes disappeared, I moved to a different part of the living room where I could get a peek into Poppy's office. He was sitting at his desk with his elbows resting on the blotter and his face cradled in his hands. It struck me all of a sudden that he looked almost as sad as he had after Grandma died. I wondered what was making him feel so terrible, and what made him need money so bad that he would sell Buccaneer's Spit. One thing for sure, whatever the problem was, it had to be very serious.

Part of me wanted to go to Poppy and try to cheer him up, but another part understood that he really didn't want me or anyone else around right then. Plankton was still in my arms where he had been the whole time stinking like a dead fish. Even though he let out a little grunt, he didn't try to squirm loose and run to Poppy, like he would have almost any other time. Even Plankton seemed to realize that Poppy didn't want company, and he didn't make a sound as we turned and crept down the hall toward the kitchen.

There, I asked Martha for some gentle dish soap, then I took Plankton outside and gave him a good washing. Once he smelled decent, I dried him off, then took him to my bedroom, where I put him on my bed, tried to read a book, but spent my time worrying about Poppy.

A short time later Martha served lunch. Even then, when Poppy came to the table, I felt his sadness like a weight. On any other day, he would have said how good the sandwiches were and peppered me with questions about what I'd done that morning, if I'd ridden my bike, or taken a long beach walk with Plankton to look for shells and maybe gone to Buccaneer's Spit. He'd have asked whether I had spotted any interesting birds or seen anything unusual on the water, because watching nature was Poppy's favorite thing to do. Asking questions was his way of trying to get me to love it here as much as he did.

Instead of talking, he sat there and nibbled his food, looking over my head into the far distance. I was dying to ask questions, but I bit my tongue. Finally, having only eaten only half his sandwich, Poppy pushed his plate away. Seeing that he was about to get up from the table, I cleared my throat. "Poppy, are you feeling okay?"

He seemed to shake himself, as his eyes lost that faraway look and focused on me. "Why sure," he said, trying to put some fake happiness into his voice.

"You *sure* everything is okay?" I asked.

"Of course! Why wouldn't it be?"

"You've hardly said a word. And you haven't finished your sandwich."

"Oh, yes, well," he smiled, but I could tell it was forced, "I've got a lot on my mind I guess."

"Like what?" I asked, when there were so many things that I really wanted to ask—*Like that guy who was in your office? Who was he? Why was he there? Even more, why was he yelling at you? And who was the big bald guy who looked like a professional wrestler?*

I held all those questions back, but even so, for a second, Poppy looked almost like a little kid who'd gotten caught by his teacher in a lie. He took a breath, then let out a fake laugh. "Ah, you know, adult stuff. You wouldn't be very interested."

I *hated* answers like that. I'd had enough of that stuff with my parents over the past couple months, and I didn't want to get it from Poppy, too. "I thought you wanted me to learn things," I went on. "Maybe I would be interested in whatever it is."

"I do want you to learn things," he nodded, suddenly looking relieved. "And that reminds me—I remember you telling me that you might be interested in learning to be a vet someday. That's why I arranged for you to go to the aquarium in Charleston tomorrow and have a special tour of the turtle hospital. I was going to take you there as a surprise, only problem is, something's come up for me, and I won't be able to go with you. I asked Mr. Finnigan if his grandson might also like to go so you didn't have to go alone, and he said yes. I hope that was okay."

I gave him my best *I can't believe you did this to me* look. "The turtle hospital with Jimmy Finnigan?" I said. "Seriously?"

"Yes," he said.

I looked at him closely. Sometimes Poppy could be a big kidder, but today was definitely not one of those times. I was still feeling sorry for him, so I tried to seem interested. "What do they do at the turtle hospital?"

"What do you think they do?"

"I guess they take care of sick turtles?"

"And injured turtles. It's a very cool place."

I knew Poppy volunteered at the aquarium and also helped with protecting beaches during sea turtle nesting. The turtle volunteers would patrol the beaches, and when they spotted a new sea turtle nest, they would mark it off with colored tape to keep people from walking over it. They would also tape off the whole beach and tell people that they couldn't have their dogs off leash because the dogs might run over the nests and even dig up the eggs. Of course, Poppy said that there were lots of other creatures that also tried to eat turtle eggs, like raccoons, possums, and coyotes, but keeping dogs under control helped a lot.

"We saw a turtle today," I said.

"Where?" Poppy asked, perking up.

"Right off the beach."

"On the spit?"

I nodded.

"That means I'll be patrolling again soon," he said, but as the words came out his face fell. I knew that instead of thinking about turtles he had to be thinking about selling his beloved Buccaneer's Spit.

"Okay," I said, wanting to get his mind off of that. "I guess going to the turtle hospital will be fun."

"Should be a lot of fun," he said, sounding fake happy again. "And you'll learn something."

I'd always wanted to see the turtles come up out of the sea onto Buccaneer's Spit at night, and watch them dig their nests in the sand and lay their eggs, but the idea of going to a turtle hospital sounded about as dorky as anything I could imagine. To my surprise, I realized that I was looking forward to seeing Finn again, but I told myself it was only so I could ask him more questions about that Granger guy.

11.

After lunch, faced with nothing to do but sit around the house and watch Poppy mope, I took my book and Plankton, and we headed back to Buccaneer's Spit. It was weird spending so much time there, especially now that it was about to be ruined, but there was simply nothing else to do. Besides, I remained really curious about what those men had been doing earlier and thought that if I hung out there I might get some answers.

When Plankton and I got to the torn-up path, the spit appeared deserted. The men who had been there earlier pushing their weird contraption were gone, but they had left their stakes pounded into the sand. I might not learn anything, but the afternoon was cloudless with the sun high overhead in a sky of perfect robin's egg blue. The air was warm and soft with humidity, and while the breeze had been light in the early part of the day, it was getting stronger by the minute and kicking up white caps out on the water.

For the second time that day, thinking about Poppy selling this place—that the spit wouldn't be the wild place it always had been for much longer—it felt like I was seeing the world around me in a different way. The spit had always been pretty, but sometimes, depending on my mood, I had found it almost too quiet. Now I understood how that silent tranquility was a critical part of the spit's perfection, and the idea of its loss brought an even deeper sadness.

I had kept Plankton on his leash, and we stopped halfway to the water's edge while I checked for migrating birds on the beach. Overhead, gulls were cutting and swooping over the sand, and farther out brown pelicans coasted low over the waves like a formation of bombers. As Plankton and I watched, one of the pelicans spotted some fish near the surface, broke from the others, started to climb higher in the air and circle back. Right away, the other pelicans began to follow the first.

The pelicans rose twenty or thirty feet into the air, then one by one they started to plummet toward the water, folding their wings and diving headfirst toward whatever school of fish they had spotted. They would hit the water with big splashes, then come up, tossing their huge beaks upward as they swallowed the fish they had caught.

I watched until they had finished feeding and took off again. As they moved out of sight, more motion in the water caught my attention. Just offshore, small black and white birds that Finn told me were least terns were diving into the water to feed on minnows and other small fish. Then, as if disturbed by all the splashing of the pelicans and the least terns, a sea turtle suddenly popped its head out of the water. It took a few breaths as it looked around, then it disappeared. Over the beach and the green band of maritime forest, swallows darted and dove, cutting sudden turns as they fed on mosquitos and other bugs.

It hit me suddenly—something that Poppy had told me more than once but I hadn't really understood—that if I kept my eyes open, really open, and I noticed everything happening around me, the spit was incredibly busy. As if seeing everything for the first time, maybe because I was older or maybe because of the coming sale, I saw that the spit was just as busy, with just as much going on as Madison Avenue a week before Christmas.

Finally, when I walked down the beach toward the end of the spit, I saw a flock of little birds that looked a bit like red knots, but smaller. They ran down to the water's edge each time a wave receded, and then after a few seconds of feeding, they would turn and race away from the next incoming wave. Plankton strained to chase them, but I kept him leashed, remembering what Finn had told me about the red knots and wondering if these birds, too, had flown some incredibly long distance to get here.

As full as I was with all the beauty of the ocean and the birds, I thought about Poppy again and tried to understand what problem could be big enough to make him sell this place that he loved so deeply. Also, it made me realize how much I still had to learn about this incredible world that I was now truly seeing as if for the first time, and even more, how much I didn't know about my own family.

Those thoughts were tumbling over and over in my brain, when motion at the very end of the beach interrupted them. A fisherman was standing out in the water. Plankton and I kept walking, and when we got closer I could see it was Finn. He was just offshore in thigh-high water and casting into some marsh grass that grew along the side of the river where it flowed out to meet the ocean.

I slowed my pace as I got closer and watched. Finn wasn't using live bait or a spinning rod like the ones most fishermen would use along the beach. Instead he was using a fly rod, longer and lighter and a whole lot harder to cast than a spinning rod.

Poppy had tried to teach me how to fly fish, and I remembered him saying that at high tide, when the marsh grass flooded, the spottail bass would swim into it, their fins breaking the water as they searched for shrimp or crabs. That was the time to catch them, he'd said.

I'd done just enough fly fishing to know how hard it was. Finn was good. He was actually better than good. I watched him cast out several times, landing his fly in small openings in the spartina grass.

He retrieved, cast again, completely unaware of me standing behind him, and on his fifth or sixth cast, when his fly plopped into the water I saw a quick flash of fin break the surface just behind it. An instant later, he jerked his rod tip up to set the hook, and then the rod bent hard as the redfish began to run. His reel sang as the redfish pulled out more line in a fast dash toward deeper water.

As soon as the fish stopped its run, Finn stripped in line. The redfish made another couple runs before Finn got it to his hand. He raised the fish out of the water to remove the hook, then placed it back in the water, where he held it for a few seconds to make sure it was fully revived before releasing it. It shot out of his hand and disappeared with one flick of its powerful tail.

For a second, I wondered if people would still come here to fish after Poppy sold the spit and there were houses all over the place. But then I tried to shake that thought and said, "Nice job."

Finn spun around in surprise, then gave an embarrassed smile. "Uh, thanks," he said. "I didn't know you were there."

"I didn't want to break your concentration."

"I'm glad you didn't. That was the only fish I've caught, but I think it's getting too windy to keep going." He paused, glancing at the clear sky to indicate the quickening breeze. "Do you like to fly fish?"

"I've done it a little, but I'm no good."

He laughed as he reeled up his line and stepped out of the water. "Takes a while to get it down. I've been doing it for years and I'm just starting to get the hang of it."

"You're being modest," I said.

He shrugged, then looked around the beach, as if still feeling awkward about the way we had parted earlier. "I'm surprised to see you. I kind of got the impression that you'd had enough of this place this morning. Or maybe me."

I held up my book. "Just figured I'd find a good spot to read."

"Oh," Finn said, sounding like I'd just suggested eating worms or pickled brussels sprouts.

At first, I thought he'd said it that way because he didn't want me around, and I was about to say something nasty right back. Before I got the words out, I looked at his face and what I saw wasn't anger directed at me but sadness.

"You don't like to read?" I asked.

He shook his head.

The way his gaze dropped made me feel like I'd asked him something I shouldn't have, so I tried to think of some way to change the subject. "Anyway," I blurted, needing to fill the awkward silence, "I wanted to get out of the house. What's-his-name Granger, that guy you mentioned earlier—at least I think it was him—was at the house when I got there."

"Desmond Granger?" Finn said, as if the name was a dirty word. He looked out at the water and shook his head. "Even if your grandfather decided he had to sell the spit, why would he sell to that jerk?"

"Why do you say he's such a jerk?"

"My grandfather says he's a crook."

I shook my head in confusion. "Why would Poppy sell to him then?"

Finn shook his head. "No one knows."

"He's got that big fancy Mercedes and a chauffeur. I thought he had to be somebody important."

"Looks can be deceiving, right?"

I shrugged. "Maybe Granger is as much of a jerk as you say, but what does it matter who Poppy sells to if he's going to sell the spit."

"I know how you feel. Maybe it doesn't matter."

I doubted he knew how I felt, but even so, I suddenly realized I needed somebody to talk to, not just about Poppy selling the spit but about all the other weird things going on in my life. I took a breath, about to tell Finn about my parents' strangeness, and how they were probably getting a divorce, and what a weird coincidence it seemed to be that Poppy was selling the spit at the exact same time. I wanted to tell him that it didn't make sense that those two things could be wrapped up together, but they seemed to be. However, before I could open my mouth and get the first words out, Finn stiffened and looked down the beach.

"What's that sound?" he asked.

I turned toward where Finn was staring. Then

I heard the same thing, a faint engine sound, and a second later the roof of a black car or truck became visible in the distance where the gouged-up path led onto the beach.

"What now?" I asked as we both started walking in that direction. After we had gone a couple hundred yards, we could make out three men standing in front of a big black SUV. A truck was parked a few yards behind the SUV. One of the men wore the same coveralls and orange vest we had seen earlier that morning, but what made the scene so strange was that the other two wore dark suits. Even from a distance the suited men looked familiar.

We kept walking and after a couple more minutes I whispered, "That's the guy who was in Poppy's office. Is he Desmond Granger?"

Finn shook his head. "I don't know what he looks like." Then he squinted at the men. "How can you tell who he is from here?"

"Eagle eyes," I said. Then I jerked my head toward the bigger man. "I also recognize the one on the left, the guy whose skull shines like a mirror."

"He's huge," said Finn.

"He's the driver. Kind of hard to miss."

"Let's see what they're doing," Finn said, picking up speed as we kept heading in their direction.

I could see the man in the orange vest pointing to each of his stakes, like he was explaining what his machine had done. "Wish I knew what they're talking about," I said.

We were close enough now that I could see the men clearly. There was no mistaking the man who had been in Poppy's office and his driver. They finished talking to the third man, who walked back to his truck and drove away, but Granger and the bald guy stayed behind. They were talking intently and staring toward the line of trees and bushes that formed the maritime forest, so they never even glanced at me and Finn. Granger pointed several times at different parts of the forest. I couldn't see what he was pointing at, but the bald man nodded at whatever he said.

We had gotten fairly close when I saw Granger reach into an inside pocket of his suit coat and pull out what looked like one of those clear ziplock bags. He removed a piece of paper from the bag, and then tucking the plastic under one arm to keep it from blowing away on the stiff wind, he unfolded the paper with great care. Something about the way he did it struck me as odd, maybe the way he seemed to hold the paper like it was something precious. From where I stood, the paper didn't appear to be anything special. It appeared dark and wrinkled like maybe someone had spilled coffee all over it, or maybe it had been folded and refolded many times. I thought it might rip in the strong wind, but it held together.

Granger studied the paper, then looked over at the forest, then back at the paper. He did it over and over like someone cramming for a

test. The big man with the bald head stood
beside him, saying nothing. Finally, Granger
folded up the paper, slipped it back into the
plastic bag, and pinched it closed. When he
finished, he held the bag between two fingers
and turned to the bald man. He opened his
mouth to say something, but in that instant
an even bigger gust of wind came out of
nowhere and ripped the plastic bag from his
hand.

12.

At first, Granger just stared openmouthed in furious shock. Twirling on the wind, the bag flew upward, rising higher and higher. It was only when the wind started to carry the bag toward the water that Granger let out a strangled cry and started running.

"Get it!" he shouted to the bald man, who was also trying to run. Both men looked pretty goofy, nearly tripping as their leather shoes slipped on the soft and uneven sand. Even if they had been barefoot, the bag had a good head start. The wind kept blowing and the bag stayed high in the air, sailing out over the water, going maybe twenty yards before it finally dropped. It floated on the surface, hard to see but glistening every few seconds as the plastic reflected the sun.

Granger stopped running, started to hop on one foot as he jerked off one of his shoes, then pulled off his suit coat and threw it on the sand. The bald man was staring at him as if unsure what to do.

"What are you staring at?" Granger demanded, pointing at the water. "Get the bag."

"I don't swim so good, boss."

Granger made a disgusted sound and started hopping around on his other leg, pulling off his second shoe. As his hopping turned him in a circle he spotted me and Finn. Not seeming to recognize me from earlier, he motioned, "Hey, you kids. Help me out. I'll pay you twenty bucks if you dive in and get me that plastic bag."

Finn shrugged. "What's in it?"

Granger threw his hands in the air. "Wha—? It doesn't matter what's in it. Just get it."

"How 'bout a hundred bucks?" I said.

"What about five hundred?" countered Finn.

"Just get that bag before it sinks! We'll negotiate a price when you get it."

Finn seemed to waver. For a second, I thought he was going to dive in the water and try to get the bag, but then he stiffened. "No," he said.

"Why not?" Granger demanded. "I just said I'd pay you five hundred bucks." He kept looking out at the floating plastic bag and then back at us.

My heart lifted when I saw the determined look on Finn's face "You could pay us five thousand dollars, and we still wouldn't get your bag," I said. "We don't want your money because we don't want you to buy the spit."

Granger looked at us in amazement, and then his eyes narrowed on me as he seemed to realize who I was. He snapped his fingers and pointed. "You were the kid standing there in Morrisey's window this morning."

I didn't reply, just looked at him, and his

face wrinkled with anger. A second later, he swung his eyes back out toward the water, checking on the bag. As soon as he did, his eyes widened. "No!" he shouted.

I shaded my eyes against the glare reflecting off the water as I tried to spot the bag, but I saw the turtle first. Then I saw the plastic bag right in front of it. The turtle seemed to stare down at the bag, and a second later, its head dipped into the water, only to rise a second later with the bag in its mouth.

Now, Finn got excited. "No!" he shouted, racing down to the shore and waving his arms frantically. Unsurprisingly, the turtle totally ignored him as it disappeared beneath the surface.

When I looked back at Granger he was staring at the spot where the turtle had gone under. He shook his head in disbelief at what had just happened, but after a few seconds he turned toward the bald man. "Call some of my men! Tell 'em to get my boat and get out here and catch that turtle."

He trotted down to the wet sand where an incoming wave washed over his socks and sloshed up his pant leg, but he ignored the wetness and stared out at where the turtle had disappeared. The ocean was cloudy here because the river washed a lot of sand and silt into it, so anything under the surface was impossible to see.

"What will they do if they catch the turtle?" I asked as Finn came walking back to me, shaking his head.

"I don't even want to think what they'll do."

"They'll kill it?"

"How else will they get that bag back?"

"We have to do something."

"I've got an idea," Finn said, pulling his cell phone from his pocket. He googled, then called the number he found. Pulling the phone away from his ear for a second, he looked at me, "I'm calling the aquarium," he said.

I couldn't hear the person on the other end when they answered, but Finn said, "I need to report a turtle that needs to be rescued."

He gave the location. "Hurry," he said. "The turtle swallowed a plastic bag, and some people want what's in that bag. They're trying to catch the turtle, and I'm afraid they're going to kill it if they do."

Granger hadn't heard us make the call because he was still slogging up and down the shore, his suit pants getting wetter and wetter. Every few minutes he would turn back to the bald man, who had retreated and was now standing beside a shiny black SUV, and shout out a demand to know where the boat was and why it wasn't there already.

"It's on its way, boss," the bald man shouted back every time. "Be here soon."

"Be here soon," Granger spat. "Christmas will be here soon. What am I paying these morons for?"

A couple minutes later a Zodiac with two powerful engines on the stern came racing along the shore and slowed as it closed in on the spit. Granger waved frantically to the man driving the boat, then pointed toward the water in the general area where he had last seen the turtle.

"What do you want us to do?" the driver of the boat shouted.

"Get a rope around its neck and drag it to shore," Granger commanded.

As the boat began to move slowly up and down, paralleling the beach, Granger continued to splash up and down through the waves, tracking its progress. One man piloted the boat, while two others stood in the stern, one on each side as they looked down, searching the water.

Ten minutes went by, then twenty. The boat continued its slow pace running up and down, staying twenty or thirty yards off the beach. Finn and I stood there watching, not talking and barely moving.

Finally, when I saw something break the surface of the water, I elbowed Finn. "Look," I whispered. When Finn turned to look at me, I nodded toward where the turtle's head was sticking out of the water about twenty yards behind the boat.

Unfortunately, Granger noticed it, too, because he shouted to the boat, "Turn around! Turn around! It's right behind you."

The boat pilot said something to the two men in the stern, then he jerked the wheel and shoved the throttle forward. The Zodiac's bow rose, the boat spun in a tight turn, and then the man pulled back a little on the throttle, causing the bow to slap back onto the water. The turtle's head disappeared, but the boat shot forward right toward the spot where it had just gone under.

The men on both sides of the boat now had loops of rope in their hands and they threw their ropes into the water. The ropes must have been weighed because they sunk right away. The men waited a few seconds after they threw then pulled the ropes back in and threw again, the boat moving in a slow circle the whole time.

"Come on, come on," Finn said under his breath. "Where are those rescue people? If they catch these guys trying to rope a turtle, Granger and his friends will get into a lot of trouble."

Unfortunately, the turtle rescue people still didn't show, and the circling went on. Finn and I were both cheering for the turtle, neither one of us trying to hide our feelings. Several times Granger stopped walking and glared at us. I didn't care. I kept hoping the turtle could just stay under water and swim a long way off.

Then, as the Zodiac made another lazy circle, one of the motors made a harsh sound and rocked up, with the propeller popping momentarily out of the water before falling back.

"Oh, no!" Finn said, his eyes going wide in alarm.

"What?" I asked.

"I think one of those propellers just hit the turtle."

"How do you know?"

"The water's plenty deep there. What else would make that engine pop out of the water like that?"

"Do you think they killed it?"

Finn shrugged. "If they hit its head, pretty likely, but if they hit its shell, they probably just hurt it."

"Bad?"

"Hard to say." He glanced at his watch. "Where are those rescue guys?" he said, talking mostly to himself.

"The rescue guys, they're not like an ambulance, are they?" I asked.

"Turtle rescue?" Finn shook his head. "I mean, they're gonna try to rescue the turtle, but I don't think they're gonna have sirens or anything like that. Normally they probably don't have to hurry that fast because they don't usually have guys trying to kill turtles." He slapped his hand against his thigh as he turned back toward the water. "Come on. Come on," he said.

I chewed my fingernails.

13.

Granger's Zodiac circled for several more minutes, but when they didn't see the turtle again, the crew went back to making long runs up and down the beach. They did five or six of those runs with no sign of the turtle. I had my fingers crossed, and hoped the turtle could hear my silent commands to stay invisible, but then its head came above the water again. This time, unlike the others, it didn't take a quick breath and go down again, and it didn't seem to notice the boat as it circled and came back toward it with a man leaning far out over the side holding a noose in one hand, getting ready to drop it over the turtle's head.

"The turtle looks like it's stunned or hurt," I said. "It's not diving."

"Come on, you silly turtle," I heard Finn say under his breath. "Dive."

The pilot cut the Zodiac's engine, and let it glide toward the turtle. The man with the noose made a lurching move trying to slip the rope over the turtle's head, but the boat was a little too far away and he missed. The boat glided past, and the pilot moved ahead, turned and came back again. The turtle still hadn't dived. It was just keeping its head above water like that was all it could manage to do.

The man was leaning over the side of the boat again, and this time the boat was going to come closer to the turtle. I knew he wouldn't miss. That was when we heard the sound of a truck engine and a horn honking. Turning toward the sound, we saw a green truck with DNR written in big letter on its doors coming down the path toward the spit. I knew the letters stood for Department of Natural Resources, which meant help had arrived just in time. It was honking its horn because Granger's SUV was parked right at the mouth of the path, blocking the truck's access to the beach.

The truck's driver honked again, then leaned his head out the window and ordered the bald man to move the SUV so he could get onto the beach.

Rather than jumping into the SUV, the bald guy shambled over to the DNR truck and talked to the driver. I knew he was acting like he didn't understand because he was trying to buy time for Granger and the men in the boat to capture the turtle.

I turned back to watch the boat and the turtle, ready to start yelling if the men lassoed the turtle, but I didn't need to worry. Granger had seen the DNR truck and was signaling to the men on the boat to stop what they were doing and get out of there.

As soon as the pilot saw Granger's hand signals, the boat's engines rose to a roar and the boat rocketed away, the guy holding the noose and leaning over the side nearly falling overboard in the process.

With the boat moving away, the bald guy climbed into the SUV. He started it up and jockeyed it to one side so the truck could get onto the beach. A second later, as the DNR truck was driving toward the water, another boat appeared, coming fast along the shoreline and curving gradually toward the DNR truck.

By the time it got closer, Granger's boat was nearly out of sight, running fast in the opposite direction. The new boat slowed suddenly, letting its wake roll beneath it, then began to approach the beach very slowly. Two men were in the new boat, one at the wheel and the other right beside him seemed to be the spotter.

The turtle's head was still out of the water, and the spotter saw him right away and pointed him out. The boat slowed even more, moving almost at a dead drift as it got closer and closer to the turtle.

On shore, two men had jumped out of the DNR truck and were now pulling on wetsuits. A third man had turned the truck around and was backing down the beach onto the hard sand and very close to the water.

Just as the driver got the truck where he wanted it, the other two men had their wetsuits on and were heading into the ocean. They waded out, moving slowly, a few feet apart, toward where the turtle's head stuck out of the water.

The turtle was in shallow water that was only about chest deep on the two men. They were able to take hold of the its shell and walk it into shore. As soon as they started bringing it in, the other man lowered the platform on the rear of the DNR truck. Something that looked like a giant soap dish was on the platform, and the man started filling buckets with ocean water and pouring them into the soap dish. Then he tossed a few towels into the ocean and got them soaked.

When the two men in wet suits had the turtle in knee-deep water, they picked it up by the edges of its shell and carried it to the truck platform, putting it gently into the giant soap dish. Right away the three men put the wet towels over the turtle, raised the platform, and slid some barriers into place on the back of the truck to keep the turtle from getting out of its container.

A second later all three men were back in the truck and moving slowly across the soft sand. As the truck disappeared down the path that led off the spit, the men in the boat waved goodbye to Finn and me then motored away.

We had forgotten all about Granger, but as the turtle rescue boat disappeared down the coast and the sound of the DNR truck engine died away, we heard an angry voice, "You kids! Did you call those people?"

We turned to see Desmond Granger coming toward us. He looked ridiculous with his suit pants soaked up to the knees and stuck all over with wet sand. As silly as he appeared, he also looked really, really mad. Fortunately, the bald man was still up by the SUV and too far away to be any threat, but Granger looked angry enough to kill.

Finn and I looked at each other, but neither one of us needed to say a word. I reached down, unleashed Plankton, then the three of us just took off, running fast toward the far end of the spit. Plankton barked with joy, because even though Finn and I were scared to death, to him it was all a game.

"Stop!" Granger shouted behind us, but we didn't slow a bit. Plankton got to the end way before Finn and I, and he jumped around happily, hoping we might race back the other way. As Finn lay his fly rod down behind the palmetto log where it was out of sight, I picked up Plankton and then we ran straight into the Raccoon River, the water coming up to our chests. My breath froze in my lungs as I felt the cold, and Plankton growled a loud complaint as his belly touched the water, even though the rest of him stayed dry in my arms.

When we reached the other side, we staggered up the bank then turned to look back. Just as we had hoped, Granger stopped when he came to the river. He looked across at us for a long moment, his eyes boiling with rage. Finally he shouted, "We're not done here. I know what you two look like, and I've got a very long memory. You kids are gonna be sorry you stuck your noses in my business."

Not knowing exactly why I did it, I looked at Granger and stuck out my tongue.

14.

With our clothes soaked and the stiff wind making us feel even colder, we made our way through the bushes that bordered the river. As we came through the thin strip of undergrowth that was thankfully much thinner than the maritime forest on the landward side of the spit, we came to a sudden halt.

We were in someone's backyard. A short distance away stood a large house with lots of big windows. The owners must have been digging a swimming pool because there was a really big hole in the ground behind the house with a huge pile of dirt beside it. Right away I tensed, expecting to hear somebody yelling at us, telling us to get off their property, or maybe even letting their rottweiler out to chase us away. I held onto Plankton, thinking right at that moment a dogfight wasn't something we needed.

I was still looking for the best avenue to get out of there when Finn said, "Weird."

I glanced over at him, but rather than crouching down like I was, he was standing in plain sight with his arms wrapped around his chest, shivering and looking up at the house.

"What?" I whispered.

"Nobody lives here."

"What?" I asked again, but then I took another quick look around, saw the long grass in the yard, no curtains in any of the windows, plus a lot of the glass panes had those tags that come with new windows but that people take off when the actually live in a house.

"Phew," I said, letting myself relax for half a second before another idea occurred to me. "If nobody lives here, then maybe there's nothing to stop Granger from coming after us here."

"Yeah," Finn agreed. "We gotta move."

We hurried out of the backyard, past the big pile of dirt and the hole where the pool was going, and as we walked down the driveway toward the street both of us were hoping to spot a person working in their yard, or maybe a car in front of another of the houses in the neighborhood indicating that people might be home. We just wanted to find people somewhere nearby who could be witnesses, so Granger and the bald guy wouldn't be able to do anything bad to us.

We were on a dead-end street with the house we'd come up behind being the last one. Immediately we hurried to the corner and turned right in the general direction of Poppy's house, but as we went past the other houses, we saw the same signs of emptiness. Almost right away, Plankton began growling for me to put him down.

"This isn't about you," I told him, but he growled again, telling me he didn't care what I thought. I put him down but leashed him.

The houses we walked past were big and new and expensive, but there were no signs of people. Everywhere the grass was overgrown, and several houses had dumpsters sitting in driveways. It was obvious that these houses were finished, or very nearly finished, but it was also obvious that they were all empty.

Finn and I were still freezing in the chilly air, and our clothes felt like icicles against our skin. We were walking faster and faster, neither of us saying what we feared, but both of us cutting frequent glances up the road as we kept checking for a big black SUV that would mean trouble. I was now regretting my decision to stick my tongue out at Granger when we'd made it safely across the river. What if that was the reason he would decide to keep chasing us?

We passed maybe thirteen or fourteen of the same big houses, all deserted. There were more houses down a couple other streets, but we didn't bother checking them out. The whole place was a ghost town. Finally, up ahead we could see where the road curved out of sight.

Finn quickened his pace almost to a run. "I bet that's the entrance where this development hits the county road," he said as I started trotting to keep up. Plankton ran, pulling at his leash, hoping we could go faster.

We came around the curve, but then Finn

stopped dead in his tracks. When I caught up to him, I could see why. Ahead we could see the front bumper of what appeared to be a big black car that was sitting in the middle of the road. Fortunately for us, a fat old live oak cut off the driver's view in our direction.

"I think that's them," he whispered.

Fear spiked in my stomach. Granger had us bottled in, and he knew it. That road was the only way out of here. Finn and I both looked into the heavy undergrowth to our right, a thick maritime forest, as dense as what grew on the back side of the spit. It was a perfect privacy screen for this development, and also a security barrier because it looked impossible to get through without a chainsaw or machete.

Plankton started to growl again, and thinking he was about to bark and give us away, I picked him up and tried to hush him. "We don't need to hear from you," I said.

"What do we do now?" I asked Finn.

"Go back the way we came," Finn said.

I nodded, even though the thought of getting back into the cold river made my skin crawl. We both turned and started jogging back toward the house we had first seen. Going up the driveway and then back around the dirt pile, a few seconds later, both Finn and I were wading back across the river, both of us uttering loud groans as the cold water rose to our armpits and soaked us anew.

When we came out of the water onto the spit, I put Plankton down and let him run,

Finn retrieved his fly rod, then we started to run along the hard sand back toward the path that would take us out to the road and from there to Poppy's house. We slowed when we neared the path, staying on the hard sand near the water until we could look down the newly gouged track and make sure no cars were waiting to ambush us.

When we saw it was clear, we raced up the path, ran along the county road and turned into the first street of houses we came to, grateful to see people out walking dogs and doing yard work. Several of the folks we passed gave us odd looks, seeing a Jack Russell and two kids who had clearly been swimming in their clothes on a day that was definitely not yet warm enough for swimming. We just waved and kept up our fast jog toward Poppy's house.

When we finally got there, we burst into the kitchen where Martha was hard at work making dinner.

"Can we p-p-please have some hot chocolate?" I asked, shivering.

Martha turned from rolling dough out on a big wooden board, looked at us and her eyes widened. "What were you two doing? Swimming?"

"We kind of fell in," I lied.

She looked through the glass door and saw the fly rod Finn had left outside. "You started to get caught in the riptide," she said, making up her mind about what must have happened. She swung her eyes to me. "You both could have been drowned. You know never to go into the water down at the tip of the spit."

"I know," I said. "I just had to grab Finn and help him get to shore. Please don't tell Poppy."

"I should," Martha said, her jaws flexing and her blue eyes burning. Then she seemed to rethink it and said, "Lucky for you he's gone to town. Besides, he's got enough on his mind that he doesn't need you two worrying him." She nodded to herself, coming to a decision. "I'll make some hot chocolate. While I do, you two jump in the shower. Callie, show your friend to the guest room. There's a big bathrobe on the back of the door. He can put that on. Bring me your clothes, and I'll put them in the dryer."

Finn and I hurried out of the kitchen before Martha changed her mind. I pointed him to the guest room, then went to my room and got into the most wonderful hot shower I had ever had. Afterward, dressed in dry clothes, I was waiting outside the guestroom door as Finn came out wearing a fuzzy white bathrobe that came almost all the way to the floor.

"You look like a polar bear," I laughed.

"Don't care what I look like. At least I feel warm," he said.

As we turned together to walk toward the kitchen and our hot chocolate, I asked the question that had been digging into my brain ever since I warmed up enough to think. "What do you think was in that plastic envelope?"

"I've been wondering the same thing," Finn said. "The guy sure freaked out."

"It looked old," I said.

"Ooooh, maybe a treasure map," Finn mocked.

"Seriously, what do you think it could have been?"

"No clue."

"Well, I know what I'm doing for the rest of the afternoon," I said.

"What?"

"Research."

"Count me out."

I looked at Finn, surprised. It was another answer he'd given me that didn't seem to make sense.

I wanted to ask him why he'd said that, but something hard in his expression made me bite back my words.

Back in the kitchen, we drank the hot chocolate. When we finished, Finn's clothes were still in the dryer, so I went to my bedroom and brought my laptop out onto the porch. "You don't have to do anything," I said, "but I'm going to try and figure out what's going on. That paper must be something about the spit, something that was so important Granger would have killed that turtle to get it back."

"How do you know it said anything about the spit?" Finn asked.

"Logical deduction," I said. "The way he was reading it right there on the beach, it *has* to be about to the spit."

Finn shrugged, seeming to agree, or at least

not disagree, and while he flipped through Poppy's latest issue of *Sports Illustrated*, I got busy on Google searching for information. After about twenty minutes of trying, I sat back in frustration.

"I can't find anything on Buccaneer's Spit," I said."

"Can't you ask your grandfather? I'm sure he knows a lot about the place, after all he owns it."

I shook my head. "He hasn't told me he's selling. You're the one who told me. He's been acting kind of weird, and I feel like . . . I don't know, like asking him would be wrong."

"What about that lady who works for your grandfather?" Finn asked.

"Martha?"

"Hasn't she lived around here for a long time?"

"I think so."

"You mind if I ask her?"

"That might be better," I said.

We took our empty mugs back into the kitchen where Martha was still working on dinner. "Thank you for the hot chocolate," I said.

She glanced around. "I just hope hot chocolate and your showers keep you from getting colds." She nodded to Finn. "I checked your clothes a minute ago, and they're almost done."

"Thank you," Finn said, then continued, "I'd like to ask a question about some local history if that would be okay."

Martha wiped her hands on her apron and turned all the way around to face us. "If I know the answer. Shoot."

"Well, it's about Buccaneer's Spit," Finn said. "Are there any stories about the place?"

"What kind of stories?" Martha asked.

Finn shrugged. "You know, interesting stories that would make it sort of different from other places around here."

Martha started to shake her head, but then stopped. "Well, during the war—if you want to go back that far—there was a small navy base. I'm pretty sure it was right there on the spit, but there's nothing left any more. Nothing ever happened there—no fighting or anything. I think they just fueled up small boats that did shore patrol. I remember playing on that beach when I was little and seeing all the old stuff the Navy left behind after the war, but it's all gone now, either buried, carted off, or rusted away. Is that the kind of stories you're talking about?"

"Exactly," Finn said. "Are there any others you can think of?"

Martha shook her head then turned back to her cooking. "I'm afraid not. This is a pretty quiet place."

"I have a question," I said. "How come the spit was cheap enough for Poppy and Grandma to afford? They're not rich."

Martha nodded, then turned back around. "Like I said, the stuff that wasn't carted off or left to rust got buried. I think that's the reason. Some say there are old fuel tanks and maybe even old ammunition buried there. It was said nobody could build on it for that reason. I guess you couldn't have people living on top of that stuff."

Finn nodded, but I could tell he had something else on his mind. A moment later, he pulled his clothes out of the dryer even though Martha insisted they weren't fully dry. Finn ignored her worries that they were still damp and hurried off to the guest bathroom to get changed.

"That is a peculiar boy," Martha said, once Finn was well out of earshot.

"Why do you say that?" I asked, feeling for some strange reason like I wanted to defend him.

"He doesn't seem to be able to relax. He always seems like he's about to rush off."

I started to say something more, but right then Finn rushed in still buttoning his shirt. "Thank you very much for drying my clothes and for the incredibly delicious hot chocolate. It was the best I've ever tasted," he said to Martha. Even though a couple minutes earlier she had told me she thought he was an odd duck, now that she'd been given such a big compliment, she beamed at him as if he was the nicest boy she had ever met.

"I think we should go to the library," Finn said to me.

15.

I tried not to show my surprise at the idea of Finn wanting to get near books. I was about to say as much when Martha, having overheard what Finn said, repeated, "Library? What a nice idea!"

Finn looked at me and shrugged. "You want to come?"

I could see from the look in his eyes that he wanted me to say "yes," so figuring I had nothing better to do, I nodded. "Don't we have to get a ride?" I asked, thinking there wasn't a library anywhere close.

Finn shook his head. "We can walk there."

We left the house a few minutes later, and Finn led the way, claiming to know exactly where he was going.

"We really are going to the library?" I asked after we'd gone about a half mile.

"Yes."

"And you're sure you know where it is?"

"Yes."

"Isn't that kind of odd for a kid who hates to read?"

"Sometimes you don't have a choice."

"Even on vacation?"

"Yes," he muttered.

Still not getting it, I asked, "Who makes you read on vacation?"

Instead of answering, Finn just looked at me. He did not slow down.

After about another half mile, we came to the library building and went inside. To my great shock, the woman behind the lending desk smiled and waved to Finn like she knew him, but he seemed not to see her.

"Finn, there's a lady waving at you."

His shoulders tensed up, but he turned his head. "Hi," he whispered, waving back, clearly not wanting to talk to her.

We headed back through the rows of books, all the way to the rear of the building where a large section was set off from the rest of the library by a glass wall. A door led through the glass wall, and another woman sat at a desk beside the door.

"This is where they have stuff on local history," Finn whispered.

Again, I wondered how a book-hater knew so much about the library, but this time I didn't ask.

As we approached the woman's desk, she looked up and smiled. "How can I help you?"

"We're looking for information on the Navy base that used to be here during World War II," Finn said.

"What kind of information?" the lady asked. "Do you want newspaper articles or books?"

Finn glanced sideways at me. "I guess we want both, don't we, Callie?"

"Yes," I said, not knowing why we wanted either one.

The lady stood, led us to the door into the glass room, then put the card that hung around her neck in front of a scanner. The door clicked, the woman opened it and stood aside as we walked through.

Inside the air was cool enough to give me goosebumps as we followed the woman to a machine that she explained was a microfilm reader. "You stay right here and let me get the microfilms from that period," she said.

She left and returned a couple minutes later with some small canisters and loaded one of them into the reader. "This is the first one. It covers our local paper for the year 1940. I also have the films for every year until peace was signed in 1945."

Finn stood and looked at me as he waited for me to sit down in front of the machine. "I guess I'm doing the research," I said.

"You are."

I shook my head and felt a rising annoyance, but I went ahead and sat. "Why is this stuff important?" I whispered to Finn. "I thought Martha already told us everything we needed to know."

"She told us what she'd heard from other people, but she doesn't really know," Finn said. "Don't you want to know for sure if something happened on the spit during World War II that explains Granger's reaction when his paper blew into the water?"

I had to admit that my own curiosity was now burning, so I swallowed my complaints and ran the machine as we went through all the war years. Unfortunately, there was nothing at all about a Navy base anywhere nearby. I was about to give up when Finn said, "You know, I bet the papers weren't allowed to say anything about military bases during the war."

"Which means if there are articles about it, I bet they're from after the war," I said.

"Good idea," Finn said. "That's why you're doing the research." He turned and went to give the lady back the microfilms we had already looked at and asked to see the ones that covered the several years after the war.

He came back a minute later with 1946-1950, and sure enough in 1949 there was an article about how the "old Navy base" was being shut down because there was no longer any need for inshore coastal patrols by small boats. Unfortunately, the article didn't say anything about exactly where the base was located, or how big it was, or what was there.

I pushed away from the machine and looked at Finn. "This is giving us less than Martha," I said.

"Yeah, I know," he muttered. "Still, that paper had to mean something big to Granger."

"But what?"

Fitz shook his head. "We still don't know anything about Desmond Granger. Maybe if you keep reading, we can find out something important."

I shot him a sideways glance. "If *I* keep reading?"

From the way he kept staring at the screen over *my* shoulder, Finn didn't seem to have heard *me*. I felt *my* cheeks turning red. Nice that I was taking on the role of his personal assistant. I wasn't the kind of girl who let boys boss *me* around, and I was going to have to find a way to let him know that. I thought about laying it out for him, right then, in all caps, bold, and italic, but I had to admit I was as curious as he was about Granger, so I bit *my* tongue and kept going through the material.

We quickly got to more recent years, when the microfilm of the local papers changed to digital, but I kept on doing the reading. Skimming through month after month of local news, stories about beach erosion, new roads being approved, a big fight about a new school building, we saw Granger's name mentioned a few times along with names of other developers, but that was it.

Then, when we were on the very last year, a headline jumped out. "Local Developer Skating On Edge," it said. I looked at the date and saw that the article, written about six months earlier, described how Desmond Granger had built a bunch of super expensive "spec" homes on the beach, but the slowdown in the economy had caused them not to sell.

I pointed to a map in the article that

showed the houses right next to a small river.
"I think those are the same houses we saw
this morning," I said to Finn.

He bent over my shoulder and looked carefully
at the picture. "They have to be," he agreed.

"I don't think people were living in any of
them," I said.

"Not the ones we saw, so I guess they're
still for sale."

"Yeah," I went on, "and the article says the
banks that lent Granger the money to build
them wanted their money back. They were
threatening to take the houses if Granger
couldn't pay them."

"Are there more articles? Keep looking"

"Oh, yes, sir," I said sarcastically.

"Please," he said, looking a little apologetic,
which confused and annoyed me even more.

I shook my head but kept going. The next
articles I found talked about how Granger was
suing the banks, claiming they were trying to
deny him credit in order to "steal" his property.
The last of the articles had been written
just a month or so earlier. It said Granger's
houses still weren't selling, and if things didn't
improve soon he would go bankrupt.

"So how does a guy who's going broke get
the money to pay your grandfather for the
spit?" Finn asked when I finished reading the
article to him.

"No idea," I said.

"So, try this on for size," Finn said. "Your
grandfather isn't some super rich guy who

could normally afford to buy a big piece of beachfront property, right?"

I nodded. "Yeah, Poppy was a school principal."

"Who did he buy the spit from?"

"The Navy, I think."

"So, the only reason that the Navy would sell Buccaneer's Spit much cheaper than all the other property up and down the coast, and the only reason bigshot developers weren't driving up the price is that Martha's right and there's something buried there that makes it impossible to build houses."

"Makes sense," I said.

Finn went on. "From the articles we read, it sounds like the Navy abandoned a whole lot of other little bases after the war. Martha said they left a lot of stuff to rust, right? Maybe they also forgot to dig up buried fuel tanks or even ammunition bunkers. Then, when they got ready to sell, they knew stuff was buried there, but they didn't remember where."

I nodded. "Which would be the reason the land was cheap."

"Exactly, because if somebody started digging around to lay a house foundation, they'd be liable to blow themselves up, or maybe puncture one of those old tanks and leak oil or diesel fuel all over the beach and the ocean. If that happened, they'd kill a lot of fish and birds and turtles, and they'd have to do an incredibly expensive cleanup."

I concentrated, trying to keep up with Finn's thoughts. Then I snapped my fingers. "So, if Poppy is selling because he needs the money, then Granger is probably paying a lot lower price than he'd pay for other beachfront because of the buried tanks."

Finn nodded. "Because if somebody wanted to build houses there, they'd have to pay for a really expensive environmental cleanup."

I went on. "Which Granger can't afford because we know from these articles that he's really hard up for money."

Finn gave me a big smile. "But if he'd found a piece of paper that showed him where the bad stuff is buried then maybe he'd figure he could sneak the stuff out secretly."

I nodded excitedly. "Because if he could dig up the fuel tanks or old ammunition secretly, then sneak them out without anybody knowing, he wouldn't have to pay for a proper environmental cleanup."

Finn nodded, and my heart started to beat faster. "I bet that was the paper that blew into the water. If we could prove there's a map showing where all the bad stuff is buried, we could tell Poppy."

"Exactly," Finn said. "So, even if he has to sell the spit, he might be able to sell it to other, nicer people for more money than Granger's offering."

But then as fast as my mood had improved, it crashed again when I thought about the words I'd overheard coming out of Poppy's office. "But I think Poppy needs the money really soon. And even if we know there's a map, we can't prove it because a turtle ate it."

"We'll keep working on it," Finn said, making an obvious effort to cheer me up. "Tomorrow we're supposed to get our tour of the turtle hospital, but after that, we can go back to the spit and maybe figure out where that stuff is buried. It's possible that if we just keep our eyes peeled, Granger will lead us to it."

I nodded, but I didn't really think Finn's idea would work. Then I thought about our upcoming turtle hospital visit. "I'm just *soooo* excited to go to the turtle hospital," I scoffed. "I'm sure that's going to be just fascinating."

"Put away your New York City 'I've-seen-everything' attitude and try to go with an open mind. If that turtle they rescued today is the same one that ate the plastic bag, maybe there's even a chance."

I felt my cheeks start to burn, unsure why I'd spoken like a cynic when, truth be told, I was actually looking forward to seeing the turtle hospital myself. "A chance for what?" I asked, trying for a nicer tone.

"A chance to get a look at that piece of paper."

"Yeah, right," I scoffed. "And how likely is it that it's the same turtle?"

"Actually, very likely," Finn said. "It's still early for the turtles to return for nesting. That one we saw may have been the first one back to this beach. That probably means there aren't very many new arrivals in the turtle hospital."

16

The next morning as he had planned, Poppy drove us to the aquarium, a large, modern building located near downtown Charleston on the banks of the Cooper River. He walked us to the ticket window, showed his membership card and told the person there that he had arranged for us to get a private tour the Sea Turtle Hospital.

"Are you coming, too, Mr. Morrisey?" Finn asked as the ticket person waved us inside.

Poppy's lips smiled, but his eyes looked sad, as if Finn inviting him to come with us reminded him of the terrible thing he was doing to the turtles by selling the spit to Desmond Granger. "Thank you," he said, his voice hoarse, "but I've got another meeting in just a couple minutes. Another time, perhaps."

Poppy left, and Finn and I followed the ticket person's directions up the ramp and into the main entrance, where we found a woman waiting for us. "I'm Pamela Ravenel, director of conservation," she said. "You must be Callie and Finn."

She gave us a quick tour of the main areas,

telling us about the aquarium, when it was built, how many different exhibits it held and how it was more focused on education than tourism. Pamela showed us the huge tank with big sharks and other large fish, but she must have noticed that both Finn and I were a bit antsy because she said, "I bet you're ready to see the Sea Turtle Hospital."

"Yes!" we both said, as we followed her to a doorway marked private. Despite what I had said to Finn a day earlier about not being interested in seeing the Turtle Hospital, I felt an unexpected surge of excitement as Pamela punched a number into the keypad in the wall beside the door, led us through, and then down a concrete staircase. At the bottom we entered a long, high ceilinged room with a number of large tanks that looked like small versions of above-the-ground swimming pools.

Pamela explained that each tank was intended to hold a single sea turtle while it recovered from whatever was wrong with it. She pointed out the filtering equipment that kept each tank's water clean and at just the right temperature.

"What's wrong with the turtles?" I asked.

"Some are ill, some are weak and malnourished, some have been hit by boats. Also during the winter we have turtles that are cold-stunned when the water is quickly cooled by a cold snap. Normally turtles move southward in fall and winter as water grows colder, but sometimes a very fast moving cold front will drop the water temperature too quickly for them to escape it."

As she talked she led us past the first tanks and told us about the specific problems each turtle patient was experiencing. "This first turtle was picked up in very poor condition. It was lethargic, and its shell was weak as if it hadn't been eating for some time. We thought it acted cold-stunned, but the water was too warm for that, so we did a CT scan."

"A what?" I asked.

"A CT scan, something they might do in a hospital on humans. It's a very advanced type of X-ray that gives us a cross-sectional image of a turtle's body. We can look for broken bones, infections, tumors, or foreign bodies."

Finn and I shared a quick glance. "What kind of foreign bodies?" I asked.

"Plastic bags and balloons are probably the most common. People who are careless with their trash sometimes throw plastic bags into the sea, or maybe let them blow away. Sea turtles have very poor eyesight, and one of their primary sources of food is jellyfish. Unfortunately, to a turtle, plastic bags very often look just like jellyfish. Even more unfortunately, when a turtle eats a plastic bag, it usually just stays in the turtle's gut, and often it blocks the turtle's ability to pass other food through its system. Plastic bags can easily kill turtles."

"Was that what was wrong with this turtle?" I asked.

Pamela nodded. "Exactly. Our CT scan showed several foreign bodies in this turtle's stomach."

"So, what did you do?" Finn asked.

"We performed an endoscopy," Pamela said. "We sedated the turtle and used a surgical device to go down its throat, then we used the same device to pull out the blockages. In this turtle's case, it was a plastic bag and also one of those shiny birthday balloons that had drifted out over the water and then lost its helium." She pointed to a glass jar on a shelf beside the turtle's tank that held a tan plastic bag and a brightly colored balloon.

"Wow," I said, thinking about how often I had gone to birthday parties where there had been tons of helium filled balloons. Some of those balloons always got away and floated up into the sky. It had always seemed so innocent watching a balloon drift out of sight, getting smaller and smaller as it rose up, but now I realized those balloons weren't really so innocent at all. They were things that could kill turtles, and maybe other creatures, as well.

"Plastic trash is a much bigger problem than many people realize," Pamela went on. "It's estimated that there are some five trillion pieces of plastic trash in the oceans today."

"Did you say 'trillion'?" I asked.

Pamela nodded. "I did. And as I'm sure you know, plastic doesn't rot or decay like organic materials. In addition to being eaten by turtles, birds, and other animals, it forms huge 'trash islands' in the Atlantic, Pacific, and Indian oceans."

I shook my head, trying to imagine how horrible a trash island must look and how terrible it must be for wild creatures.

"But while that's a big problem, it's not the only problem," Pamela went on. "Over time, while the plastic does not decay, it does break down into tinier and tinier pieces, and some of it is eventually eaten by lots of species of sea creatures, such as shrimp and clams and all kinds of game fish."

Finn nodded. "Which means we end up eating that plastic, if we eat shrimp, clams, or fish."

"*Exactly!*" Pamela said. "You also eat that plastic if you eat predator fish like tuna or swordfish that have eaten those same shrimp, clams, or other smaller fish."

As she talked, she led us past several more tanks, telling us in each case what was wrong with the turtle inside it. When we were approaching the back of the room, Pamela pointed out one of the last tanks and said, "Here is a turtle we just got in yesterday. It looks like the shell has been struck by something like a boat prop."

I felt a quick flutter of excitement in my belly. "Can I ask where the turtle came from?"

"Near a beach a few miles outside of Charleston where turtles often nest."

"Was the beach called Buccaneer's Spit?" Finn asked.

"I'm pretty sure it was," Pamela said.

Finn and I looked at each other again. "Finn is the one who called it in," I said. "We were on that beach yesterday. We saw the turtle's head come out of the water, and a minute later we saw a boat running close to shore. Suddenly, one of its engines hit something and jumped out of the water. Finn knew what it was right away."

I might have told her more of the story, all about the piece of paper in the plastic bag, the boat and the horrible man who was going to ruin Buccaneer's Spit, but I remembered that my grandfather was a member of the aquarium board. It was possible that whatever we said here would get back to him, so I bit my tongue.

Pamela didn't seem to realize my story had been cut short because she was smiling at Finn. "You called for this turtle's rescue? Really?"

Finn nodded, but he looked embarrassed by all the sudden attention.

Trying to take the pressure off Finn, I pointed to where the cut on the turtle's shell was all closed up. "What did you do?"

"We gave it antibiotics because the flesh beneath the shell needs to heal cleanly, and we need to prevent infections. Then, because this cut was pretty bad, we used a special epoxy and some bonding material to glue the split sections of shell back together, just like gluing a crack in a fiberglass canoe."

In the next instant Pamela seemed to get

another idea, because she said, "We're also going to do a CT scan on this turtle, and we're just about ready. Since you were such good Samaritans, would you like to watch?"

"Yes!" we both exclaimed.

Pamela told us it was going to take a bit of time for the hospital vets and technicians to prepare the turtle for the procedure, so she suggested we walk around the rest of the aquarium and she would come get us when they were ready.

Finn and I went upstairs and spent a good bit of time gazing into the huge ocean tank in the center of the building. Big sharks glided slowly along the glass walls, along with snook, grouper, barracuda, tuna, and other large fish. At one point a diver entered the tank and fed some of the fish by hand.

By the time Pamela came to get us and brought us back to the Turtle Hospital, they had already moved the turtle to the CT scan room. She showed us the machine and explained how it worked, then we all stood behind a big shield while the vet took X-rays of the turtle's stomach and digestive tract.

As the computer was finishing up the X-rays, I asked, "Can you tell whether the turtle is male or female?"

The vet, who Pamela had introduced as Dr. Cribb, turned to us. "This turtle is female. She weighs three hundred sixty pounds, and she is probably thirty to thirty-five years old."

"Is that old for a turtle?" I asked.

"It's old, but not ancient," Dr. Cribb said. "We believe loggerheads can live fifty years or so."

"How old do turtles have to be before they start laying eggs and breeding?" Finn asked.

"Good questions," Dr. Cribb said with a smile. "Probably twenty or twenty-five, but nobody really knows for sure. Some scientists say earlier, but some say even later."

"That must have something to do with why they are endangered," Finn said. "If a turtle has to survive twenty-five years before it can help make baby turtles, then that seems like a long time."

"When you think of all the risks a turtle faces, it is a very long time," Dr. Cribb agreed.

As soon as the X-rays were ready, it took only a second to spot the problem. Dr. Cribb pointed at a dark shape on the screen. "Right there," she said. "That's the turtle's stomach, and that square thing I'm pointing at is almost certainly a plastic bag or something similar. No food can get past it."

I felt a shiver of worry for the turtle. "What can you do?" I asked.

"We'll have to do an endoscopy, and hopefully the thing that's in there will come out as easily as it went down."

We watched as four technicians lifted the turtle off the CT scan table and carried it to the treatment room next door. The treatment table looked a lot like the one in my own doctor's office, only about four times bigger. In fact, everything in the room seemed oversized, but that made perfect sense when they were taking care of three-hundred-pound patients.

Dr. Cribb gave the turtle a shot to make it calm, then examined the repair on its shell for a moment while she waited for the anesthesia to take effect. Once the turtle appeared to be sleeping, she brought out a long contraption that she told us was an endoscope. She worked it into the turtle's mouth, then very carefully pushed it farther and farther down the turtle's throat, the whole time looking at a screen on the wall that showed what the end of the endoscope was seeing.

"Does this hurt the turtle?" I asked.

"It could," Dr. Cribb said. "The camera helps me make sure that if I hit resistance I don't push too hard and puncture something." As she talked, she pushed the endoscope deeper along what looked like a wet, pink tube. "The camera also lets me see the thing I need to get out," she went on, speaking slowly and pausing as she concentrated on her procedure.

After several more seconds, she nodded and said, "Yup," speaking to herself.

We watched the scope get closer and closer to a large, shiny object. When the camera appeared to be right up against the object, Dr. Cribb moved a different set of controls, doing what looked like the same movement over and over.

"What are you doing?" I asked after the third or fourth try.

"Trying to snag the thing," Dr. Cribb said. "I need to grab the plastic without snagging the stomach lining." She finally let out a little, "Yes," as her scope got a grip on the object.

"Strange," she said after a few more seconds.

"What's strange?" I asked.

"This plastic—and I think that's what it is— isn't as shapeless as most of the bags we find. I'm going to have to be really careful getting it out."

Working slowly and very carefully, Dr. Cribb used the controls to get the plastic thing folded roughly in half, then backed the scope out the turtle's throat. It took several minutes, and she had to stop a number of times to make sure that the edges of whatever she was pulling weren't cutting into the soft skin of the turtle's throat.

Finally, she brought out the last of the endoscope, then reached in with her fingers and pulled out a plastic bag. She gave it to one of her helpers, who took it over to the sink, rinsed it off and gave it back to her.

Unlike the crumpled plastic grocery bag and the collapsed balloon we had seen in the jar near the first turtle's tank, this bag was flat. Also, there was something inside the bag, and seeing it made my heart beat really fast.

The vet looked at the bag for a few seconds, then shrugged. "You never know what a turtle will eat. They're not the smartest creatures on the planet."

Following the technicians as they once again

carried the turtle back to its tank and gently lowered it into the water, the vet turned to look at us. "We still have one very important task to perform," she said with a smile.

"What's that?" Finn asked.

"We give a name to every turtle that comes in here, and this one doesn't yet have one. I think since you two called in the emergency, you should name it. Got any ideas?"

"You said it was a female, right?" Finn asked. The vet nodded.

"And you said she was bigger than average." The vet nodded again.

"How about Big Bertha?" Finn said.

The vet looked at me. "How do you feel about Big Bertha?"

"Sounds great," I said.

We thanked everyone again for giving us such a great tour and got ready to leave, but then I hesitated as if I was just thinking about it for the first time. "Do you think . . . would it be okay if we kept the plastic bag?" I asked.

"The one we just took out of Big Bertha?" The vet shrugged. "It's pretty gross and discolored, and we usually keep the objects we remove to show people." The vet raised her eyebrows and gave a shrug. "But since you're the ones who called it in, if you really want it." She walked over to the jar where one of the techs had put the plastic bag and pulled it out. She sniffed it and made a face but held it out. "Here," she said. "Your souvenir."

"Thank you."

I held the bag tight in my fingers as we went outside the aquarium and sat in the park where we waited for Poppy to pick us up.

"Great job getting the bag," Finn said. "I was afraid they'd want to keep it."

"Me, too," I said. "I didn't want to steal it, but I would have if I had to." I looked down at the plastic bag. "Should we open it here?"

"No," Finn said. "I think we should wait 'til we get back."

When Poppy pulled up to the curb and we jumped into his car, I made Finn sit in the front while I sat in the back, keeping the stinky plastic bag out of sight and as far away from Poppy as I could.

"What's that smell?" he asked when we had only gone a short distance.

"I think I stepped in something in the Turtle Hospital," I said, thinking whatever was on the bag smelled like rotten fish guts.

"Well, wash your shoes before you go in the house," Poppy said, shaking his head at the awful odor.

Poppy had invited Finn to eat with us. When we got home and Poppy went inside to see if lunch was ready, Finn and I stayed outside to supposedly wash the stink off our shoes, but my pulse was pounding with excitement at the promise of finally seeing what Desmond Granger had been so upset about losing.

17.

We hurried around the side of the house to where a solid wall of azaleas made an almost perfect hiding place. I took the plastic bag and carefully opened the top, nearly gagging as I made the mistake of breathing in. "It really does stink," I said.

Finn laughed. "I was worried your grandfather might even tell you to throw away your shoes before we got to the house."

"It really was a stinky trip," I said with a laugh. "Now let's see what all Granger's excitement was about."

Worming one finger into the bag, I ran it along the folded paper inside. As I did, I felt the dampness.

"Oh, no," I said. "There's a hole in the plastic."

Finn's eyes went wide with fear. "Is it ruined?"

"I can't tell yet, but it's definitely wet."

"Can you get the paper out without tearing it to bits?" Finn asked.

"I don't know. What should I do?"

"Just do your best."

I gently pushed my fingers into the bag as

far as they would go, then worked my thumb down on the other side of the paper. Pinching the paper between my thumb and finger, I tried to pull it out as gently as I could.

"I can't get my fingers in all the way. The paper's still stuck to the plastic," I said when it wouldn't budge.

"We need something long and skinny," Finn said. "Can you ask Martha if she's got something?"

I ran to the kitchen and asked Martha if she had a butter knife I could borrow.

She gave me a funny look. "What do you need a butter knife for?"

"I'm trying to clean something smelly off my shoes," I said because it was the only thing I could think of.

"We use butter knives for food." She reached into the garbage and came out with a used popsicle stick that she rinsed and dried off. "Try this," she said.

I rushed back outside to where Finn was holding the plastic bag, still wrinkling his nose at the smell. "Here," I said, using the stick to gently pry the paper away from the bag's sides. After a minute, I was able to pull the paper out of the bag.

"It didn't rip at all," Finn said.

"It's heavy paper," I said as I unfolded it carefully on the grass.

"What the heck?" Finn muttered as we stared in confusion. I had been expecting to see some kind of US Government document, but what we saw instead was a crude hand sketch drawn by somebody who wasn't much of an artist.

Along the top of the paper lay a wavy line. "If this is somebody's map, is that supposed to be the shore?" I asked.

"I guess." Finn said.

"Then here's the river," I said, running my finger along the bottom of the page where what had to be a river was bordered by a thick fringe of what looked like a third grader's idea of bushes and other maritime forest growth where several palmetto trees stuck up taller than everything else.

"You think that's really Buccaneer's Spit?" Finn asked, sounding very uncertain.

"It's impossible to know," I said. "This could have been drawn by a little kid. It could also be any spit of land anyplace warm enough to have things like palmetto trees."

"I think we have to assume it's Buccaneer's Spit because of the way Granger was using it. That means whatever was so special must be here." Finn pointed to a single palmetto tree that stood out from the others because it was drawn darker and taller. A line of small Xs ran from the palmetto tree to a bigger X.

"X marks the spot," Finn joked after a long silence. "What do you think is there?"

"No idea," I said.

"How old do you think it is?"

"Who knows," I said. "It looks to me like the kind of map somebody might have drawn if they were trying to remember where something was buried. Like, maybe some old sailor who was stationed here during the war."

Finn nodded, then pinched his nose like he was deep in thought. "Okay," he said. "That makes sense."

"And if your idea about the Navy leaving something buried is right, that must be what this is."

"And maybe it means there's just one big gas tank or ammunition storage place rather than a bunch of smaller ones. I don't know why, but I thought there would be a bunch of them. This actually makes more sense from Granger's point of view. If he's only got one thing to get rid of, it's a lot better for him, right?"

"Whatever's buried down there, it's a big deal to Granger," I said.

"So, what do we do with this map?"

I hesitated, thinking.

"Should we tell your grandfather?"

I shook my head. For some reason I hated the idea of telling Poppy that I knew about the sale of the spit. I knew he hated selling, so it had to mean that he really needed the money. Telling him about Granger's map would make him feel even worse, but it wouldn't save the spit.

"We need to try to understand what this map means before I talk to Poppy," I said at last.

"How're we gonna do that?" Finn asked.

"Simple. We use the map to beat Granger and we dig up whatever is buried under the big X."

Finn just looked at me in amazement. "You do realize that if Granger comes back onto the spit and sees that we're digging some kind of huge hole, he's gonna know exactly who has his map."

"So what?"

"Well, if what the paper said about Granger is accurate and he's about to go belly up, then he's probably pretty desperate. That means if he's trying to do something sneaky with your grandfather's land, he'll do anything he can to keep other people from knowing, especially if he intends to dig up something dangerous or dirty and sneak it off the spit so he can build houses here."

"We didn't steal his map. We found it. Even if he doesn't like that, what can he do?"

"For starters, he could sic that huge guy with the bald head on us."

Finn was right. That was a big problem, but no matter how afraid we were, we couldn't let Granger get away with what he was planning. "Okay," I said. "We have to let Granger buy the spit so Poppy gets the money, but then we have to do something." I asked. "We can't let Granger get away with whatever he's planning. Right?"

Finn looked at the ground and kicked some dirt with his shoe. "I guess not."

I thought for a few seconds, then nodded. "Okay, here's the plan. What time do your grandparents go to bed?"

"Ten or eleven?"

"Pretty much every night?"

"I think."

"Could you sneak out of your house without waking them up?"

Finn shrugged. "Probably. My bedroom's at the other end of the hall from theirs. Why?"

"We'll dig up whatever Granger's trying to find and figure out what it is without Granger seeing. Then we'll fill the hole back up before we leave so he doesn't know."

"What are we gonna dig with?"

I had to think for a moment. "Poppy has a couple big shovels in his garage. I'll sneak them out and hide them in the garden this afternoon."

"What about flashlights?" Finn asked.

"I can't carry everything. Do your grandparents have some?"

"I think so," Finn said.

It was obvious to me that he wasn't as eager to do this as I was, but then the spit wasn't *his* grandfather's property. I just hoped that I could keep him interested because I hated the idea of sneaking out all alone. "Well, try to hustle a couple flashlights out of your house before dinner and put them someplace where it'll be easy to find them in the dark. I mean, that shouldn't be too hard, right? They're small."

Finn nodded, but then he screwed his face up. "You know, in addition to sneaking out and bringing all the stuff we need, there's another problem. The map goes from a palmetto tree to some big X, right?"

"So?

"So, how many palmetto trees are on the spit? You have any idea?"

I shrugged, trying to picture the spit in my head and count the trees. I hadn't ever looked very closely. "More than one," I said.

"Try like ten or twelve, at least."

I ground my teeth in frustration, knowing Finn had to be right because he noticed stuff like that a lot more than me. I didn't say anything for a few moments, but then an idea came to me. "Okay, look, if Granger already knew where the thing was buried, he wouldn't have freaked out about losing his map, right?"

Finn looked at me, clearly not sure where I was going. "Yeah, I guess."

"Well, aren't most of the palmetto trees closer to the beach side than the river side of the spit?"

"Yeah."

"And that guy with the X-ray machine already went over all the beach side of those trees, right? So, we don't waste our time digging anywhere near the beach side. We work around the trees on the river side. How many do you think that would be?"

Finn shrugged. "Maybe two or three."

"And the extra bonus is that we'll be digging back in the bushes. That will make it even easier to hide what we've done."

Finn seemed to brighten at that. "Okay, so, if we find what's down there, we let Granger buy the spit from your grandfather, then we make sure we tell people about what we found, so Granger can't sneak it out."

"Exactly," I said.

"But what if it's something really bad?"

"Like environmentally bad?" I asked.

He nodded. "Like oil tanks that are about to leak, or maybe even an unexploded bomb. I mean, who knows what it could be, right?"

"As long as we let people know, we'll be doing a good thing. And we'll be protecting the spit."

Finn looked at me and shook his head. "This is pretty intense."

I shrugged. "Definitely, but it's also kind of fun, right? I mean aren't you curious?"

A slow smile spread across Finn's face. "Yeah."

18.

With our plans made, we put away the map, and I snuck the shovels from the garage and hid them behind the azalea bed. We went into the house for lunch, and afterward, Finn went home. I spent the rest of the afternoon reading and trying to ignore how slowly the clock seemed to move as I thought about the night's special plans.

Poppy and I finally sat down to another of Martha's delicious dinners. Poppy was still as strangely silent as he had been ever since I arrived in South Carolina, maybe even more so. He seemed to grow sadder and sadder with every day that went by, and I knew that it had everything to do with selling Buccaneer's Spit.

A part of me wanted to be angry with him for keeping it a secret, but another part was scared. What terrible problem did he have? What had happened to make him lose so much money? If selling the spit made him this miserable, he had to *really* need that money. Those thoughts made me even more determined to try and find out what Granger thought was buried there.

Even Plankton seemed to sense Poppy's sadness because he didn't bark or run around the way he usually did when nobody was paying him enough attention. He just lay curled up at Poppy's feet, where every couple of minutes he would look up with questioning eyes, as if checking to see if Poppy had gotten any happier.

I wished that I could call my mom or dad and ask them what Poppy's problem was, but of course I couldn't. I didn't even know if they were home in New York or somewhere else. I only knew that they had needed to "have some time to themselves to work some things out." Which meant I couldn't call them up in the middle of their divorce discussions and expect them to tell me anything.

After dinner, when we went into the family room to watch TV, I kept a careful eye on Poppy to make sure that he followed his normal schedule. Nervous that he might stay up later than usual because his mood had made it impossible for him to sleep, I was relieved when he got up from the couch earlier than normal. "You don't mind putting yourself to bed, do you, Callie?"

"No, Poppy, I'm fine. If you're tired you should go to bed."

"Good because I'm a bit more tuckered out than usual tonight. I'm sorry to be poor company." He shot a look down at Plankton, as if hoping the Jack Russell would come with him that night, even though he usually slept with me because I was the only one who let him up on the bed.

"Go ahead," I told Plankton, but the dog just gave me a look that suggested I mind my own business.

I tried not to show the nervousness I felt because I was afraid that if Plankton ended up coming to bed with me, there would be no way I could sneak out without having him make a lot of noise and probably waking Poppy.

Poppy stood there and looked at Plankton for a few more seconds, as if giving him a chance to change his mind. "I guess Plankton has decided to sleep with you tonight," he said, tossing us both a wave and heading off to bed.

As soon as Poppy disappeared, Plankton hopped up on the couch and cuddled beside me. I looked down at him. "I've got things to do tonight, and you can't come," I said softly.

Plankton looked up at me, twisted his head slightly as if questioning how I could be foolish enough to think I could keep him from doing whatever he wanted. Then he seemed to shrug and settled back down for a short snooze.

I turned off the TV and read a book until I started to yawn, then I let Plankton out one more time and turned off the lights. On my way down the long hallway to my bedroom at the far end, I stopped in front of Poppy's door and looked down at Plankton, who had followed at my heels. Through the thick door, I could hear the sound of Poppy snoring, which meant he was sound asleep. "Want to go in?" I whispered to the dog.

Plankton just gazed up at me as if he knew *exactly* what I was planning and had no interest in being left behind. I scowled down at him, but after a few more seconds, I gave up and headed to my room. Plankton's claws clicked behind me, making an almost happy sound, as if he couldn't wait to sneak out.

19.

That night in total darkness, I woke to a strange beeping sound. For several seconds I didn't know what it was, until I suddenly remembered I had put my phone under my pillow. Without raising the pillow, I slid a hand underneath and pushed on the screen until the alarm went silent. It was midnight.

Propping on my elbow, I blinked sleep from my eyes, then turned on the bedside lamp only to see Plankton sitting up beside me on the bed, his ears pricked and his dark eyes glittering with what seemed like excitement at the promise of an adventure.

"You're not coming," I muttered.

Plankton appeared to disagree, and he pawed my shoulder to let me know he was eager to get moving.

I scowled at him, but I climbed out of bed, pulled on blue jeans, sneakers, a long-sleeved shirt, and heavy sweatshirt to ward off the night chill, then opened my window. Earlier, just before dinner, I had loosened the screen to make sure it wouldn't make too much noise, and now I removed it, leaned it against the wall, and got ready to climb out.

As soon as I put one leg out the window, Plankton let out a low growl. When I looked back at him his head was cocked to one side like he was making sure I understood the threat; he was going to make an unholy racket if I dared to leave him behind. I sighed, pulled my leg back inside, but before I could even walk to the bed and pick him up, he leapt into my arms.

"You are a criminal dog," I whispered, as I swung him outside and let him jump to the ground where he turned in small circles to show his excitement. Fearing he might start barking with joy, I put my fingers to my lips and made a loud hushing noise. Plankton turned his head to one side again, seeming to sense my concern. Fortunately, he remained silent.

I dropped to the ground beside him, pulled the window back down, leaving just a crack so I could get my fingers under it and wedge it open again, then we started out. Right away I realized my mistake because I hadn't brought a leash, but it wouldn't have done me much good even if I'd remembered because the two shovels I had snuck out of the garage earlier were pretty much all I could carry.

Fortunately, most of the people where Poppy lived were retired, and they seemed to go to bed early. I didn't see a single light on in any of the houses other than outdoor lights, and there wasn't a bit of traffic. If a cop had come by, it would have been hard to explain why a kid my age was carrying two big spades down the road at one in the morning, and they almost certainly would have taken me home and woken up Poppy.

Adding to my nervousness, Plankton used his freedom to run into every yard we passed, lift his leg on a tree or bush and generally sniff his head off. Twice he set dogs barking inside the houses he was sniffing, and one time somebody even turned on their porch light to see what was going on. I didn't start to relax until we were past the last house and heading down to the public beach.

After a few more minutes of fast walking, I came to the path through the thick undergrowth that led to Buccaneer's Spit. Given the way the men in the truck had gouged it up, it was easy to spot even in the dark. I hurried along the path for a little way to get Plankton and me out of sight of any cars that happened to come along, then stopped. For a few seconds I thought I was totally alone, but then Plankton started growling.

Up ahead a shape stepped away from the bushes and into the path. I could barely see the person's silhouette in the moonlight. "You brought the dog?" Finn asked in amazement.

"I had no choice. If I left him he was going to bark and wake up my grandfather."

"I hope he doesn't do anything bad out here."

As if Plankton understood what Finn was saying, he let out another low growl.

"It's okay," I whispered, resting the spades on the ground long enough to give Plankton a pat on the back. "Did you bring the flashlights?"

A second later I saw a quick explosion of light as he turned one on and then off right away. "Better if we don't use them unless we absolutely have to," he said. "People might notice the light, and it also ruins our night vision."

We started down the path, letting the dull glow of moonlight on the churned-up sand show us the way. When we got to the beach, the light was brighter with moonlight reflecting off the water and the white sand. I could see the silhouettes of palmetto trees against the sky and realized Finn had been right. There were a number of them scattered throughout the maritime forest along the beach.

As if he was reading my mind, Finn whispered, "Not those. Over on the river side like we talked about."

I nodded. "Do you remember the number of Xs from the tree?"

"Twenty-five," he said.

"Even if we can find the right tree, how will we know what direction the Xs go?" I asked.

"They go toward the river."

Finn had definitely noticed more things than I did. I felt silly asking questions now that I should have thought of earlier, but I couldn't stop. "What if the tree in the map was here during World War II, but isn't here anymore?"

"Then we've got a problem," Finn said.

What Finn said gave me a bad feeling. "Maybe that's why Granger had that man run his X-ray machine all over the beach. Maybe he's already checked around all the trees that are still here and found nothing."

Finn stopped walking and turned to look at me. "Granger's guy only did the beach, right?"

"Maybe he did the other parts of the spit when we weren't here," I said.

"I don't think so. Like you said before, if he'd found what he was looking for he wouldn't have cared that his map blew into the water."

"I guess."

"So, like we talked about before, Granger did us a favor. He eliminated the beach as the place we need to look."

Earlier that afternoon, I had been the one trying to make sure Finn was willing to help, but now, I seemed to be the one losing heart because there were so many places where something could be buried. "It still leaves a big area to search," I said, gazing at the dark band of maritime forest with the silhouettes of palmetto trees sticking up.

"Boy, are you negative," Finn said. "You need to be a little more positive. Otherwise we should just quit and go back to bed."

He was right, but my hopes were still plummeting. Now, in the middle of the night everything seemed much more impossible than it had earlier. In the moonlight, with the wind coming off the sea and whispering loud across the sand and even louder through the thick wall of bushes that ran along the river, the spit looked so much bigger than it had in my imagination. I realized we probably didn't have a chance of finding what we were looking for. "We're just two people," I said. "Finding whatever is buried here could take months."

Finn shook his head. "Well, absolutely nothing's going to happen if we just stand here and find reasons why we won't succeed," he said, his tone suggesting he was running out of patience.

He turned and pointed toward the maritime forest. "Almost all those palmetto trees are close to the edge of the sand. I'm counting only three palmettos that grow farther back. "Like we agreed earlier, those are the ones we need to check out."

I wanted to stop being negative, but I had to point out one more problem. "Uh, even if we can get to them, there are, like, hundreds of bushes all around those trees. How are we gonna dig through the roots?"

He looked at me like he couldn't believe what a pain I was being. "One of them has to be different."

"Different? What are you talking about?"

He waved an impatient hand, grabbed one of the shovels from me, and started trudging down the sand. "Just come on."

The moment Finn started moving, Plankton took off, racing joyfully along the water's edge, then cutting up through the loose sand before turning sharply and shooting back toward the water. I shrugged, feeling none of Plankton's happiness, but I followed. After all, Finn was losing as much sleep and taking as much risk of getting caught as me. Even though it didn't seem like we had much chance of finding anything, I needed to see if his idea was any good.

We walked to the end of the spit, where I handed Finn a shovel, then picked up Plankton before we followed the land back along the river bank. Keeping a lookout for gators with every step, I was relieved not to see any, even though I also knew that not seeing gators didn't necessarily mean they weren't close by.

Finn came to a stop when we were opposite the first of the palmettos that grew deep in the forest of beach scrub. He walked back and forth, looking for some way to get through the bushes.

The branches here were stiff and incredibly tangled. They were too thick to push through and too stiff to break, and they wove together until they were like a wall. And some of them had big thorns.

"How do we get in there?" I asked after Finn had paced up and down a few times. "And even if we do, it's so thick. How are we ever going to count off twenty-five paces?"

"Forget that one. Next tree," he said and took off walking. I hurried to catch up.

The next palmetto offered the same problem, protected by an unbreakable rampart of hard branches. Even if we could somehow manage to get through the branches, we'd be unable to see anything, such as a poisonous snake before we stepped on it or a nasty spider before we stuck our hand in its web. The whole thing gave me the willies.

Finn had already headed off toward the last palmetto and was walking up and down looking for a way in. For my part, I held Plankton close and was pretty much back to where I had been a few moments earlier—out of hope and convinced we would never uncover Desmond Granger's tricks. I was about to suggest that we should quit, however, just as I opened my mouth, Finn stopped walking.

"I think there's a way in," he said.

20.

"You sure?" I peered over his shoulder at what appeared to be a solid rampart.

Finn took a step toward the gnarled branches. I thought that would be as far as he got, only to my amazement, he slipped through and disappeared. I still didn't move, expecting to hear him come to a dead stop a couple feet in.

Instead, I heard, "Come on, follow me," his voice faint, but sounding farther ahead than I would have thought possible.

Tucking Plankton under one arm, I pushed between the branches where I had seen Finn go in. I was surprised I could move forward without getting stabbed by thorns or having to claw my way with major effort. "Finn?" I called.

"Just keep coming," he said.

Following his voice, I moved through what had looked as impossibly thick and tangled as all the other scrub, until with one more step I stumbled free of the bushes into a small, hidden clearing. I came up behind him just as Finn, keeping his hand over the beam, turned on his flashlight, letting just enough light leak through his fingers to show just how big the clearing was. "This has to be it," he whispered.

Despite having convinced myself we weren't going to find anything, I felt a buzz in my stomach as Finn's light showed a long but narrow clearing in the middle of the maritime jungle. A lone palmetto stood at one end of the clearing. *We had found the tree on the map,* I thought. For the first time since we had gotten to the spit I was truly excited.

I watched as Finn went to the spot where I had come out of the bushes and partly broke a branch. "What are you doing?" I asked.

"Marking the place where the path is, so we can find our way out."

With a shock, I realized he was right when I turned in a circle and looked at the wall of greenery all around us. We might never have found our path again. "Why do you think this clearing is here when the bushes are so thick all around it?" I asked.

"Only one reason I can think of," Finn said, his voice full of excitement. "There's something underneath this sand that keeps bushes from rooting."

"Then we should start digging," I said.

Finn turned off his flashlight. I started to tell him to turn it back on, but then I realized there was just enough moonlight reflecting off the sand to let us see the clearing. I could also see Finn's face well enough to tell that he was frowning.

"What's the matter?" I asked, thinking he

should be excited to have found the right place.

"There's a problem. This tree is on the wrong end of this little clearing," he said.

"So?"

"So, the Xs go toward the river, not away."

"Maybe you were wrong about that."

"I don't think I'm wrong," he muttered.

"Or maybe the map was drawn upside down, and we didn't realize it."

"I guess we have to hope that's the case."

Finn put his back to the tree and started counting his steps. When he hit twenty-five, he chunked his shovel blade into the sand to make it stand up. "If that tree is the right one, this is where we should dig," he said.

I walked a few feet from where Finn's shovel stuck out of the ground, put Plankton down and told him to stay close, then I slammed my shovel into the sand. Standing about five yards apart, we began separate holes.

For most of the next hour, I threw out shovelful after shovelful of sand, until my arms and shoulders began to burn, and I felt blisters beginning to rise on my fingers and palms. In spite of my hard work, I found nothing. When I was about three feet down and hadn't hit anything at all, I stopped digging and looked over at Finn. From the way he was digging, it was clear he hadn't hit anything either.

I opened my mouth to tell him we were wasting our time, but instead of words, the first thing that came out of my mouth was a huge yawn. That was when Finn stopped digging, as well.

Only, he didn't stop because of me or because he wanted to give up. In fact, in the faint glow of moonlight I could see he had his back turned to me and was staring toward the other end of the clearing. "There," he said.

"What?" I asked.

He pointed one finger, and I squinted at where it was aimed but saw nothing.

"I should have checked there first," he said.

With no more explanation, he climbed out of his hole and walked to the far end of the narrow clearing. Standing close to the wall of scrub, he turned his flashlight back on and bent over like Sherlock Holmes studying some clue nobody else had noticed. I headed over to stand behind him, unable to see what he was staring at.

"What is it?" I asked after several seconds of watching Finn stare at the ground.

"A rotten stump," he said, turning the flashlight back off.

At first, I didn't understand, but then it dawned. "A palmetto stump?"

"I'm pretty sure," he said. "A really old palmetto stump. There was a tree here when that map was made." He turned, put his heels against the old stump and started counting off steps, going a good fifteen steps past the farthest of our two holes.

"Here's where we should be digging," he said.

Hearing the certainty in Finn's voice gave me goosebumps in spite of my tired muscles and the blisters on my hands. We started digging new holes right away, once again a few yards apart. Plankton worked his way around the clearing sniffing at things on the ground, and then every few minutes he would come over and look into my hole as if silently asking me what I thought I was going to find.

For about ten minutes, the only sounds in the clearing were the rough hisses of shovel blades going into sand and then the plop as Finn and I threw our shovelfuls out of our ever-deepening holes. I was breathing hard. The shovel felt heavier and heavier with each load of sand, and the wooden handle rubbed a couple of really big blisters.

My back ached, and my shirt was soaked with sweat by the time my hole was thigh deep. I was starting to think that this hole was as much of a lost cause as my first hole and there was nothing but sand beneath me. My body wanted to quit in the worst way, but my brain kept reminding me that I was doing this to help Poppy and also help the spit. I kept digging.

"You found anything?" I whispered to Finn.

The sound of his shoveling stopped. "No," he huffed, sounding almost as tired as me. But almost right away he started digging again.

I did the same, trying to ignore my growing sense of failure. Even if there were other places to explore, or even if we were just a couple feet to one side or the other of the X and needed to dig more exploratory holes, I didn't think we could. One of my blisters was close to popping and my arms were so tired I could barely throw the sand out of the hole. I wanted to cry with frustration, but that was when my shovel blade slammed into something hard.

Suddenly, the pain in my hands disappeared. I forgot about my burning muscles. Raising the shovel, I stabbed it down again about a foot to the side, and I heard and felt the same solid *thunk*.

"Hey," I called to Finn.

He must have heard something in my voice because he climbed out of his hole and hurried over. "What?"

"I hit something."

"Metal? An oil tank?" he asked, sounding excited.

I shook my head. "I think it's wood."

"Careful," he said. "Maybe it's an ammunition case." But then he shrugged, and his voice fell. "But probably the trunk of an old palmetto."

I chopped the shovel down several more places, forward and back, and then side to side. Each time I hit the same thing. "It's too wide for a tree or a box," I said.

"Hey! Maybe it's a roof they built over an oil tank," Finn said, sound excited all over again. "I bet that's it! That has to be what it is."

"How big do you think it is?" I asked with a groan.

"Hop out a second, and let me have a turn,"

Finn said.

Happily, I did as he suggested, shaking my aching arms as I watched Finn tap his shovel into the sand all around the area where I had been digging.

"Sure seems like a roof," he said, scooping up shallow loads of sand and tossing them out of the hole as he tried to reveal whatever we had hit. "I can feel the shape of logs," he said. "At least I think they're logs. Each one is laid parallel. I bet they're half-logs because whole logs would have been too heavy."

"What's a half-log?" I asked.

"One that you saw in half lengthwise."

"Oh . . . duh," I said. "So, why did they build a roof over the oil tank?"

"It was a war, right? They had to bury the tank to hide it in case of an air attack or an enemy ship offshore shelling them. And probably some logs to protect it beneath the sand made even more sense."

"How do you know all that? You must have read it somewhere."

Even in the dark I could see the way Finn's face suddenly turned sour. "Heard it on the History Channel," he said.

"So, what do we do now?" I asked, changing the subject.

"We cover it back up so Granger doesn't find it. This *has* to be what he's been looking for."

"But what if we're wrong? What if it turns out to be an old cabin or something? Granger won't care, and we'll look like we cried wolf when there wasn't anything here."

"You're saying we should look underneath the logs?"

"Yeah."

Finn climbed out of the hole, and I could see that he was as tired and sore as I. "We can't do it tonight. I'm too beat to keep digging."

He started shoveling sand back over the logs.

"What are you doing?" I demanded.

"We have to try and cover this up, just in case Granger's guys try to search in here."

"You're going to fill the whole thing back up?" I asked in alarm.

"No, just a little, then we'll throw some dead branches around the hole to try and make things look normal. If somebody really searches hard they'll find it, but if they just walk through, they probably won't."

I nodded, then in spite of how much my arms, hands and shoulders were killing me, I grabbed my shovel and helped. Fortunately, putting the sand back took a lot less effort than digging the holes in the first place.

After we finished and then tossed some dead branches on top, I leaned on my shovel. "So, what now?"

Finn threw his arms back in a huge yawn. "Now, we go back to bed and get some sleep." He looked around the clearing. "Given how hidden this place is, we should be able to come back here in daylight. As long as we work quietly, no one will know we're here."

I looked at my hands. "I think I need a day to recover."

Finn laughed. "I think you need a pair of gloves. We both do," he said, looking at his own hands.

I nodded, then let out a sigh.

"What's the matter?" Finn asked.

I shrugged as the excitement I had felt moments earlier collapsed. "We still don't know if we found anything important, and I just want to be able to help Poppy."

"You are helping. We made a lot of progress tonight, but you were right—we have to come back and get our proof."

"Then what do we do?"

"Just like we talked about. When Granger buys the spit from your grandfather, we go to the police and the press and the state environmental people and tell them what's under this sand. Your grandfather will have his money, but Granger won't be able to build a thing. The spit will stay just the way your grandfather wanted it."

"Yeah, but I just feel bad with all our sneaking around. If we told my grandfather what's under here and that Granger is probably planning to secretly dig it up and get it out of here—"

"What's that going to accomplish? And what if you told your grandfather what Granger is planning and he refused to sell no matter how badly he needs the money?"

"Well . . . I guess you're right. Poppy can

be really stubborn sometimes."

Finn clapped me on the back, trying to reassure me. "We're both tired and need some sleep. It'll all make more sense in the morning, and we'll figure out the right thing to do."

I nodded, hoping he was right. Needing to take the shovels back before Poppy noticed they were missing, Finn carried them while I picked up Plankton and we made our way out the nearly invisible path Finn had found. As we dragged ourselves back down the spit, I put Plankton down and let him run along the beach. He was the only one who still had energy. Back on the road, Finn handed me back the shovels. Just before we headed off toward our houses, he smiled. "Thanks for the adventure," he said. "That was fun."

21.

I didn't get up until after ten the next morning. Despite how tired I was and how exhausted my muscles felt from all the digging, I'd had bad dreams, and I climbed out of bed full of doubts.

When I wandered into the kitchen to grab a bowl of cereal, Martha glanced up from her chopping, took one look at me and seemed to sense my mood. "Feeling okay?" she asked.

"I'm good, thanks," I said. "I guess I didn't sleep very well."

"Something troubling you?"

I shrugged. "Kinda."

She turned back to her knife and cutting board, and for a few seconds all I could hear was the crunch of celery being chopped. Martha swept the celery bits into a bowl, then looked up again. She seemed to be reading my mind, but it might have been the fact that I'd been standing with the cupboard open, staring at the breakfast bowls but not making any move to grab one. "Maybe talk to your grandfather about it. He's a pretty smart guy."

I nodded. "I think I'll try that," I said, as I

finally managed to move and grab a bowl.

Once I finished breakfast, I went looking for Poppy and found him out in the yard planting flowers in the pots on his front porch.

"Well, sleepyhead, looks like you're finally awake," he joked.

"Can I help you?" I asked.

"Sure," he said with a pleased smile. "Why don't you use the trowel to put new dirt into the pots and then mix in some fertilizer. I'll come behind you and plant the flowers."

I did as he asked, holding the trowel as gently as possible to avoid popping my blisters, and we worked in silence for some time, while I worked up the nerve to start talking. At one point, when I let out a big sigh, Poppy turned to me, "What's up, Callie? You seem to have a lot on your mind. In fact, you've seemed to have a lot on your mind ever since you arrived."

I wanted to say that made two of us, but instead I stuck the trowel into the dirt and looked at him out of the corner of my eye. "A couple things have been bothering me," I admitted.

"Do you care to talk about them?"

"Well, Finn said that you're selling Buccaneer's Spit. Is that true?"

Poppy's shoulders slumped. He stopped working, turned and sat on the edge of the porch. "I thought you might have heard about that. I know I probably should have told you myself, but . . . well it's complicated."

"Are you going broke?"

"No, sweetie, I'm not going broke."

"Then why would you sell? You've always loved the spit. That's why you and Grandma bought it."

Poppy had gardening gloves on his hands, but what I'd said had made him forget them, because he rubbed the bald part of his head with one hand and smeared dirt all over it. He barely seemed to notice. "I *do* love the spit," he said. "It breaks my heart to sell."

"Then *why* are you?"

"Because somebody else needs the money."

I thought about what he was saying for a long minute. Finally, I turned all the way around and looked at him. "Mom?"

He nodded.

"Cause she and Daddy are getting divorced," I said. "I know that's why they sent me away. It's the same way it's happened with some of my friends at school."

Poppy closed his eyes and pinched the bridge of his nose, getting even more dirt on his face. "They're not getting divorced, Callie."

"Then why do they need money? They both have good jobs, don't they?"

"Yes."

"Then why? Did they lose their jobs?"

He made a soft groaning noise, and after a few seconds I realized he was grinding his teeth. I just kept staring at him, waiting.

"Your mom is sick," he said at last in a very low voice.

I had a sudden terrible bubbling in my

stomach. "What do you mean?"

"She's . . . got a disease."

"Is it serious?"

He took a deep breath and sighed it out. "Well . . . I'm afraid . . . yes. That's the reason your parents wanted you to come down here without them. Your mom is going through treatments, and she was afraid that if you stayed home, you would be upset."

I felt tears welling in the corners of my eyes. "I *am* upset," I said, hearing the way my voice shook when I said it.

Poppy gave a sad nod. "I know you are. I'm upset, too." He held out his arms and I went over and let him hug me. I didn't care a bit about whether his gloves were filthy. We stayed that way for a very long moment, until finally I broke away.

"Is there something about Momma's disease that costs a whole heap of money?"

"Yes." He nodded, considering his words. "That's actually the good news. There are treatments that are very expensive, but they will help her."

I almost didn't want to ask, but I had to. "What kind of disease does she have?"

"Cancer."

I felt more tears break loose from my eyes and roll down my cheeks. "Is she gonna die?"

"No!" he said, his voice growing loud. "Not if I have anything to say about it. We're going to make sure she gets the best possible medicine."

I nodded, suddenly getting it. "So, that's why you're selling the spit, to get money to help take care of Momma?"

"Yes."

I shook my head, still not getting it. "How much does it cost?"

Poppy made a face. "Your parents didn't want me to talk to you about any of this, but I can see that you're smart enough to be worried, so it better if you know the truth. Can we keep this between us, and not let your mom and dad know that we talked?"

"Yessir."

"Okay," he said, taking another deep breath. "Your mother's cancer is rare. A lot of times when a disease is very rare, drug companies don't do much experimenting to discover potential cures because there are too few patients who would take the drug for them to make a profit. Can you understand what I'm saying?"

I nodded. "I guess it costs a lot to develop new drugs, so if hardly anybody takes them, the drug companies lose a lot of money."

"Yes, but in this case a company has developed a drug, a very powerful one that is the best possible treatment for your mother's cancer."

"How much does it cost?"

"That's the problem." He paused, then shook his head as if the thought of what he was about to say disturbed him. "It's going to cost nearly two million dollars for all the doses your mom needs."

My jaw dropped. "How can *anything* cost that much?"

Poppy shrugged. "Doesn't seem right to me, but that's what it is. Your mom's insurance company won't pay it, so if our family can't come up with the money, she can't get the treatments." He looked so sad that for a second that I thought he might start to cry. "Sometimes, life sure isn't fair," he said.

At that point, I think we were both so full of our own sadness that there seemed to be nothing left to say. We lapsed into silence and didn't talk any more as we finished potting the flowers. Afterward, we washed our hands and then ate lunch together on the porch, but we still didn't speak. If Martha noticed how silent and unhappy we appeared, she said nothing.

After lunch, Poppy said he had to take a nap. As far as I remembered it was the first time when I had been around that he had ever slept during the day. I just assumed that he needed some alone time, just like I did.

Instead of napping, I leashed Plankton and took him down to Buccaneer's Spit to walk the beach and be alone with my thoughts. I watched the pelicans crash into the sea as they tried to catch fish, listened to the cry of gulls overhead. Finn had taught me the names of more kinds of birds, and I watched sandpipers, dowitchers and sanderlings race along the tide line, and noticed crabs of all kinds as they scuttled along in the shallows. My grandfather loved the spit, and he wanted to protect all the creatures that made their homes there, but now he was selling because he loved something even more . . . my mom.

It made me think Poppy had been right when he'd said life wasn't fair, and how terrible it was when somebody had to make a choice between a person they loved, and a place with all the wonderful creatures that lived there. It was a terrible choice. To get a good outcome one way, Poppy had to accept a terrible outcome in another.

Thinking about all that unfairness put me in such an angry mood. I thought more about Mom and Poppy, and also about Desmond Granger and all the houses he would build on the spit, and if he did, how the dolphins would no longer be able to strand here, and the turtles would no longer dig their nests on this beach, and the birds would have to find other places to rest from their long migrations. At some point, I guess I started to cry because the next thing I knew I was sitting on a fallen palmetto at the far end of the spit, and I had tears running down my cheeks in big, fat rivulets. That was why Finn and I had to figure out what Granger was doing so that once Poppy got the money, we could stop Granger.

That was how Finn found me a short time later. "Hey, Callie," he said from just a foot or two behind me. I hadn't heard him approach, and Plankton had given no warning growl.

Taken by surprise, I wiped my wrists across

my eyes to mop up my tears, and as I spun around I tried to give him a happy smile. "Hey," I said.

"I went to your house, and the cook lady said she thought you were here."

"Yeah." I kept that fake smile plastered on my face because I couldn't think of anything else to say.

Finn was squinting at me with a funny look on his face. "Did something happen? Did you, like, get caught when you went back home last night?"

I shook my head.

"If you're not in big trouble, what's wrong?"

I sat for a long time not answering.

"Come on, you look like somebody died."

That was all I needed to hear. I started crying all over again, and when I'd coughed out four or five sobs, I whispered, "I found out why Poppy's selling the spit."

"Why?" Finn asked in a soft voice.

"My mom's sick, and she needs some super expensive drug. If she doesn't get it, she'll probably die."

He looked at me, and his face changed and became softer. He didn't look a bit like the cocky kid he always had been up until then. "I'm really sorry."

I shrugged. "Well, now I know the truth."

Finn slumped down on the log beside me. "What do you think we should do?"

"You mean about the map and what we found?"

He nodded.

I shook my head. "We have to keep it a secret, because we can't do anything to screw up the sale. Mom needs that money. Whatever we do, we need to be absolutely certain Granger pays Poppy for the spit."

"But once he buys it, we can still show everybody what we found."

I nodded. "But we have to be super careful. What if we did that and then Granger found some way to get his money back? Then my mom couldn't get her treatments."

"How's that possible Granger could get his money back if he was going to do something illegal?"

"I don't know, but we're not lawyers. Who knows what he could do?"

"So, you're saying we can't say anything." Finn's head slumped.

"No. We have to do something, but I can't risk letting Granger get his money back.

Finn shook his head. "It would sure be terrible to have such a big secret and not be able to use it." He sat up and looked around with an angry expression. "If it turns out we can't use it, I'm just glad I'll be gone from here when this whole place starts getting bulldozed."

"Yeah. If that happens, I guess I'm lucky I'll be back in New York," I said, feeling like I was being torn in two.

22.

I said goodbye to Finn, wondering if, after this year, we would ever run into each other again. I was pretty sure he wouldn't come back to the spit if it got ruined, just like I didn't think I ever would. It made me too sad to be in the middle of so much wild beauty and think that very soon it was liable to be destroyed. It seemed better to just stay away.

"We'll have to find a new place to go walking," I said to Plankton as we headed down the path that led away from the spit.

He looked up at me and twisted his head sideways the way he did whenever I said something he didn't agree with. Choosing to have no further discussion with Plankton, I walked home in silence, with him pulling me to a stop every ten or fifteen yards so he could smell something important. I was in a terrible mood and a couple times I felt like jerking on his leash to make him move faster, but I didn't.

When I got to Poppy's house, my bad mood got even worse because that same black Mercedes was parked in the circle in front of the house with the same muscle-bound guy polishing the metal. The guy gave me a hard look, like he wanted to run after me and give me a good shaking when he caught me, but I refused to hurry as I went past him. Acting like he felt the same way about the guy that I did, Plankton let out an angry growl.

"Little dog thinks he's tough," the man said.

"He is," I said, and kept on going.

Inside the house I picked Plankton up to keep him quiet, then tiptoed into the living room, squatted low behind the couch, and tried to eavesdrop the way I had the first time Granger was there. This time when I overheard Poppy's voice, I understood the words and they chilled me to the bone.

"What do you mean you're walking away?" Poppy cried, sounding older and more frightened than anything I'd ever heard from him.

"Just what I said. Your price is too high."

"But you signed a contract! I'll sue for enforcement."

"I don't care what I signed. You know I'm probably going bankrupt thanks to those houses that haven't sold just across the river from your precious spit. You can sue me all you want, but the banks are already standing in line. You won't get a cent."

"But . . . but what's changed? I knew you had financial problems, but the spit is right across the river from your other properties. You said it made good financial sense for you to own it. And you swore you had the ability to get the money to buy it. In spite of what other people say about you and your business ethics, I was willing to work with you and sell you my property."

"Let's just say the property no longer satisfies my needs."

"But you can't just walk away from our deal."

"Can't I?"

"No! Please. I . . ."

"You what?" Granger demanded.

"I need the money."

"Well, I'm sorry. You'll have to find yourself another buyer. I'm in a difficult financial position myself, and I won't be able to honor the contract."

Granger's voice was becoming louder as he spoke those final words, and I realized it was because he had turned around and was about to walk out of Poppy's office. I squatted lower even though every part of my brain wanted to stand up and scream that he couldn't walk away, that he *had* to pay Poppy that money so Mom could get her cancer medicine.

Those thoughts went nowhere because in the next second Granger opened the library door and walked out. I stayed stone-still, my stomach roiling like a swimming pool full of acid. I was drowning in guilt because I had a terrible feeling that Granger's sudden change had a lot to do with his missing map. This *couldn't* be happening, but it was, and it might be all my fault.

Granger's footsteps faded as he walked to the front door and let himself out. Still in his library, Poppy was as unmoving as a statue. As long as he stayed at his desk, he couldn't see my hiding place, so I risked standing up and sneaking out of the living room. I didn't want to face him because I knew how bad he was feeling, and it was my fault.

I walked to the front door, where I put Plankton down then squeezed through the door, leaving him in the house. He barked a few times to let me know he wasn't happy, but I didn't care.

Granger's car was already gone from the driveway, which was a relief. Forcing myself to keep my movements slow as if I had no place special to go, I headed slowly toward the end of the street. I kept walking until I was about a block away then I started to run.

My heart was pounding, and my thoughts were a tangled mess. Why had we kept that map? It wasn't mine to keep. Why hadn't Finn and I given the map back to Granger when we first found it? If we had, I was sure Granger would still want to buy Poppy's property.

I had no idea where Finn lived, but I had to find him and tell him what had happened. Two brains were better than one. Together we needed to make a plan to somehow make Desmond Granger buy Buccaneer's Spit. Mom's life depended on it.

Racing back toward the Spit, I stopped at the opening of the path that led through the bushes to the beach. With my chest heaving, I closed my eyes and tried to recall the direction Finn had gone when we came off the spit. I had always turned right toward Poppy's; he had always turned left.

Starting in that direction, I found myself on a long winding road with marsh on both sides but no visible houses. Not knowing what else to do, I kept running. After what seemed like a mile, the ground finally rose a little, and I started to see some mailboxes and then houses going back off the road I was on.

None of the mailboxes said Finnigan, so when I came to a cross street, I turned into it then slowed a little to catch my breath. The houses here were neat, and surrounded by yards full of big trees, palms, and flowering bushes. In one yard a man was riding a mower, but I was pretty sure he didn't live there because a truck with a lawn service logo was parked in the street with its tail gate down and its ramp lowered. I waved to the man and when he stopped the mower, I trotted over.

"Excuse me," I said, as he took off his headphones. "I'm looking for a boy about my age. His name is Finn. He's visiting his grandfather for spring vacation. Do you know him?"

The man shook his head. "Nope."

I tried to remember what Finn had been wearing when I saw him on the beach before lunch. "I think he's wearing a purple tee shirt. Have you seen anybody like that?"

"Sorry."

"Thanks anyway," I said, then turned and started running again.

The next house looked empty and had a For Sale sign in the front yard. The one after that had no car in the driveway, and it looked like whoever lived there was away. The next house was the last on the street, and when I ran toward it, I spotted Finn sitting on the front porch with a fly rod laid across his lap, tying something on the line.

"Finn!" I called to him.

He looked up in surprise as I came racing up. "What's going on?"

It took me a few seconds to get my breathing under control enough to talk. "It's Desmond Granger," I huffed out. "There's a big problem. You gotta help me."

23.

Fifteen minutes later I had told him everything I had overheard.

"That's terrible," Finn said.

"I know. We need a plan. Somehow, we have to make sure Granger buys the spit at Poppy's original price."

Finn shook his head. "But how can we possibly do that?"

"We'll go to Granger's office, give the map back to him and swear we'll never say a word."

Finn threw up his hands. "I just don't know if that would work."

"Okay, here's another idea. We won't give him the map, but we'll tell him what we found. And then we'll offer to show him where it is, but only if he promises to go ahead and buy the spit at the original price."

Finn gave me a look. "You're the kid from New York City."

"What's that supposed to mean?"

"You're supposed to be the one who thinks everybody's out to cheat you, but I think you're being a sucker. You really think Granger will keep his promise?"

"We'll draw up a contract."

"We're just kids. Who's gonna care if he doesn't do what the contract says?"

I nodded because Finn was making a good point. "He already told Poppy to go ahead and sue him, but I've got a couple ideas. He says he's in financial trouble, but that means he needs people to be nice to him and maybe do him some favors. If we let the world know he cheated a girl out of the money for her mom's cancer treatments, it'll make him look terrible. Nobody will want to give him a break. And when he signs our contract we'll take his picture so we can prove what we're saying."

Finn chewed the side of his cheek for a few seconds as he thought it over. "Okay," he said at last. "That might work."

"And there's one more thing," I went on. "Poppy can't know."

"Why?"

"I don't want him to know that I spied on his meetings with Granger. Also, if he doesn't know anything about this, he can't possibly get into trouble."

"What kind of trouble could he get in?" Finn asked.

"I don't know, but what if Granger gets caught? And then what if we get accused of helping Granger sneak some bad stuff off the beach? I don't want Poppy involved."

"You're saying we could get in trouble by helping him?" Finn asked.

"I'm guessing whatever he's doing isn't legal,

so maybe we could," I said. I took a breath, then went on. "Look, you don't have to do any of this. I'll go see Granger by myself. I know it's not fair to ask you to stick your neck out for somebody you don't even know."

"Your *mom*?" Finn said.

I nodded.

Finn grimaced and shook his head. "Boy, this really stinks. If this wasn't about saving your mother, there's no way I would even think about it. I think Granger's a horrible person, and it bothers me to even think that we might help him ruin the spit." He paused. "But I can't let you do this by yourself."

"Seriously, think about it," I said.

Finn shrugged. "I have. I'm in."

I looked at him, and for a second, I had to fight off the urge to throw my arms around him. The fat little kid who had walked around wearing his baseball mitt had turned into a smart kid with a lot of guts, and I really liked him. "Then I have one more favor to ask," I said. "Can you get us a ride to Granger's office tomorrow?"

Finn thought for a second. "I can tell my grandmother that we'd like to go into Charleston because you want to do some shopping. She's been after me to buy some new clothes 'cause she thinks I'm too casual." He looked down at his tee shirt. "Just so you know, I *hate* shopping, but I'll make an exception just this once. I'm pretty sure she'll jump at the chance to take us in."

24.

That night at dinner, I watched Poppy play with his food, barely saying a word, and taking only a few bites. Unable to let on that I knew what the problem was, I pretended to be so interested in my own dinner that I didn't notice. Actually, because Martha was such a good cook and had made some kind of grilled pork loin with an amazing sauce it wasn't too hard to pretend.

I gobbled down my food, and because I was pretty exhausted from all the running around I had done that day and not getting much sleep the night before, I asked to be excused so I could go to bed early. Poppy glanced up from playing fork hockey with his pork, tried to give me something like a smile, and said, "Certainly. See you in the morning."

I went to my room, and just as if I had a big paper due for school the next day, before I turned off my light I wrote down my ideas for what I was going to say to Desmond Granger. Then, after what seemed like only a few minutes of sleep because of strange dreams about being a lawyer in a huge courtroom and having Desmond Granger as the judge, I woke up to see that the sun was already up.

A glance at my watch showed that I had very little time to grab breakfast because Finn and I had agreed to meet at eight, which meant that in only a few minutes I'd have to head over to his house. I brushed my teeth, dressed, and hurried down the hall, seeing that Poppy's bedroom door was still closed.

When I got to the kitchen, Martha gave me a big smile. "I made you a special treat for breakfast this morning," she said.

I could smell freshly cooked bacon and a quick glanced at the stove showed a bowl of batter beside the already warmed up griddle. I felt almost too antsy to eat, but I forced myself to smile and nod. "Pancakes?" I asked.

"You got it!" Martha said, heading over to the stove and pouring out the first batch. Pancakes were always a special treat in Poppy's house because he had a recipe that he said was "top secret," and anybody who had ever had his pancakes admitted that they were the best. However, I also knew that Martha would never let me get out of the house with just one batch in my stomach.

Given the fact that it would only hurt Martha's feelings if I tried to get away too fast, I settled down to eat at least two helpings. Despite how nervous I was about what Finn and I had to do, it wasn't really hard to eat those two plates full of delicious pancakes with maple syrup and butter.

A few minutes later, with my belly stuffed, I asked Martha to please tell Poppy that I was going out to meet my friend, Finn, and that I wouldn't be around for several hours because his grandparents were taking us shopping in Charleston. When I raced out of the house a few seconds later, Plankton tried to go with me, then started to growl when he realized I was leaving him.

"Sorry, Plankton. I'll take you for an extra-long walk later on," I said as I closed the door.

Running with two batches of pancakes in your stomach isn't easy, but I had no choice. Finn's grandfather had an early doctor's appointment in town, which meant he would have to leave a couple minutes after eight if he wanted to be on time, and there was no way I was going to miss our ride to see Desmond Granger.

When I got there, Finn was waiting outside and gave me a relieved look. "Grampa's ready to go. I was afraid we were going to take off before you could get here."

"I came as fast as I could. I had to eat pancakes before I could leave."

He gave me a weird look and I just said, "Long story."

We went into his house where he introduced me to his grandmother, who was wearing a tennis dress and getting ready to head out for a match. "Your grandfather has told us so much about you," she said as we shook hands. "He's extremely proud of your fine grades and all your other accomplishments."

"That's very nice of him," I said.

"I understand you're going to take Finn downtown for some shopping," she said. "I think that's a wonderful idea, because he needs some new clothes. I've given him money, so he can buy whatever you help him pick out.

I glanced at Finn, whose expression had soured with the mention of shopping. Fortunately, we didn't have to spend much time talking about it because right then Mr. Finnigan came rushing out of his bedroom. "Ready to go?" he asked as he whizzed past us, grabbed the car keys, and headed out the back door.

"Coming, Grampa," Finn called after him. Giving his grandmother a quick peck on the cheek, he looked at me. "Ready?"

I nodded and said goodbye to Mrs. Finnigan, then followed Finn as he hurried out the door behind his grandfather. I climbed in the backseat, while Finn rode up front. We didn't have a chance to talk in the car, but Mr. Finnigan filled the silence by talking nonstop about Finn's baseball—how great he was at pitching, at batting, at every part of the game. Finn sat looking out the window as if he wanted to be someplace far away.

As we got close to town, Finn's grandfather seemed to realize that we were going to get there before most stores would be open. "Where do you want me to drop you?" he asked, suddenly concerned that we would have no place to go.

"How about the library?" I suggested.

"*Wonderful* idea!" he said.

I saw Finn slide lower in his seat, and right away, I regretted the suggestion, but it was too late to take it back.

Mr. Finnigan brightened, seeming not to notice Finn's sudden dejection. "I'm sure you like to read, don't you, young lady?" Mr. Finnigan said, turning his head to ask me the question.

"Yes, sir," I said.

He nodded. "Yes, yes, Finn's grandmother and I love to read, as well. We find books to be *so* important in our lives."

I glanced at Finn who was staring out the side window with a tired, sad look on his face.

"Yes, sir," I said softly.

A moment later Mr. Finnigan pulled up in front of the library to drop us off.

"Thank you for the ride," I said, even as Finn got out of the car without saying a word. As we went inside I couldn't help but notice the scowl on his face. He followed me in plodding silence as I found us some comfortable chairs to sit in, and then he immediately grabbed a sports magazine and started flipping through looking at the pictures.

"I don't mean to be nosey, but why do you hate reading so much?" I asked.

Finn flashed a look at me that was pretty much equal parts of anger and hurt, and for several long seconds I watched his jaw muscles flex. "'Cause I can't do it," he said at last.

I just looked at him, not understanding.

"'Cause I've got a learning disability."

"You're dyslexic?"

"Yes."

"So, what's the big deal? One of my best friends back in New York is dyslexic, and she's still one of the smartest kids in our class."

Now it was Finn's turn to look at me like he didn't understand. "My grandfather thinks I can't read because I'm dense. That's why I knew where the town library is. He sends me over there a couple times a week to work with a reading tutor."

"A person who specializes in reading differences?"

He shook his head. "Just a basic tutor."

"Your grandfather is the dense one," I said. "People can help you learn to overcome dyslexia. Also, there are ways to read other than a book."

"What are you talking about?"

"Audiobooks, books on tape. You ever heard of them?"

He shrugged. "Yeah, but my family wants me to read books."

"Doesn't matter how you get the words, as long as you get them." I pointed to a section of the library that held a whole wall of recorded books. "The library can loan you talking books or printed books. What's the difference if you like one better than the other?"

His eyes drifted to the floor as he seemed

to think over what I'd said. Finally, he nodded and sat up taller, looking almost as if a big weight had been lifted off his shoulders. "Thanks," he said quietly. "I'll try them."

We sat there in an awkward silence, and I tried to fill it. "I'm going read you the contract I wrote last night before I went to bed," I said. "Tell me if it makes sense."

"Okay."

"Upon receiving my lost map and directions to the hidden item, I irrevocably promise to complete the purchase of the land known as Buccaneer's Spit at the original agreed upon price from Mr. James Morrisey of Spinnaker Island, SC."

When I finished, Finn smiled. "You called it an 'item'," he said.

"If we ever had to take it to a lawyer, I figured it would kill the whole deal if the contract talked about a hidden oil tank or ammunition."

"Good idea." He thought for a second, then asked. "Got your phone to take a picture of him signing?"

I nodded. "I'm all set." Then, glancing at my watch, I asked, "You think he's in his office now?"

"I think it's time to find out."

25.

I had already looked up the address for Granger Enterprises. With the location in my phone, we left the library and followed the mapping app's directions several blocks to a fancy looking glass and metal building with a big sign—*Granger Enterprises.*

Taking a deep breath, I led the way through the front doors and up to a desk where a man in a security uniform sat watching us. "Can I help you?" he asked.

"Yes, sir," I said. "We're here to see Mr. Desmond Granger."

The guard's eyebrows went up a bit. "And is he expecting you?"

"No, sir."

"Well, I'm afraid Mr. Granger is a very busy man, and doesn't have time for surprise visits."

Finn cleared his throat. "We have something he wants."

The guard smirked. "Are you selling something?"

"No, we have something Mr. Granger lost on the beach the other day."

"I see," the man said, clearly not buying it.

"Why don't you leave it with me, and I'll make sure Mr. Granger get it."

I shook my head. "That's not possible. We need to see Mr. Granger personally. Otherwise, we won't hand it over."

The guard looked back and forth between us for a moment. "Wait a moment," he said with a sigh, then picked up his phone and hit a couple buttons.

I could hear a ringing tone, then a woman's voice said, "Granger Enterprises."

"Mary, this is Jed at reception downstairs. I've got a couple kids here who claim to have found something Mr. Granger lost on the beach the other day. I asked them to leave it with me, but they say they won't give it to anybody but Mr. Granger."

I heard the woman say, "Hold on," in a testy voice.

The guard kept the phone to his ear but gave us a nasty look. At least a minute went by, but then the woman came back on the line. This time her voice sounded different. "Keep them there. Mr. Granger wants to see them. I'll be right down."

"Will do." The guard put down the phone then said in a much nicer tone, "Someone will be right down to take you up."

We didn't wait more than a few seconds before one of the elevators opened and a thin, blonde woman came straight toward us. "Hello," she said in a voice that sounded about as sticky-sweet as cotton candy. "I'm Donna,

Mr. Granger's executive assistant." She wore expensive looking clothes, and her haircut, nails and makeup were all very nice, but a tightness around her eyes told me that Desmond Granger probably wasn't any nicer to her than he'd been to Poppy. "Mr. Granger has a few minutes free right now," she went on. "Would you like to come up and see him?"

"Yes, ma'am," I said.

"This way." Donna led us toward the elevator, stood to one side, and ushered us in. Holding her identity card up to the elevator keypad, she pushed the button for the top floor, then turned to us as the doors closed. "What are your names?"

We introduced ourselves, and Donna asked, "Do you know Mr. Granger?"

"Not really," I said.

"I see."

It was clear to me that she was confused about why Mr. Granger would want to see two strange kids, which probably meant she didn't know about his map. Also, while I'd never talked to Desmond Granger, I would have bet that he was the kind of man who had absolutely no use for kids. No wonder Donna was trying to figure out what was going on.

When the elevator stopped and the doors opened, I expected to walk into a typical building corridor with offices opening off of it, but it looked like most of this entire floor was Desmond Granger's office. Donna led us across a thick Oriental carpet, past a wall filled with lots of pictures of Mr. Granger with famous people, then pointed us toward a grouping of chairs and a couch on the far side. Through a floor-to-ceiling glass window just behind the couch, I could see all of Charleston stretching out beneath my feet.

On the opposite side of the room stood the biggest desk I had ever seen, while the middle of the room held long tables with miniature houses and streets that I guessed were buildings Mr. Granger had built or planned to build.

Beyond the huge desk in a glass-walled conference room, I could see Mr. Granger along with two other men. One of the men was the big, muscle-bound, bald guy that drove his car. The other was more normal sized and looked younger than Granger, maybe in his thirties.

The room's glass walls must have been very thick, because Mr. Granger was waving his arms and appeared to be shouting in an angry way, however, not a sound escaped the room.

"Mr. Granger will be right out of his meeting," Donna said, pulling my gaze from the conference room. "Please make yourselves comfortable. Can I get you some water, juice, or soda?"

Finn and I both asked for water. Donna left and came back a few seconds later with glasses full of cold water and wedges of lemon. Then, saying she would be back to get us when Mr. Granger was free, she went to sit at another desk that wasn't too far from Mr. Granger's.

Finn and I sat in the chairs, and I could tell by the way he kept running his eyes all over the office that he was as nervous as I was. Everything about the place screamed that this was the office of a Very Important Person. Seeing Granger yelling at those two men behind the glass walls and having heard the way he talked to Poppy, I also knew he wasn't a nice man. How would he react when he realized we were the same two kids who'd been on the beach the day he first lost his map and that I was the girl who'd stuck out her tongue at him when we got away? We were right to be scared.

I took a deep breath and blew it out. In order to stop my brain from freezing up, I silently ran through all the things that I wanted to say. When I thought I'd gone over all the points I needed to make, I checked the time and saw that nearly ten minutes had passed since we first sat down. Granger was still in his conference room and he still looked angry.

"You know what's weird?" Finn said in a near whisper. "This whole place makes Granger look like some kind of super rich guy, but the paper said he's going broke. My grandfather said Granger still hasn't sold even one of those beach houses across the river from the spit. How he can come up with the money to buy your grandfather's land if he's almost broke?"

"What are you saying?" I whispered back.

"How can he buy more land if he doesn't have any money? He shouldn't even care about the map. Something about this doesn't make sense."

I remembered what I'd overheard Granger telling Poppy the day before, how even if Poppy sued him and tried to force him to buy the spit it wouldn't matter, because he didn't have any money. I hadn't paid much attention to that because I had wanted to believe that the map would make all the difference. Only, now I looked at Finn with a sense of sudden panic thinking maybe no matter what we did, Poppy wouldn't be able to sell the spit in time to pay for my mom's treatments. I opened my mouth to tell Finn he was wrong, that he *had* to be wrong, but just then a different voice broke the silence.

"Terribly sorry to keep you waiting."

26.

Whipping my head around, I saw Desmond Granger, his face that had seemed so angry just a few seconds earlier now with a welcoming smile. For a second, I couldn't come up with anything to say because he was beaming at us like we were his long-lost niece and nephew.

"No problem, sir," Finn said, saving me from looking totally lost.

"Donna tells me that you may have found something I've been looking for."

"Yes, sir," I managed.

"Well," he said, plopping down on the couch across from our chairs, "tell me all about it."

Finn and I looked at each other for a half second. It was obvious from the expression on his face that he was as shocked as I was at how nice Desmond Granger was acting. It almost couldn't be the same person who had been so nasty to Poppy and who just moments before had been yelling at his men.

Donna hurried up, bringing fresh glasses of water for Finn and me, and what looked like iced tea for Mr. Granger.

"Okay," Granger said once the drinks had

been handed around, "let's start with your names."

When Finn said his name, Mr. Granger had little reaction, but when I told him my name was Callie Long, he squinted his eyes. "I could swear I've seen you before."

"Maybe around town," I said, playing innocent.

"Yes . . . maybe."

He looked back and forth between us for a few seconds. "So, this thing I've been looking for. What is it?"

I cleared my throat. "Something you lost."

"What would that be?" he asked as if he had no idea what we could be talking about.

"A plastic bag."

He wrinkled his brow. "A *plastic* bag?"

"With an old paper inside."

"Oh, yes, that," he said as if he was recalling some embarrassing joke. "It's just an old piece of paper with a drawing. It blew away when I was on the beach." As he said that, his eyes narrowed, and he looked at each of us again and snapped his fingers. "That's where I've seen you two. On that beach the day my . . . bag blew into the water."

"You wanted me to jump in and try to swim out to get it," Finn said.

"Yes," Granger said with a smile. "I apologize. It was too cold to swim, and I had lost my perspective. You know how some people get when they lose something, even if it's a silly nothing."

"Yes, sir," Finn said. "You offered me five

hundred dollars to get it. You sure did seem to want it back pretty badly."

"Well, yes, because it's personally important to me. It's a *memento*. Sort of an antique that was in my family for years." He held out his hand. "May I have it, please?"

Finn and I sat there, neither of us making any move to hand over the "paper."

"We sort of looked at it," I said.

For the first time Mr. Granger's face lost its happy smile. "You did? Even though it wasn't yours."

"We didn't know whose it was, of course."

"How could you not," he said, his tone growing sharp. "You saw it blow out of my hands into the water."

"But we didn't find it on the beach or in the water," I said.

Finn nodded. "Actually it was given to us by people at the aquarium."

Mr. Granger looked back and forth between us again. "Did you come here to waste my time with some kind of joke?"

"No, sir," Finn assured him. "We went for a tour of the Turtle Hospital, and the bag was taken from the belly of a turtle that had been brought in sick."

"Sea turtles eat plastic bags," I explained. "They mistake them for jelly fish, but when they eat them they can't digest the plastic, and it clogs up their stomachs and their intestines, and they die."

Granger was watching us much more carefully

now, as if he feared that we were working some kind of terrible plot on him. "Was the plastic damaged?"

"Don't you want to know if the turtle was damaged?" I asked.

"You came here to tell me about the bag, not the turtle."

"No, sir," I said, "the bag wasn't damaged."

"And you say you opened the envelope and looked inside?"

"Yes, sir," I said.

"Was the *paper* damaged?"

"No, sir," I said.

He seemed to take that in. After a second, he nodded and held out his hand again. "Can I see it?"

"It's a map, isn't it?" I asked.

Granger blinked in surprise, but he recovered fast. "It's a very old map. I use it as a personal good luck charm. It's not a map to anyplace real."

"Well," I said, "we came here to make a deal. We'll give you the map, but you have to promise that you'll still buy Buccaneer's Spit."

Now, Granger's eyes narrowed. He sat back in his chair and stared at me again for a few long seconds. "You're Leland Morrissey's granddaughter." He nodded to himself before I could answer. "You were standing in the window watching me when I left his house."

I just stared at him, my heart pounding. *Please, please, please say you'll buy the spit if we give you the map,* I was thinking, but I kept my face blank.

"Did your grandfather put you up to this?"

"No!" I snapped. "He would never do that." I shot a sideways look at Finn. "He doesn't even know we're here."

"I see," Granger said, as if that was important somehow. "So, you've come here all on your own, and you want to know if I'll still buy the spit if you give me the map."

I nodded, not daring to speak.

He looked at me for what seemed like a very long time. "How old are you, if I may ask?"

"Twelve."

"You're certainly a piece of work for a twelve-year-old. Why do you care do much about this?"

"Because my mother is sick and Poppy needs to sell the spit to pay for her treatments."

"Well, that's a sad story, but I'm very sorry to say that I no longer have any interest in Buccaneer's Spit."

Upon hearing that, I felt a sob well up in my throat. I choked it back, unwilling to let Granger see how much those words hurt. But no matter whether I showed it or not, I knew we'd been beaten.

I was about to stand up and walk out of the office when Finn said, "We know what the map leads to."

This time Granger's expression changed

completely. He jerked as if he'd been shocked by a cattle prod. But almost right away he caught himself. "Like I said before, it's a very old map. Just a personal good luck charm. It's not a map *to* anything." He shrugged again. "Maybe it was once, but not anymore."

"What Finn means is that we *found* what the map leads to," I said.

Granger looked back and forth between us for what seemed like a long time. Finally, he made a face and shook his head. "Come on, kids. Don't kid a kidder."

"We did," Finn said.

"I don't believe you," Granger said, his eyes once again darting back and forth between Finn and me.

I nodded. "We know exactly where the map leads. We followed it, then dug down until we hit the roof, then we covered it up again."

Granger's face was changing, the skin seeming to tighten around his eyes, until his cheekbones stood out over deep hollows where his cheeks curved inward. "I see," he said quietly.

"If we agree to give you your map and show you what we found, you have to agree to buy the spit from my grandfather for the original price."

"That sounds like blackmail."

"Not a bit," I said. "It sounds like deal making, something you're supposed to be good at."

"Is that right?"

"Yes."

"Well, then here's a deal for you. You show me what you found, and if it's . . . interesting to me, I'll agree to buy the spit at the original price."

I reached into my pocket and pulled out the paper I had brought. "You have to sign this first."

Granger raised his eyebrows. "What's this?" he asked in a scoffing voice.

"It's a contract. You swear that if we show you where the oil tanks are buried, you'll pay my grandfather's original price."

"Oil tanks?" Granger said in a soft voice. "You've seen them for yourselves?"

I glanced at Finn, who jumped in. "We didn't actually see the tanks, but we dug down to the log roof that covers them. There's no question that's the spot on the map."

"I see." Mr. Granger was looking at us with a strange expression. It reminded me of my chess club back home when my opponent suddenly thought they were about to put some big move on me and take my queen or even get me into check. I had that terrible feeling that Finn and I had missed something important. "So, let's say I sign this 'contract' and then it turns out there's nothing beneath those logs you found."

Finn looked at me, and I looked back at him. Finally, I said, "If we can't show . . . if there's nothing there, then . . . then I guess we don't have a deal."

Granger smiled and nodded, and he reached

for my paper. When he took out his fountain pen and got ready to sign, I pulled out my cell phone and clicked off several pictures. When he sensed me moving he looked up at me with a sudden glare. "What do you think you're doing?"

"Making a visual record of you signing, just in case you try to say we forged your signature."

"My, my, my you're not a very trusting person."

"Like one of our Presidents said, 'trust, but verify,'" I said, feeling a little bit smug.

"Good point," Granger responded. He paused a second, then snapped his fingers, turned and called over his shoulder. "Donna, please bring me two copies of our standard non-disclosure." He turned back and smiled at me. "You just reminded me of something important."

"What's that?" I asked, feeling a little buzz of uncertainty.

"'Trust, but verify,'" Granger said, as Donna handed him two documents, each one consisting of several sheets of paper stapled together.

Granger handed one copy to me and one to Finn, and I looked at long paragraphs of heavy, legal-looking language. "Just as the two of you are trusting me to go through with the original deal if you can show me the tanks, I'm trusting you both to keep everything we have discussed totally secret. Forever. Do we understand each other?"

I looked up from the document to Granger. "What happens if we don't?"

He smiled, but not pleasantly. Above the smiling lips, the eyes were hard as marbles. "You go to jail. You go straight to jail. You do not pass Go. You do not collect two hundred dollars. This is serious stuff. No games."

I glanced over at Finn, who just shrugged. "I sort of expected this," he said.

Granger held out a pen, and after a second's hesitation, I took it and signed where he showed me on the back page, and then I had to initial each page at the bottom. Finn did the same.

When we handed the documents back to Granger, he took his pen and got ready to sign my contract. "Take your picture if you wish," he said, as he signed.

27.

After we met up with Finn's grandfather and he drove us out of Charleston, we each went home for lunch knowing we had to get to Buccaneer's Spit as soon as we were finished. Poppy was still moping and didn't say much while we ate our sandwiches, but it seemed to cheer him up a little when I told him I was going to meet Finn at the spit after lunch.

I got to the spit several minutes before Finn arrived. All during my walk there, something had been bothering me about the way Granger had acted. It was obvious that he thought he was so much smarter than two kids, and I was trying to figure out what kind of trick he had up his sleeve. I had no idea what it might be, but I was going to be on my guard.

When Finn showed up, I could tell he was worrying about the same thing because he kept his head down as he walked toward me, absently kicking at lumps of sand, the way someone does when they're trying to figure out a big problem.

We had no chance to talk about our suspicions, however, because almost the moment Finn arrived, the shiny black **SUV** came down the path and stopped right where the sand became soft.

A window came down, and Granger stuck his head out. "Show me what you found," he ordered.

"It's all the way at the other end," I said.

Granger put his window back up, and the **SUV** drove quickly across the soft sand, down to the hard sand that had been recently washed by the tide. It accelerated there, heading down to the end of the spit where it idled until we caught up.

When we did, Granger rolled down his window again. "Where to now?"

"We have to walk from here."

The man with the bald head got out from behind the wheel. He went around to the rear and pulled two spades as Granger climbed out of the front passenger seat. A third man, the other one I'd seen getting yelled at in the glass-walled conference room, popped out of the backseat. All three men still wore the dark suits they'd had on earlier that morning and also the same shiny leather shoes. They were terrible choices for where we had to go, but neither Finn nor I said a word.

Granger signaled for us to start walking, so Finn and I took the lead with Granger and the two men behind us. We headed around the end of the spit, then up the narrow strip between the river and the thick forest of bushes that ran between river and beach. As we came off the loose sand and onto the muddy soil of the riverbank, I glanced back at Granger whose fancy black loafers already looked like they had filled up with sand. I hoped he had a few sand burrs in his socks, too.

Finn was in the lead, and he came to a stop as he reached the nearly invisible path that led toward the old palmetto stump.

"This is going to ruin your suits," I said as I came to a stop next to Finn.

"I have lots of suits," Granger said.

The big guy stood beside Granger and eyed the bushes with an unhappy expression. Granger shot him a sideways look. "You have enough suits, too, Serge."

Finn went first, and I followed as we slipped and shoved our way through the narrow opening in the tangle of branches. Behind us Granger grunted as he forced his way through. Behind Granger the bald man he had called Serge sounded like a wild hog as he muscled his huge body along the tight path. Several times I heard sticks snap and clothing tear and some ripe cuss words. The third man came last, but he seemed to have an easier time.

By the time Granger and his men were through, Finn was already standing atop the sand where we had been digging. "Right here," he said.

Granger looked around, seeing the tree on the south end of the clearing, then glancing at the distance of the hole from the tree. "That's the tree?" he scoffed, making it sound like he was sooo much smarter than a couple of kids.

"No," I said, pointing. "It's there."

Granger scowled. "I don't see a tree."

"There's none now, but if you look close you can see where one used to be," Finn said, indicating the rotten palmetto stump he had spotted the previous night.

Granger glanced at the big guy who was carrying the shovels and at the smaller man. "Dig," he commanded.

As Finn moved out of the way, Serge and the other man stepped into the small depression where our hole had been. They tossed aside the dead branches then began throwing out shovelfuls of sand. It took less than two minutes before one of the shovels chunked into wood.

I glanced at Granger, who had already paced off the twenty-five steps from the old palmetto trunk and was now standing perfectly still, his eyes riveted on the hole where both men were shoveling the last of the sand off the wooden roof. After a few seconds, he seemed to realize that I was watching him, and he made a noticeable effort to appear relaxed.

Shrugging like it was no big deal, he cleared his throat. "Mark off the length and width," he told the two diggers.

Obeying, the two men widened the hole and cleared off sand until their shovel blades came to the edge of the wood. Granger appeared to study the size of the roof, as if that in itself was important. Finally, he gave a small nod.

Once the two diggers had found the edges

of the roof, Granger nodded to Serge. "What's it sound like?"

Serge moved around the roof tapping the blade of the shovel against the wood. As he did, I heard the sounds change and realized thumps along the edges showed something hard was underneath, but those in the center had a hollow tone.

When Serge finished tapping, he and Granger exchanged a long look. There was something they weren't saying out loud, and it bothered me because I had no idea what it could be.

"You and Stevenson get the other tools," Granger said.

The two men stood their spades in the sand, then started back through the narrow space in the bushes, the sounds of ripping cloth and a few more choice curses telling us it wasn't any easier to get through a second time. Once they were gone, Granger stepped down onto the top of the wooden platform, walked to its center, took out his cell phone and appeared to concentrate hard for several minutes. I was working up the nerve to ask what he was doing when the sound of snapping branches and tearing cloth interrupted. The younger man, who Granger had called Stevenson came struggling through the path carrying a pick, a crowbar and a heavy-duty flashlight. Serge came behind with an axe, a thick coil of rope thrown over his neck, and a sledgehammer.

Dumping the tools on the ground, they turned without a word and headed back through the bushes, returning minutes later with a big metal stake that looked like a peg for a circus tent, another coil of rope and a silver gizmo that had a handle and some wheels. Granger called it the "come-along."

I looked at the growing pile of tools, thinking Granger had brought way more than he needed to tear off the roof of an old lean-to that covered an oil tank. Also, it was midafternoon. The sun overhead was bright. I gave the flashlight a questioning look but didn't say anything. Later on, I would think back to that very moment and realize how wrong Finn and my assumptions had been.

28.

Maybe I would have started to think about it then, but I was distracted by Serge tying one end of the rope around Stevenson's waist, wrapping the other end around his own waist, then standing about ten feet from the edge of the uncovered roof and bracing himself like a guy who was belaying a mountain climber.

Finn glanced at me, seeming as amazed as I was. "What are they doing?" he whispered.

"Just being careful, I guess."

"I guess there could be a couple feet between the roof and the old tanks," he said.

"And if they're rusty and he breaks through, he could get his legs all cut up."

We watched as Stevenson took off his suit coat, hung it on a branch, and then tried to jam the end of the crowbar between the outermost logs as he tried to pry one loose. I could see that some kind of old brown chinking had been shoved into the seams between the logs. It must have been pretty hard because it took a bunch of hits before Stevenson broke up the chinking and actually got the crowbar down between the logs.

Even when he did, the old wood did not give easily, and Stevenson had to move down the length of the log, using the sledgehammer to break up the chinking and pound the bar between the logs over and over as he tried to loosen them.

Finally, when he got down to the other end and pounded the crowbar in for maybe the seventh or eighth time, the log moved a little. When it did, Serge tightened the rope a bit as if he was worried about Stevenson falling in. Granger moved to the edge of the hole, and without stepping down onto the wooden roof, he tried to jimmy the pointed end of the pick between the logs as Stevenson crowbarred the other end.

The surprise came when the log broke free and the end rose. It turned out not to be a half-log but rather what appeared to be an entire palmetto trunk. The outer part was punky and rotten, like anything that had been buried in the sand for a long time, but the inner part still appeared to be firm and strong.

Once Stevenson had pried one end of the log a few inches above the others, Granger looped the second coil of rope around the raised end. After slowly lowering the pick handle so the log settled back into place, Stevenson knotted the rope tight on the log, then climbed out of the hole.

With Stevenson off the log roof, Serge let go of the safety rope, grabbed the stake and the sledgehammer and pounded the stake deep into the ground. Then, hooking one end of the come-along to the stake, he picked up the rope that was tied around the log and fed the loose end into the come-along's gears. A second later as Serge cranked the come-along, I watched the rope tighten and begin to pull the log away from the rest.

I held my breath as the log groaned under the pressure. For a second, I thought it might snap right in half, and if it did, I realized the broken part would whip toward where we were standing. If somebody got hit, they'd be badly hurt, so I grabbed Finn's arm and pulled him away.

Luckily, instead of breaking, the log gave one last squealing groan and popped free from the rest. When it did, Serge and Stevenson strained hard to roll it out of the way.

Once it was totally clear, Finn and I hurried over to see what lay underneath. Serge waved us back, because Granger was already there, right on the edge of the hole, using his powerful flashlight to shine a beam down into the opening.

Granger got down on his knees and looked for a long time, shining the light back and forth into the darkness between the logs. When he turned to look back at me and wave me over, he had a look on his face that made my stomach twist.

I walked to the edge of the hole and took the light Granger held out to me. "Take a look," he said.

With a shaking hand I held the light over the blackness and tried to see down. Musty air smelling like it had been closed up for ages hit my nose. My face wrinkled in disgust because the odor made me think of a grave.

I saw nothing, so I dropped to my knees and stuck the light even closer to the opening. Even then, I could see only blackness until I shined the light along the side of the hole and saw the ladder. It was an old wooden ladder, ancient and irregular, with rope holding the cross pieces in place. It seemed totally out of place, because it was the kind of ladder that would have been used in a time much earlier than World War II.

I shined the light on the ladder, following it as it descended until it faded away in the darkness. Then I shined the light around the rest of the hole, seeing nothing but what looked like a bottomless pit going down and down forever. There were no gas tanks here. There was nothing at all.

29.

I stayed where I was for a long time, shining the light with increasing desperation as I searched for anything that I thought should be there, like ammunition boxes or an old gas tank. At some point I felt Finn take the light from my hand as he got on his knees beside me and began to shine the beam around.

"Jeez," he muttered after nearly a minute, "how far does this thing go down?"

"Kids," I heard Granger say after a time. I turned around to see him giving me a regretful smile. "Sorry," he said.

When he said it, the meaning of his words hit me like a punch. My face crumpled, and I felt hot tears spilling from my eyes. "You . . . you're not going to buy the spit?"

He shrugged. "Are there any tanks down there, like the ones you promised?"

"But we found . . ." My words trailed off.

"You found a hole in the ground." He shook his head. "It changes nothing. The spit just doesn't work for me anymore."

"But the map . . . even at a lower price?" I

said, the words coming out almost like I was choking.

Granger shook his head.

I felt as if my body was falling, plunging into that black hole we had just uncovered. Poppy had planned to sell the spit to pay for Mom's treatment, and now he wasn't going to get the money, not any of it. My mother was going to die.

Granger looked as if he actually felt bad. "Look, kid, I probably shouldn't have gotten your hopes up. I was pretty sure there wasn't anything down here that was going to change the value of this spit. I discovered that old map, and I'll admit I was curious of what it was all about. When you said you found something, well, I just wanted to see what you'd found. I'm going to give you and your friend some money to thank you for showing us what you uncovered, but I'm sorry to say I won't be buying your grandfather's land."

I could barely see him through my tears, but I coughed out, "Why did you say you wanted to buy it in the first place?"

Granger threw up his hands like someone admitting something very embarrassing. "I'm having a lot of money troubles, which is no secret. I just thought—it was a wild idea I'll admit—but I thought if I could buy the spit pretty cheap and build more houses, then maybe I could cut my price on all the houses I haven't been able to sell. Now, I realize it's never going to work, and I'm just going to look even more ridiculous if word gets out I was even thinking about it."

He pulled out his wallet. "Here," he said taking some bills and handing a couple to me and a couple to Finn. "Take this for your trouble. I sure would appreciate it if you would do me the favor of keeping this little adventure secret. And remember the non-disclosure agreement you both signed. I don't want to have to take any legal action against you, but it would embarrass me greatly to have people find out I was playing around with old maps when I should have been working hard to save my business."

I took the money and shoved it in my pocket without even glancing at the bills. I didn't care about the money because the world had gone black. There was no hope. I just nodded and then moved out of the way as the men went back to work, pulling the log they had jerked free back into place and onto the opening. Afterward, they shoveled sand back over the logs, but I hardly paid attention.

Without saying anything to Granger, I pushed through the bushes and started back around the end of the spit, heading toward home.

I had gone only a short way, when footsteps came up behind me, and I heard Finn's voice. "I'm really sorry."

I shrugged but kept walking. "It's not your fault."

"Yeah, but I know how much that meant to you. I feel terrible."

"I probably never should have thought I

could change anything. I just got my hopes up. It was silly."

"It wasn't silly," Finn said.

The way he said it, with so much force and confidence, made me angry enough to stop and turn to look at him. "Yeah, it was."

"It wasn't silly," Finn repeated. "Not a bit."

I shook my head and started walking again.

Finn came up beside me, his footsteps making soft thuds in the sand. "You want to know why?"

I stopped, not looking at him. "Go away, Finn."

Finn ignored what I said and continued. "You're so upset you don't even see it."

"See what?" I snapped, starting to cry again, in spite of trying not to. "See that my mom's going to die?"

Finn held up his hands in a sign for peace. "I'm talking about Granger. He was lying to you."

"What, he's gonna buy Poppy's property?"

"No," Finn shook his head. "It's not that . . . it's something else."

"What else is there to lie about?"

"What's buried under those logs?"

"There's nothing. It's just a huge hole."

"Yeah," Finn agreed, "but Granger went through that whole song and dance, *'I was so silly. Please don't tell anybody I was looking at maps when I should have been saving my business.'* Does he strike you as the kind of person who says those kinds of things about himself?"

"No," I admitted.

"And did you see the other guys' faces?"

"What are you talking about?"

"When there was nothing but that . . . that hole."

"What, they thought it was a big joke?"

Finn shook his head. "No, you know the way people look at each other when they've got some big secret that they don't think anybody else knows about?"

I shrugged. "I guess."

"Well, that's exactly the way Serge and Stevenson looked at each other, like they had just pulled a huge trick on us."

I shook my head. "*What* kind of trick could it be?"

"I don't know, but don't you think we have to find out?"

"How?"

"We have to come back when those guys are gone and figure out what that hole really means."

I shrugged, sure he was just saying all this stuff to make me feel better.

"Look," Finn said, "go home and get some rest. I'm going to find a place where I can keep watch on those guys. When they leave I'll come straight to your house, okay?"

I nodded. "I guess."

"Callie, I don't know what's really going on,

but I know there's something fishy." Finn stuck his hand in his pocket and pulled out the bills Granger had given him. "Five hundred bucks!" he said, waving the bills in my face. "Did you even look at what he gave you?"

I put my hand in my pocket and pulled out my money. Five hundred dollars for me, too. Under any other circumstances I would have been insanely happy about five hundred dollars to go shopping and spend on anything I wanted. Now, thinking about my mom's expensive treatments, it wouldn't even make a dent in the cost.

"Callie, listen to me. *Nobody* gives five hundred bucks to kids, especially when they didn't find anything. Especially not somebody who's supposedly going broke. Something's going on!"

I looked down at the money in my hand then up at Finn. He had to be at least a little bit right. "Okay . . . and thanks. I'll lie down for a little bit, and when you get me, we'll come right back here."

Finn broke into a big smile. "Good!"

"And Finn?" I said, "I really appreciate you doing this."

"No sweat," he said. "It beats school all to pieces."

30.

I spent the next few hours in my room resting and trying to read a book, but unable to concentrate. My eyes went over the same paragraph again and again, but the sentences wouldn't stick in my brain. I thought about my mom, about cancer, about Poppy trying to sell the spit to Granger and how Granger was walking away.

Finn was convinced that something else was going on and there was some kind of mystery to solve, but Finn was a boy and his imagination was fired up. It was a game to him, but something very different to me—literally life and death. The fact that he never came to the house that afternoon told me he'd already gotten tired of the game or maybe even forgotten about it and gone fishing.

A short time before dinner, Plankton jumped on my bed and started to jam his wet nose into my cheek. When I put down my book and looked at him he tilted his head as if he had just asked me a question and was waiting for his answer.

"You want to go for a walk?" I asked.

Plankton barked in response.

I closed my book on the same page where I'd opened it several hours earlier, got off the bed, grabbed the leash and some poop bags, and went outside. As I was heading toward the street a whisper came from a nearby azalea bed. My head whipped around as Plankton froze, his hackles going up and a deep growl coming from his throat.

A second later Finn rose up. "I thought you'd never come out," he said, scratching at a mosquito bite on his neck.

"How long have you been here?" I asked.

"A while."

"Why didn't you just come up and knock on the door like a normal person?"

"'Cause I'm really sandy and gross. I thought your grandfather would either get ticked off that I came looking so dirty, or he'd start asking me questions I didn't want to answer."

He stepped out from behind the bushes and I could see that he really was a mess. He had managed to get grease or dirt stains all over his clothes, and his shirt was soaked with old sweat. "What have you been doing?"

"After those guys left, I went back to my grandfather's, loaded up his golf cart with tools and equipment and brought them out to the spit. The golf cart wouldn't go across the sand, so I had to carry everything from the path to the hole."

"What kind of tools?"

"A drill, a saw, some rope, a pry bar, a

sledge hammer, a pick, a couple flashlights—a bunch of stuff."

"Why?"

"We have to go down that hole."

"Are you serious? We can't get those logs out of there."

"If we saw them into smaller pieces, we can."

I shook my head. "This isn't an adventure game."

Finn's expression hardened. "I know it's not. You didn't see those two guys when they looked at each other after Granger gave you his big 'I was so silly' line. Granger's blowing serious smoke up your rear end, and that means there's something else going on. You owe it to yourself . . . and to your mom to find out what it is."

Finn's words were like a slap, and I looked at him more closely. His eyes were sparking with energy, but he wasn't playing. He was dead serious and totally believed what he was telling me. If Finn had been willing to work this hard and get this sweaty for me, I needed to play it out.

"I can't go now," I said. "Dinner's pretty soon."

Finn nodded. "Then we need to sneak out again, before my grandfather notices all the stuff that's missing."

"Tonight?"

He nodded.

I took a deep breath and looked down at

Plankton. I knew he would insist on going, either that or he'd wake up Poppy. "Okay," I said. "Same as last time?"

"Yes."

A short time later when Poppy and I sat down to dinner, I could tell he was sadder than ever, and I knew it was because Granger had refused to buy the spit. I was pretty darn sad myself, but I decided not to make things worse by telling Poppy about my visit to Granger and his trip to the spit with Finn and me, and how he had weaseled out when I'd thought we had him in a box.

Martha served our food, and I could tell from her eyes and her expression that she had noticed just how sad we both were. Of course, Martha didn't say anything, but she knew. It was a very quiet dinner.

After we ate, I told Poppy I was tired and wanted to go to bed early. He said he was heading to bed early, too, and because I already knew that Plankton was only going to cause big trouble for me if he didn't get exactly what he wanted, I took him to my bedroom after his night walk and let him sleep on my bed. He put his head on the pillow right beside mine and started to snore. Fortunately, I was tired enough that his dog breath didn't keep me awake.

A couple hours later, my phone alarm went off, and I jumped into my clothes and slipped on my daypack, which I had already loaded with a couple breakfast bars, bug repellant, a small first aid kit, and some bottled water. Then, having remembered it this time, I snapped on Plankton's leash, leaned out the window and lowered him to the ground, then climbed out right behind. The night was chilly and cloudless, and a mostly full moon made walking easy. We hurried toward Buccaneer's Spit, Plankton straining at his leash as if he knew exactly where we were headed and was eager to get there.

Reaching the path, I hurried toward the beach, thinking I must have beaten Finn by at least a few minutes, and I nearly jumped out of my skin when he stepped out of the shadows. Plankton knew Finn by now, so he barked and turned in circles to show how excited he was and to remind me that I needed to let him off his leash.

"Any trouble getting out?" Finn asked as Plankton streaked into the darkness.

"No, how about you?"

He shook his head as we turned and set out at a fast walk down the beach toward the end of the spit. Surprised that he wasn't being a bit more talkative, I shook my head but kept up.

When he reached the end of the spit, Finn didn't slow down. I picked up Plankton in case of gators, then followed Finn's fast walk along the river, as we quickly reached the narrow path that led to the wood-covered hole. Carrying Plankton as I snaked through the bushes behind Finn, I found all the tools that he had talked about earlier lying in a big pile.

"How many trips did you have to make to get all this stuff here?" I asked.

"A bunch," he admitted, as he picked up a shovel and started digging down to the wooden roof.

"No wonder you got dirty."

"Yeah."

"You have another shovel?" I asked.

"No, I had too much other stuff to carry."

I hated standing there, and I wasn't going to let him think that I was letting him do all the work just because I was a girl. "Then move," I said, jumping down into the hole and grabbing the shovel, ignoring the pain from last night's blisters. "You've already done a lot of the work, so let me do this."

"Just be careful," he said. "Now we know how deep this thing is."

"No, actually we don't," I said with a shiver, remembering how earlier the flashlight beam hadn't been able to show us the bottom of the pit. "We just know it's *really* deep."

I let Plankton off his leash, which I stuffed into my daypack, and he sniffed around the clearing while I started on the hole. The work went fast because the sand was loose, and I knew exactly where to dig. As I worked, Finn was rummaging in his pile of tools, and when I looked up, he had an electric drill in one hand and a saw with a pointy blade in the other. He laid them by the hole, and a moment later he reappeared with a length of rope that he'd run around his chest and then down and around each thigh. He'd tied the other end of the rope to a long steel pry bar that he laid on the ground between two sturdy bushes that held it in place.

"What's that for?" I asked as I felt the shovel hit log.

"It's a safety harness, in case I fall through the wood when I'm cutting it," he said. "Since you're not heavy enough to hold me if I do fall, this bar will do it."

Amazed at how much planning Finn had done, I asked, "You really think we can get those logs out of there?"

He waved me out of the hole, giving me a hand up as I climbed out. "Watch me," he said, picking up the drill. It was battery powered, and it held a very thick drill bit, the kind used for making holes big enough for cables or ropes. He stepped down into the hole and walked along the edge until he was near the middle.

Placing the drill bit in the center of one of the logs a couple feet from its end, Finn pressed the button. The drill whined as the bit chewed down into the wood. It went all the way through really fast, and he pulled the bit out, then put the pointy saw blade into the hole he had made and started cutting.

The sawing took longer than the drilling, and Finn was grunting by the time he finished making two cuts, each one going from the hole

in the center of the log to the edges. When
he finished, he used the pick to dig along both
sides of the log until the cut piece broke free.
Finn and I looked at each other and smiled.
Next, Finn put the end of the pick into the
hole he had drilled and was able to pry up
the log, and I reached down and helped him
toss it out of the hole.

Finn picked up the drill and was about to
make a hole in the next log, when he froze
and cocked his head.

"Something wrong?" I whispered. I looked
around, but I couldn't hear any sound other
than the rough cry of some bird that called
out over the river every few minutes. "Is
someone coming?"

Finn held up a finger, then held perfectly
still for a few seconds. Finally, he put down
the drill and knelt, lowering his ear to the
opening we had just made. He listened for a
moment, then straightened.

"I hear noises coming from down there," he
said.

"You can't be serious," I said. "What could
be down there?"

"I don't know, but come here."

I stepped into the hole, then grabbed the
rope that was tied around Finn's waist, so I'd
have something to hold on to just in case.
When I knelt over the hole and got my ear
close, I could hear it, too.

"What is it?" I asked.

Finn shook his head, and we put our heads

together and kept listening. After a few more moments he said, "Sounds like somebody digging, doesn't it?"

I heard what he was talking about, a very faint sound like "chunk" pause "chunk" pause. "Yeah but it can't be. I mean, how would they get down there?"

"Even more, *why?*" Finn asked.

"Maybe it's an animal," I said.

"What kind of animal would make that noise?" Finn asked.

I shook my head, but a shiver went up my back as I tried to imagine.

After a few more seconds of listening Finn shook his head, straightened, and grabbed the drill to make his next hole. When he finished, he used the pick to hammer out the chinking that bound the logs together, then he went to work making two outward cuts. This time, before he got all the way through, he had me lie on my stomach at the edge of the hole and hold one hand under the nearest edge of the log. Then, holding one of his hands under the other end of the log, he finished the cut. When the log came loose, we rolled it on top of the other logs so it didn't fall.

Finn stood, ironed out the cricks in his back from being bent over, then tossed the log out of the hole. The opening he had made was now several feet across, plenty wide enough for either of us to slip through, and Finn had planned his cuts so the old wooden ladder we had spotted earlier that day was directly below us.

Also, with the opening larger, the sounds coming from below seemed louder, although strangely, they also sounded farther away. As Finn shined a light downward, I grabbed a nearby shell and dropped it. We both listened and heard a splash several seconds later.

"Water," Finn said as his light picked up faint ripples that appeared to be thirty or forty feet below. He shook his head. "Who dug this thing?"

"Not the Army or Navy," I said. "And not during World War II. The ladder's too old-timey for that."

"What do you want to do?" Finn asked.

"We need to go down, but I think we should go home, get some sleep and come back in the morning when we've got better light."

Finn nodded, and we agreed to meet the next morning at ten. He took the drill and saw back to his grandparents' house but left the rest of the tools in case we needed them tomorrow. I walked home with Plankton, my stomach bubbling with nerves as I thought about the next morning when I would be going down that rickety old ladder into the shaft of darkness.

31.

After another night of weird dreams, I woke up before it was even light. Still dead tired but too stirred up to go back to sleep, I hung out in my room until it wouldn't look too weird to be up, then I got dressed and headed past Poppy's closed door to the kitchen where Martha was already busy.

"Feel like eggs this morning?" she asked.

"Thanks, but I think I'll just have some cereal," I said, since my stomach felt all jangly with nerves.

Martha poured some corn flakes into a bowl, put some fresh fruit on top, and it took me only a minute or so to eat it. A glance at my watch showed it was only eight. Two hours to go. Two hours with nothing to think about but going down that skinny, creaky ladder. What was down there? And who or what had been making those sounds last night?

The next hour and a half seemed to take forever. At nine-thirty, I loaded my daypack with all the usual stuff and left the house, asking Martha to let Poppy know that I was meeting Finn at the spit. Plankton followed

me to the door, pulling his leash off the
doorknob where it usually hung. I would have
preferred to go alone, but knowing he'd bark
his head off if I left him, I gave in. I walked
fast, not letting Plankton have his usual long
sniffs, and even though we made it to the
hole about fifteen minutes early, I found Finn
already waiting.

The moment he saw me, he started tying
the rope around his waist. I noticed that he
already had a flashlight dangling from a thin
cord knotted through one of his belt loops.

"Take off the rope," I told him.

"Why?"

"I'm going first."

"That's ridiculous."

"No, it's smart. First of all, the ladder's
really old, and I'm lighter. I'll put less strain
on it. If it breaks you're stronger and you can
help pull me out. When I get to the bottom,
I'll untie the rope, and you can haul it up and
tie it to yourself."

"I've almost got it tied. I'll go first."

I shook my head. "No. I got us into this. I
go first. Period."

He looked like he wanted to argue, but finally
his lips tightened into a flat line. He took off
the rope and tossed it to me. "Okay, bossy."

"Flashlight, too," I said, as he scowled but
took the cord off his belt loop

Tying the rope around my middle, I knotted
the flashlight cord to my wrist since I had
no belt loops. I worked fast, so Finn wouldn't

see how badly my hands were shaking. Finally, I slipped on my daypack then moved to the edge of the hole. Glancing nervously at the total blackness, my imagination flashed images of snakes, spiders, and alligators all waiting at the bottom of the shaft. And while I told myself there were no such things as ghosts, I thought again about what had been making that noise the night before.

Think Laura Croft. Think Indiana Jones, I told myself. *You can do this.*

Holding the rope with one hand so it was tight against the two bushes where Finn had wedged his pry bar, I backed to the hole and let the slack pool at my feet. Reaching with one leg, I took a shaky breath then felt around until my toes found the first rung of the ladder. Slowly, I let more and more of my weight rest on the old wood, hoping it wouldn't snap under me. It held, and I lowered myself further until my other foot rested on the second rung.

When I got down to the third rung, I let go of the rope and gripped the top rung with my hands. The wood felt skinny and dry as a matchstick, but it was holding my weight.

Before I could go any farther, a frantic growling noise came from above, and a bunch of loose sand began to fall into my hair and onto my shoulders.

"Hold on a second," Finn said. "We have to do something about the dog."

I looked up at where Plankton was hanging

way too far over the hole, looking down as if he wanted to jump in after me.

Letting out a soft curse, I went back up the ladder until my head was back in the sunlight. Plankton began to lick me furiously.

"Where's your leash?" Finn asked.

"In my pack," I said, struggling to turn me face away from Plankton's tongue. "But we can't tie him up here. "He'll bark his head off, and that's liable to bring other people."

"So what do we do?"

I came up one more rung. "Can you stuff him into my pack?"

I leaned over so the pack wasn't hanging over the hole, as Finn picked up Plankton, unzipped my daypack and loaded him inside.

"Leave his head sticking out, but make sure it's too tight for him to escape," I said.

"Roger that," Finn said. When he finished he patted the pack. "All set. Good luck with your wild little friend."

"Thanks."

As I started down the ladder again, I wasn't so worried about falling since it had held me the first time, so I relaxed enough to look around. I realized I was climbing down into something that looked more like an elevator shaft than a simple hole. The sides of the shaft were made of logs. Nearer the top, the logs were covered by a fine layer of dust that had drifted down over many years, but down a little farther, even in the dim light I could make out their shape. They looked sturdy, which made me feel a bit safer.

Even so, my stomach bubbled like a tea kettle on full boil. When I looked up, I could see Finn's face set with a nervous expression, framed against a square of blue sky that grew smaller and smaller as I went lower. I wanted to keep my face pointed upward at that shrinking bit of light and safety, but as the rope pulled over the edge, it loosened bits of dirt and sand from around the hole that fell on my face.

The deeper I went, the thicker and staler and more awful the air seemed, so I made myself think about Mom. If there was any way of saving her, it would make all the scariness worth it. Even Plankton must have been a little frightened, because for once in his life he was totally quiet.

"Use the light," Finn whispered down to me. "Tell me what you see."

Despite my fear of the spiders that might be attracted to my light, I halted, gripped the ladder tight with one hand, then pulled the cord that held the flashlight across the knee of my upper leg until I was able to grab it and turn it on.

Fortunately, I saw no spider webs, and when I shined the light straight down, the beam reflected off what looked like water maybe twenty feet below. It made me think of the strange noise we had heard the previous night, but also of snakes and gators.

"There's nothing but straight walls, and then gross water at the bottom," I whispered to Finn. Maybe because of the stillness and the heaviness of the air, whispering seemed smarter than talking in a normal voice.

"You doing okay?" he asked.

"Fine," I lied as I clicked off the light and continued deeper into the shaft. Now with each step, I paid more and more attention to the pool of water at the bottom. It smelled like something rotten, and I was starting to fear that some giant tentacle would shoot out of the darkness and wrap around my ankle.

I was looking so hard at the water that I nearly missed the opening. It was on the side of the shaft facing the river, probably ten feet above the pool of stagnant water, a black square even darker than the barely visible walls.

I quickly grabbed the flashlight and turned it on, then descended a few more feet until I was even with the opening. When I shined the light into it, it looked just like the shaft I was in, a square tunnel lined on all sides with logs. It appeared to go straight ahead; I couldn't see an end.

"There's another tunnel down here," I whispered up to Finn. "It goes toward the river."

"Can you get into it?" Finn whispered.

I stretched out my leg and tried to get my foot onto the ledge where the tunnel began. I barely touched it. What a bad idea, I thought, putting the tunnel entrance so far from the ladder. "Maybe."

"Be careful."

If I were careful, I never would have come down this creaky old ladder, I wanted to say, but didn't. Getting into the tunnel was going to require letting go of the ladder and taking a long step. With nothing to hold onto there seemed to be an excellent chance of slipping.

I took a deep breath and got ready to jump, but that was when I spotted the grip set into the wall right next to the tunnel opening. It was made of the same skinny, old looking wood as the ladder, but it was clearly meant to be a handhold that a person could grab as they went from the ladder into the tunnel. The ladder had held me; hopefully, the handhold would work, too. I thought about Mom one more time. I thought about the safety rope. Finn could always pull me up if I fell.

"Here goes," I whispered, as I reached for the grip with one hand and stretched my foot toward the tunnel lip.

As my foot came down on the tunnel's lip and my fingers grasped the handhold, I realized belatedly that getting back onto the ladder was going to be extremely difficult, maybe even impossible without the rope.

"Are you in?" Finn called down, no longer whispering.

"Yes," I whispered. "But be quiet."

"You hear any of those noises from last night?"

I'd managed to forget about the noise as I worried about other things, but now as I stepped into the tunnel I stopped and listened. To my relief, I heard nothing. "No," I whispered back.

"Send up the rope when you're in."

I untied the rope from around my waist and let Finn haul it up. As he did, I looked around. The tunnel's opening was framed with big logs that formed a solid looking square. Underfoot, the floors were made of the same wood that lined the sides of the vertical shaft. Whoever had built this place had taken a lot of care and spent a whole lot of time, but for what purpose? It might have been used to store ammunition or gasoline in World War II, but the people would have needed an elevator to get the stuff up and down and there was no sign there had ever been one. And wouldn't they have used concrete rather than wood to make an elevator shaft? A lot of things made no sense.

A moment later, sand and dirt started to break loose up above, and I looked up to see Finn step onto the ladder. I leaned out of the tunnel and shined my light up as he came down.

Finn was on the sixth or seventh rung when it happened. He lowered his foot onto the next crosspiece and it snapped. Even so, that shouldn't have been a problem because his other foot rested on the rung just above, and he still had good handholds. But whether it was the sudden tug of extra weight, or something else, the rungs he held with his hands broke at the same instant.

Finn cried out and tumbled backward until the rope snapped tight, jerking him like a ragdoll. I stared in horror as he dangled ten or fifteen feet below me, the lower part of his legs in the nasty, dark water. For several seconds he didn't move, but then he let out a groan.

"Finn?" I whispered.

He looked up and blinked at the flashlight beam.

"Are you hurt?"

"My ribs," he rasped.

I felt a sudden shot of panic. "Are they broken?"

"No, they just hurt a lot. This rope wasn't exactly a professional harness."

"Can you climb back up the ladder?"

"I think so." He used his legs to move his body back and forth like a clock pendulum until he finally touched the wall where the ladder was. He grabbed but missed, swung away, then back again, grabbed again and missed again.

"Shine you light on the wall," Finn whispered.

I had been shining the light on him like a spotlight, but now I painted the wall with light. When I saw it clearly, I let out a gasp. There was no ladder down where Finn dangled.

32.

A long silence followed as we tried to get our heads around this sudden disaster. I panned the light up the shaft and saw that the ladder ended about six feet above where Finn hung. It gave me a horrible suspicion that his fall might not have been an accident, and this shaft was a trap. It sure looked like one. Maybe, the ladder was supposed to have broken, leaving whoever climbed down to fall into the water, where presumably they would drown. Maybe out of pure luck I had been light enough to get down without breaking it.

But why? There had to be a reason. Was something down here worth killing people over? That thought filled me with fear but also curiosity. I had no time to dwell on it, because right then Finn started trying to shinny up the rope. He could only climb with his hands and arms because the rope didn't reach to his legs. He made it a few feet only to slip back.

"I don't think I can get up," he said after a second and then a third try. "The rope is too slippery, and my ribs are killing me."

"Don't try again," I said. "You need to save your strength."

"For what?" he rasped, his voice tinged with fear. He kept looking down at where his legs disappeared in the black water. It was impossible not to dread what might live under its surface.

"Try this," I said. "Go to the wall, put your feet against the logs and try to walk them up the side while you pull yourself up the rope with your hands. If you can make it to where the ladder starts, you can hopefully get to where I am."

He tried, making it three or four feet out of the water before his feet slipped and he fell again.

In the beam of my flashlight, I could see him starting to shiver from the cold water. I had read somewhere that when people got cold they got weaker. We needed to come up with a better idea fast, and if it didn't work, I was afraid Finn wouldn't have the strength to try anything else.

"Get over as close as you can to the wall where I am," I told him.

Once again, he raised his knees and used his legs to swing toward my side of the shaft and then away. On his third or fourth try, I was able reach out and grab the rope. I hadn't counted on now heavy he was, and as the rope started to swing back, I had to let go because he nearly pulled me off my feet and out into the shaft.

"Sorry," I said, taking off the daypack with Plankton still inside and resting it against the side of the tunnel. Plankton growled to be let out, but I ignored him. "Try again," I said.

Finn did, and this time as soon as I grabbed the rope, I threw myself backward, sitting on the ground and digging my heels into bumps in the wooden floor. Despite how hard I pushed, Finn's weight began to drag me toward the tunnel lip. With only another foot before my feet would be off the edge and I would fall into the water, I was in full panic mode, but then my heels caught and held. I gripped the rope with all my strength, dug my heels and leaned back.

"Try to walk up the wall again," I grunted.

Right away I felt the pressure on the rope change as if Finn was giving it hard tugs. My arm muscles burned but I held on. My hands and fingers, still blistered from our night's digging, were on fire, and Finn seemed to be taking forever.

It felt like there was no way that I could keep hanging on, but Finn's life depended on me finding more strength. If I let go, he'd fall back and we'd both be too tired to try again. It was either get him up now or we would be trapped down here.

My arms felt like they were pulling out of their sockets. If my heels started to slip, I would shoot over the edge like a rocket and fall into the black water below. A voice in my head told me to let go because it was hopeless, but I didn't. For some reason I kept trying, my eyes clamped shut, tears streaming down my cheeks.

In another instant, the pressure vanished, and I fell backward, my head thumping hard against the wooden floor. My first thought was panic that the rope had broken. There was no pull. I couldn't feel Finn.

I shot upright in a frenzy of dread, and that was when I heard Finn say, "Man, I didn't think I was going to make it out of there."

My flashlight had rolled to one side of the tunnel, but it still threw enough light for me to see him sitting on the tunnel floor, pulling the rope over his head and tossing it onto the ground.

"I didn't think I could keep holding the rope," I croaked.

"I was amazed you could. I'm at least twenty pounds heavier than you." Finn looked at me for a few long seconds, nodding slowly like he was really impressed. "Thanks."

I rubbed the back of my head, then took my cell phone from my pocket and looked for a signal. Zero bars. "Now, we just have to figure out how to get out of here."

Finn looked back toward the dark shaft. "We need to keep the rope," he said, piling it in a tight coil so it's weight would keep it from sliding back out into the shaft. "We can't risk the ladder, but maybe one of us could shinny up to the top. Not me, though. I'm way too exhausted to even think about it now."

"One of us?" I looked at the ruptured blisters on my hands and shook my head. "Not me."

He huffed out a bitter laugh. "Probably neither of us, which means we need to figure another way out of here. Maybe that sound we heard."

"You think there could be another way out?" I said, and then I shivered remembering those noises the night before. If some kind of animal burrowed all the way down here, I was sure it was one we didn't want to run into.

Finn stood, turned on his flashlight and shined it into the tunnel, which seemed to go on a long way. Plankton let out another growl, reminding us that he was stuck in the daypack.

"We should turn off one of the flashlights to save the batteries," I said, hating to think that if we were stuck down here long enough we would eventually be in complete darkness.

A quick glance at Finn's face told me he found that prospect as unpleasant as I did. However, he clicked off his light, and instantly the darkness closed in around our one puny beam.

"You know," I said, "I think it's possible the ladder was rigged to break and drown whoever tried to climb down."

"Yeah," Finn said. "I've been thinking that same thing."

"Then don't you think it's possible that there are more traps?"

After a pause, he said, "Yeah."

"I should go first," I said, struggling to sound

braver than I felt. "I was too light to break the ladder, so maybe if there are other traps down here, I'll be light enough to get past them."

"That won't do a lot of good if I set them off right behind you."

"At least, now that we know they might be here, we can look for them," I said. "I might have a better chance of spotting them."

"You know who might have an even better chance," Finn said, pointing to Plankton.

As if he knew exactly what Finn had said, Plankton let out a soft bark. I wasn't happy about Plankton going first, but the Jack Russell was dying to get free. The moment I let him out, he lifted his leg, then trotted down the tunnel, his claws clicking on the wood floor.

I followed behind him, shining my light up, down, and sideways. I didn't know what to look for—something that seemed out of place, something that could move, a piece of ceiling that could collapse and crush us. My imagination had blowguns coming out of the walls and shooting poison darts, or maybe huge boulders suddenly careening toward us.

It all seemed unbelievable, the idea of why anyone would go to the incredible effort to build this place and then set booby traps. There had to be a rational explanation we just hadn't thought of yet. I had almost convinced myself of that when I heard it, the hollow sound just ahead as Plankton crossed a section of wooden floor.

I stopped and ran my light over the floor

ahead, but it looked no different. But when I studied it again more closely, I could see where the pattern of the wood altered slightly. Behind me Finn whispered, "What?"

"There might be a trap."

Plankton had continued trotting ahead, but his claws sounded normal now. I called him back. As he turned and came to me, the sound changed once again, going hollow as he came over the same section of floor.

Finn came up beside me, and we shined both lights down. Where Plankton's paws had tracked through the thick layer of dust, the floor *definitely* looked different. Finn sat down next to the strange piece of floor, then gathered Plankton in his arms. "Hold my shoulders," he said.

It felt strange kneeling down beside Finn and putting my arms around his chest and my face right up against his ear. For some reason my thoughts went to Tommy Bluestein, the only boy that I had ever kissed, who was in my sixth-grade class back in Brooklyn. He had been a slobbery kisser and smelled bad, and it wasn't something I looked forward to doing again. Even so, despite how much work and sweat and fear we had gone through already that night, Finn actually smelled kind of good.

I shoved all that out of my mind as Finn raised his heels and slammed them down on the hollow sounding section of floor. The first time, the floor bounced slightly. The second time, a loud crack sounded, and a piece of floor almost as wide as the tunnel fell in.

Finn and I threw ourselves back from the sudden hole. We ended in a tangle, Finn lying on top of me, Plankton between us. Finn pushed himself off as if I was on fire, and we both sat up quickly, grabbed our flashlights which had rolled to either side, and shined them into the hole.

I sucked down a frightened breath at the sight of the savagely pointed wooden stakes lining the bottom. The thought of what would have happened if one of us had fallen in twisted my stomach.

"Who would do this?" I exclaimed. "It's cruel!"

"It's like a movie," Finn muttered as he stared down into the hole. "But it's real."

"There's a way around it," I said, pointing my light toward the narrow ledge just a little wider than a person's foot that ran along one side of the tunnel.

"Want me to go first?" Finn offered.

"No."

My heart went into my throat as I looked again at the cruel stakes. Sweat streamed from my armpits, but I steeled myself and stepped out onto the ledge, then I jumped, clearing the pit by a good margin. Finn put Plankton down on the floor, and he trotted along the ledge without a problem. Finn came last, stepping on the ledge as I had, then jumping. All safe, we turned off the second flashlight and started forward.

Plankton went first again with me behind,

but nothing more happened. We'd gone maybe twenty or thirty yards when Finn whispered, "Stop."

I did, immediately, wondering if Plankton and I had walked right past something dangerous.

"What's that up ahead?" he asked.

I'd been focused so hard on the space to either side and directly in front that I had paid no attention to what lay farther ahead. Now, as I shined my light down the tunnel's length, my heart sank. At the farthest reach of my beam, the tunnel ended.

How was this possible? What was the point of digging a huge shaft and tunnel, putting in horrible traps, and then having the tunnel just end? Like everything else about this place, it made no sense.

We crept ahead, Plankton first, me examining every inch of tunnel, Finn right behind. I saw nothing dangerous, but with each step, I was more and more certain that we hadn't seen the last of the traps.

"We have to be under the river," Finn said as we neared the dead end.

"Why did you have to say that?" My knees began to shake as my brain pictured the ceiling caving in, tons of river water choking and drowning us in pitch blackness.

That was when I spotted the big iron door handle. It was right there in front of us, set in the wall like an invitation or an exit sign.

"Thank heavens," Finn said from just behind me. "I bet this is the way out."

He stepped around me, and started to reach for the door handle, but I quickly shoved him back. "Don't touch it!" I snapped.

33.

Finn gaped at me as if I wasn't making any sense. "Why not?"

"It *has* to be another trap."

"It also might be the way out."

"No," I said, holding him back.

"How—?" he started to ask, clearly anxious to open the door and escape.

"You just said we're under the river."

"Yeah, but—"

"Assuming this place is booby-trapped why put a door right under the river?"

"You think—?"

"Don't you?"

Finn said nothing, but he took his hand away from the door and stepped back. I ran my light up and down along the door. "There aren't any heavy wooden beams around the door here like there are at the other end of the tunnel."

Finn still didn't want to listen. "What are you talking about?"

"If we move this door out of position, and there's no framing to hold up the roof, what's going to happen?" I asked.

Finn stepped back from the door as if he'd been burned. "Jeez," he said in amazement. "You're right, but it makes no sense. After all these traps, the tunnel can't just end here. What's the point of all this?"

"I don't know," I said, fighting down a fresh wave of panic at the thought that there was no way out.

"There *has* to be something on the other side of this door," Finn said. "Nobody would waste their time building this if there wasn't." He turned on his light and started looking around. I could tell he was as freaked out as I was and trying hard not to lose it.

I stood back. Sharing Finn's need to find an answer, but with a growing feeling that if we rushed, we would make a terrible mistake. I shined my light to either side of the door, searching for clues that there might be another way to go. Unfortunately, the walls seemed as solid here as they had everywhere else.

"Callie, we can't get out any other way," Finn said, his voice wavering with emotion. "We *need* to open this door."

"No," I said.

"I don't think either of us is strong enough to shinny all the way up the rope. What other choice do we have?"

"We need to keep looking," I said.

"These are *walls*. You can't get through them."

"Maybe there's a way," I muttered.

Over and over, I ran my fingers over the

wood on both sides of the door feeling for cracks, moving logs, anything. I found nothing.

Finn watched my fruitless search. Finally, he took a deep breath and snapped, "I'd rather die fast than starve to death down here." He was next to the big iron door handle, and I was too far away to stop him as he grabbed it and tried to give it a hard push down.

"Don't do it!" I begged.

Nothing happened.

I felt an immediate surge of relief that the handle hadn't budged.

Finn ignored me, grunting as he pulled up with all his might. I watched in terror as the handle moved, going from horizontal to vertical in one squealing motion.

Somewhere inside the walls we heard a loud *thunk* that made me shudder with fear. It sounded like something very heavy sliding into place, or out of place, and I held my breath waiting for the ceiling to collapse or the walls to burst inward with the power of the river.

Finn stood in a fighter's crouch, as if bracing for an attack. Neither of us spoke. Finally, after a minute, he took a shaking breath and reached again for the handle. Knowing he was preparing to force it open, I shouted, "No!" and grabbed his arm, hoping I was strong enough to keep him from killing us.

Finn stopped and turned on me. "We have no other choice!"

"There *has* to be another choice!" I swung my head groping desperately for some new idea, and that's when I saw it. Something was different. At first, I thought it was just some splinter of wood that had fallen off the wall, but it was more than that. Something had moved.

"Please wait," I said. Something in my tone got Finn's attention. He froze, his gaze going where my finger was pointing. "What is it?" he said.

It might have been a crack and nothing more, but I could see a faint line in the wall to our left. Barely visible, and not very long, it didn't go all the way up to the ceiling or down to the floor, just through a couple logs. It was so small that I'd barely noticed, but I was sure it hadn't been there before Finn turned the handle.

I stepped to the wall and scraped my fingers along the wood where the crack had appeared. A few dusty chunks broke loose, and I scraped harder. After only a few minutes, I had exposed a crack running from floor to ceiling.

Finn saw what I was doing, and he added his light to mine as I worked. "We've got to find another crack. It could mean there's a hidden door," he said.

We looked and looked, going up and down the tunnel in both directions. I ran my fingernails over the wood, hoping to knock loose more of the same stuff that had covered the first crack. I found nothing. We both put our hands against the wall next to the crack and shoved with all our might. Nothing moved.

When he quit pushing, Finn stared back at the door.

"No way," I said.

"We're out of options. We gotta try it."

"One more idea," I said.

Finn sighed. "What?"

"Try the handle again. Just the handle. Don't push or pull the door."

"Try what with the handle?"

"Try turning it down like you turned it up."

"I tried to push it down. It wouldn't go."

"Well something happened when you pulled it up, so maybe something will happen now when you push it the other way. At least try, okay?"

He shrugged, but he grabbed the lever and pushed it back to its original position, then tried to shove it down. It groaned, barely moving. But then, as Finn kept pressing, with a slow grinding noise, followed by another *thunk,* the handle moved down.

As soon as that happened, I shined my light along the wall where the first crack had appeared. My heart sank. No change. Again, I tried to dig my fingers into the wood to uncover another crack, but it was hopeless. I shined my light on the opposite wall, hoping to see a crack there, but it too was totally unmarked.

Finn shook his head. "Only one thing left to try," he said.

"No," I said. "There has to be something else."

Before he could turn back toward the door, I slammed my shoulder into the wall next to the crack. This time it moved slightly.

Finn saw it, too. "Wait," he said, furrowing his brows in concentration. "I think I get it." Then, instead of pushing next to the crack where I had, he went to the corner, and right where the wall ended, he pushed.

Next came a sound like something breaking free after many, many years, and the wall began to move. It pivoted on a central point, the part nearest Finn going outward and the part where I was standing swinging into the tunnel. I jumped toward Finn, then he and I stared ahead at the opening that had been revealed.

"What *is* this place?" he muttered as we shined our lights into the gloom. At first, we could see only a couple feet because our lights reflected off the dust that had been kicked loose when the wall moved. As we breathed it in, we both started to cough and sneeze. I had forgotten about Plankton, who had been unusually quiet, but he started to sneeze, too.

When the dust cleared enough for us to breathe again, I put my hand out to block Finn. "I'll go first." It took several careful steps before I could see clearly, and that was when the gasp escaped my throat.

34.

"Are you okay?" he asked as he hurried up behind me. That was when he, too, stopped dead. "What the—?" he said in a choked voice.

For several seconds there were no words to describe the sight before us. We were in something like a big room, the ceiling higher than the tunnel by several feet, held up by thick timbers that supported heavy looking beams.

The room was not empty, not by a long shot. I moved my light slowly, from one side to the other. "Is this what I think it is?" I finally managed.

"Unbelievable," Finn whispered. He started forward intending to get around me, but I put out a hand to stop him.

"We have to be really careful," I said. "Remember the traps?"

"Okay," he said, suddenly as still as a statue.

I crept forward, looking for trapdoors in the floor, for things hanging from the ceiling. I half expected something like a giant blade to swing out from the wall and cut off our heads. I'd seen stuff like that in movies when somebody raided a treasure room, and that's exactly what we were in.

What must have been centuries of dust covered everything, but there was no mistaking the things that lay underneath. I could see chests and what looked like big candle sticks. Atop the chests, just lying loose, were helmets and things that looked like crowns, as well as swords and other weapons. In other places we saw piles of stacked blocks that from their shape seemed likely to be bars of gold or silver. From what we could see, there were hundreds of them.

I forced myself to stop staring at the huge piles of loot and kept my light moving in search of traps, for bits of rope or string that might be trip wires, anything that looked dangerous. Seeing nothing, I took a hesitant step toward the pile, softly running the toe of my shoe over the ground to uncover anything in the floor that might harm us.

After more careful steps, I reached out and picked up what looked like a ball from the top of a closed chest. Surprisingly heavy for something so small, I blew the dust off to reveal what looked like a human head with a bird's beak. It had beautiful red stones for eyes but everything else appeared to be gold.

I handed it to Finn. "You think that's real?" I asked.

He hefted it in one hand then nodded. "Real gold is heavy, just like this." He squinted at the red eyes. "And I bet these are rubies," he said.

"What do you think it's worth?"

Finn closed his eyes for a couple seconds, continuing to raise and lower the statue. "Gold is something like thirteen hundred bucks an ounce."

"How do you know that?"

"My grandfather watches those stock market shows on TV. There are sixteen ounces to a pound, and I'm guessing this weighs close to five pounds." He opened his eyes. "A hundred thousand dollars."

I gaped at him. "That one little thing?"

He nodded. "It might be worth even more 'cause it's a statue and it's old, but I don't know anything about that."

I smiled. "And you told me you were supposed to be dense."

He shrugged. "In reading."

"But not in math."

"No, I'm actually kind of good in math."

I shook my head.

"What?" he asked.

"You're actually really smart, Finn. I think you're the one who tells you you're not. Stop listening to that voice."

He looked at me for a long moment but didn't say anything. Finally, he turned back to the huge pile of dusty treasure. "If this little thing is worth that much, think about this whole pile."

"That's exactly what I'm doing."

Finn slipped the head into his pocket, then reached down and used both hands to pick up one of the block shaped things from the top of a stack.

"Maybe twenty-five pounds," he said hefting it. Blowing off a lot of dust, he cleared a spot along the top. "Same color as the statue. Sure looks like gold to me," he said. He glanced at the ceiling and calculated. "If I'm even close to right, I've got like half a million dollars right in my hands."

"But who put this here?" I asked.

"It's pretty obvious," Finn said. "We should have guessed when we first saw that shaft and then the tunnel, and all the traps to keep us from getting here. This is pirate booty."

"No way!"

"What else could it be? It sure isn't something the Navy put here in World War II, and when you think about Granger's map and how it was drawn by hand, it's logical."

"Pirate stuff sounds like a fairy tale."

"It's not. Some of the most famous pirates raided ships and even cities in the American colonies before the Revolution."

"Finn, pirates were scoundrels and drunks, and this," I waved my hand taking in all the treasure, "is too much. It can't have been put here by some drunk ship stealer."

"Pirates who captured Spanish treasure ships and looted whole cities?" he shook his head. "They were really rich."

"I guess it doesn't matter who put it here.

Who does this belong to, now?"

"If it's on your grandfather's land, it belongs to him. At least I'm pretty sure it does."

"We got in here through the spit, and the spit belongs to Poppy."

Finn nodded. "Yeah, but what if we're not under his property anymore?"

"You said we're under the river."

Finn shrugged. "I think we are. I don't know if anybody can own a river."

"So, who owns this stuff?"

"Maybe the state, or maybe whoever finds it first."

I looked around at the room full of dusty treasure. "I'm pretty sure that we're the discoverers."

"Me, too," said Finn.

That was when we heard it, the same sound from the night before. Only now it was louder and a lot closer than it had been then.

Thunk—pause—*thunk*—pause—*thunk.*

35.

"What is that?" I whispered.

Finn closed his eyes, listened another second, then said, "I'm almost positive it's somebody digging."

That answer made everything click into place. "It has to be Granger," I said. "I bet he's trying to dig his own tunnel to get here."

Finn gave me a questioning look, so I kept talking, "Remember how upset he was when he lost his map, but how it didn't seem to bother him a bit when the man who ran the X-ray machine all over the beach didn't find anything?"

Finn's eyes widened as he got it, too. "And remember how Granger tried to act like it was no big deal when we showed him the log roof. You missed it, but I saw Serge and Stevenson react. Finding that shaft *was* a really big deal."

I nodded. "And how Granger said he wasn't going to buy the land even though we showed him what he'd been looking for? *Of course* he wasn't going to buy it." I pointed in the direction of the digging, also the direction of the fancy houses Granger hadn't been able to sell. "He was digging a tunnel in here from his houses across the river, so he could steal all of this. He was *never* going to pay for the spit!"

Finn's eyes widened as our predicament hit home. "So, what do we do? We're trapped until those guys dig their way in, and once they get here, what do you think they're gonna do? They're not gonna help us!"

Finn was right, but hearing him say it made me feel like I had a brick in my throat. Granger would never split his treasure, not with us. That meant he wasn't going to let us walk away. "Do you actually think he'd . . . ?" I couldn't finish my question, but I didn't need to.

Finn just nodded. "What other choice does he have if he wants all the money?"

"And according to the paper, he's desperate."

"Which means we need a plan."

"We don't have much time to make one," I said. "They sound really close."

"We could put on some of the helmets and armor," Finn suggested, pointing at things lying atop some of the piles. "Then, when the diggers break through, we'll run at them screaming and yelling. It might make them panic and run away, or at least panic enough to let *us* run away."

"Who do you think is doing the digging?" I asked.

Finn shook his head. "Does it matter?"

"If it's Serge or Granger, do you think they would panic?"

Finn's hopeful expression faded. "Maybe Stevenson would, but not Serge," he agreed. "You really think Serge is the one digging?"

"Who else would Granger trust?" I asked. "The more people that know, the greater the risk of a leak. Also, the more who would demand to share in the loot. I bet the diggers are the same three that came to see the shaft."

"Okay," Finn agreed. "My idea's bad. What's your idea?"

"We wave to them when they come in."

His eyes went wide. "That's ridiculous!"

I shook my head. "No, it's not." And then I told him the rest of my plan.

"If we do that we're dead. They'll get us for sure," Finn said when I finished.

"Not for sure."

"For sure," he repeated.

"Then give me a better idea."

"That's the problem," he said after a few seconds.

"Look on the good side," I said. "Maybe they won't even find this room."

"That's not the 'good side,'" he replied. "If they don't find it, we'll starve to death down here."

"If they don't find us, but they get close, we can wait until they stop digging, then we can dig to their tunnel. When we get there, we can escape."

"Dig with what, our bare hands?"

I moved my light across the huge stacks of

loot. "There has to be something we can use."

He pointed his light at the wooden walls. "I bet we can't even get through those walls to start digging." Finn paused and looked down at the beam his flashlight was throwing. It was dimmer than it had been at the start, and my own beam was dimmer, too. "We also need to conserve our batteries," he said.

He clicked off his flashlight, and the darkness stretched in toward us like some hungry thing that wanted to eat us alive. I felt my stomach clutch. The *thunk*—pause—*thunk*—pause—*thunk* suddenly became an even scarier sound, but after taking a deep breath, I switched my light off, too.

Instantly, the dark became total. It was terrifying to sit there in *real* blackness, while other than our own breathing, the only thing we heard was the *thunk*—pause—*thunk*—pause—*thunk* of diggers who when they finally got to us would try to kill us.

For a long time neither of us spoke. Time became impossible to gauge in the dark, but at some point, I realized the sound of digging was louder.

"How long 'til they get to us?"

"No way to tell."

"But they're close?"

"Real close, I think."

As if to add his two cents, Plankton let out a low growl from where he lay curled on my lap. "Sshhh," I said, putting my hand on top of his head. "We can't let them know we're here."

Plankton let out a much softer growl, letting me know that he didn't like it, but he'd go along with my suggestion, at least for now.

We lapsed into silence, our senses focused on the steady sound of digging. It felt like we were waiting for doom.

I had no idea how long we had been sitting there when the digging stopped, and then we heard the growl of an engine. It came closer for a time, seemed to move back and forth, then faded away.

"I bet it's one of those really little bulldozers," Finn said. "They're using it to clear out the loose dirt."

A long silence followed, but then I heard voices. They sounded very close, almost on top of us, and then something slammed into the wooden wall.

36.

The crack of splintering wood nearly made me jump out of my skin. A second later, another loud crash, then a blinding light on the far side of the room shattered the darkness.

Plankton let out an angry bark. I froze, afraid we had given ourselves away, but someone had fired up a chain saw on the other side of the wall. As its engine revved and then the person started to cut away the wood, it drowned out the sound.

I tightened my arms around Plankton, holding him tight to my chest, whispering "sssshhhh," into his ear and praying that for once in his life he might decide to obey.

Finn clicked on his flashlight, clamping his hand over the beam so just enough light leaked through to let us make out general shapes. We crept toward the swinging door that had brought us into the treasure room, but rather than go back into the tunnel, we stayed in place, right where the swinging door swung outward into the tunnel.

My heart was beating so hard that I feared the thumping might give us away. Finn hated my plan. Even I hated my plan, but it was the best we'd been able to think up. We had to hope that when we drew the attention of the diggers, their surprise would keep them from noticing the other part of the door where it swung into the treasure room. Everything depended on that. If they saw how the door actually worked, we were dead. We were probably dead anyway, but if our plan worked, we at least had a chance.

For the next couple minutes, we waited. All we saw was the bright light and the whirring chain saw blade as one of the diggers cut a big hole in the far wall. When it was big enough to step through, the saw stopped, and a dead silence seemed to descend into the underground room. I was shaking with fear as I held Plankton tight in my arms, and that was when he started to let out a low growl.

"You will get us all killed," I whispered in his ear.

Amazingly, Plankton fell silent.

More seconds passed, then we heard Granger say, "Go in, but be careful."

A hand reached in and gripped the cut wall. A leg followed, and then a man stepped partway into the room. He was hard to see because all the cutting had stirred up a thick cloud of dust on that side of the room. A pair of bright lights directly behind him made his head and face a dark silhouette. The man coughed and sneezed several times, and I was pretty sure it was Stevenson.

He finally stopped sneezing and stepped all the way into the room. Right away, he began shooting his flashlight beam toward the ceiling and the walls on both sides, as if he was frightened and expected the exact same things I had—blowgun darts, or a huge blade coming out of the ceiling. My heart slammed in my chest like a kettle drum. I squeezed Plankton even tighter.

After several seconds of looking around, Stevenson's shoulders relaxed, and he took another step forward, now aiming his beam at the piles and piles of treasure that filled the room.

"Speak up, Stevenson. What do you see?" came a gravelly voice from outside the treasure room. That had to be Serge, the bullet-headed chauffeur.

"Un-unbelievable," Stevenson stuttered, his voice hoarse with amazement. "There's so much . . . it's like a king's treasury."

"I told you it would be, but we have to be very careful," said Granger. He had come into the room behind Stevenson, and he placed a second light over the wall right next to the hole they had made as he began tapping the wood with a small hammer.

"A king's treasury is exactly what Black Jack Burton stole," Granger went on. "He was one of the worst pirates, both highly intelligent and demonically cruel. Over a period of two years he captured three massive Spanish galleons, each of them packed with gold and silver from

Spanish colonies in the New World."

"You've already told us the pirate history," Serge said, as he stepped into the room. "Let's forget about that and figure out what we got here."

"What you need to not forget is who's running this operation," Granger snapped. "You'd still be an ex-con with no job and no hope of getting one if I hadn't put you in a suit and given you a chance to get rich, so knock it off and learn something."

"Yeah, right," Serge grumbled.

"Uh, boss, what are you doing?" Stevenson asked.

"Looking for traps," Granger replied, continuing to tap with his hammer as he moved slowly around the wall. "You should stay very still until I finish."

Until then, Serge had been shifting his feet, but now neither he nor Stevenson moved as Granger inched along and continued his tapping.

"Most other pirates' loot, if they had any, was discovered years ago, but not Black Jack Burton's," Granger said. "Do you boys know why?"

"I guess you're gonna tell us again," Serge said.

"Very true." *Tap, tap, tap.* "Legend has it that Black Jack and two of his most trusted lieutenants made twenty captured Spanish sailors dig a secret hiding place for his treasure. The hiding place was not only incredibly hard to find, it was also full of traps so that anyone who tried to break in and steal the treasure would probably die a horrible death."

"That's why you're tapping the wall?" Stevenson asked with a nervous quaver.

"Exactly," Granger replied. *Tap, tap, tap.*

"And why he let you walk into the room first," Serge said with a laugh.

"Wha-what, exactly, do you think could be here?" Stevenson asked.

"If I knew I'd tell you," Granger said. *Tap, tap, tap.* "But since this room is under the river, I would guess whatever traps are in this room probably involve water."

"Like . . . the river coming down on us?" Stevenson asked, shining his light up at the ceiling.

"Exactly," Granger said. *Tap, tap, tap.*

"Oh, jeez."

"Gimme a break," Serge said. "This place has been sitting here for hundreds of years. You think some booby trap will still work after all that time?"

"Probably not, but why take the chance," Granger said. *Tap, tap, tap.* "The more you know about Black Jack Burton, the more you should understand my caution."

"We already know all about him," Serge muttered.

Granger appeared not to hear. "After he built the hiding place for his loot," he went on. *Tap, tap, tap.* "He murdered all of the sailors who had helped construct it, and then, according to legend, he also poisoned the two trusted friends who had helped him."

"So he was the only man alive who knew where the treasure was," Serge said in a bored voice.

"Yes." *Tap, tap, tap.* "Then he was either murdered by his crew or went down in a shipwreck, so no living person knew where the treasure was buried. There were only the rumors and legends and stories, and a few tantalizing clues." Granger paused for a moment to cough, probably from the dust. "But I did my research. I studied the man and read everything I could find about him. I went to antique book dealers and junk shops. I wasted money buying sea chests, books, and cutlasses Black Jack supposedly owned. I tore the chests apart, searched the books for secret codes and hacked apart the handles of his old sabers to see if some mysterious clue was hidden inside.

"I found nothing, but I kept going. I listened to fools tell stories about pirate lore, hoping to hear one or two tiny nuggets of truth in the lies they told. I never stopped searching. Rumors said the treasure was in Bermuda, or Antigua, or somewhere near Nassau. I went to all those places and found only dead ends. Finally, I bought that map in some thirdhand antique store in Charleston. It showed nothing but a tree and some Xs and a narrow spit of land, really nothing at all. But I had researched Black Jack Burton enough to think I recognized the somewhat unusual way he wrote the letter

X. Then I did a computer search of all the spits of land that might have a similar shape, all the way from the Chesapeake Bay, down the American East Coast, and throughout the Caribbean.

"Surprisingly, there are very few spits with a shape like this one, so I was able to use my detective skills to figure out that it was *this* spit of land. *I* did that, gentlemen. *I* saw the opportunity when no one else did. *I* persevered when others would have quit. And now you have only me to thank for your newfound wealth."

As he finished speaking, Granger seemed to remember what he was supposed to be doing, and he resumed his tapping along the walls.

If Finn and I hadn't been so scared, I would have laughed out loud at hearing anybody say such egotistical stuff. But we weren't laughing because as Granger kept talking and tapping, he was getting closer and closer to where we were hiding.

"H-how much do you think all this is worth?" Stevenson asked.

"Fifty, sixty million, maybe even a hundred million," Granger said. "Not a bad reward for getting a bit dirty, right?"

"Yeah," the man responded with a nervous laugh.

"Still, we won't get that much because we'll have to be careful when we sell it." *Tap, tap, tap.* "We can't afford to raise suspicion about where this came from and what it might be.

Old man Morrisey would have us in court in thirty seconds if he had any idea."

"We'll be lucky to get twenty percent of the value," Serge grumbled. "And what about those two kids? They found the shaft."

"Just luck on their part," Granger said. *Tap, tap, tap.* "I stood on that wood and set a waypoint in my GPS. It confirmed to me that we had dug our tunnel in exactly the right direction, and those kids didn't have a clue. They'll be on a shopping spree for the next couple days spending the money I gave them, and they won't be in our hair."

Beside me, I felt Finn stiffen in anger, and I gripped his shoulder to keep him quiet.

"Lucky or not," Serge went on, "what happens if they show other people what they found?"

Granger let out a mocking laugh as he kept tapping. "They found some old logs with a hole below it. So what? And how long are they here, a couple weeks? In no time they'll be back in school wherever they live, and they'll forget all about this. Even if they don't, when we get the treasure out, we'll blow the tunnel and cave it all in. There won't be anything to find, even if they come back next year."

Granger kept moving toward us, tapping the wall as he came. The men's flashlight beams moved around the room, several times coming very close to where we squatted. Each time, my nerves went taut as piano wire, and I flinched away as if the light could burn me. Without realizing it, I had kept my hand on

Finn's shoulder and my fingers were digging into him like talons. "Ready?" I whispered, forcing my grip to relax.

"Yes," Finn whispered back.

I stood up from behind the piles of loot that were now barely hiding us and shouted, "Run!" Then I turned on my flashlight as I darted toward the swinging door and into the tunnel. I kept Plankton in my arms, and he started to bark furiously, adding to the chaos.

Finn's feet slapped the floor right behind me, and in the next instant I heard one of the men cry out in shock as we shot through the door, then slammed it back in place.

Moving down the wall close to the fake door with the iron handle, we waited.

"Get 'em!" boomed Serge.

"Who . . . who were they?" asked Stevenson.

"Those kids. They must've gotten down here somehow," Granger cried.

"Just get 'em before they ruin everything!" Serge cried, no longer sounding like he was working for Granger, but more like the one giving the orders.

In the next instant, the door flew back where we had just pushed it shut, and it swung outward where Finn and I were standing on the other side of the center hinge. Wasting no time, we bolted, knowing it would take only seconds for the three to figure out what we'd done and come after us.

We had a head start, but only a slight one. I knew it might not be enough, because even if we got out of the tunnel, we probably weren't going to know exactly where we were—or the fastest way to safety.

We raced through the treasure room and out the hole that Granger's men had cut in the wall. Spilling into the black tunnel, Finn pushed me into the lead, and I ran as fast as I could given how small the tunnel was.

Behind us came angry yelling, but muffled as if the men were still on the other side of the swinging door. It meant we still had a chance. Then I thought, if they saw the fake door and in their rush to catch us, they pulled it open, the river would soon be rushing through the tunnel. Fresh fear made me run even faster. That was when I came around a corner and slammed into something hard.

Plankton let out an angry bark as he jumped to the ground. Whatever I hit also made a grunting sound, as I bounced back a step or two and sat on my butt.

"Keep going!" Finn whispered. "We're almost out."

My breath froze in my throat as my light pointed up at the thing that had stopped me. It was Serge, his huge body blocking the narrow tunnel. He held a flashlight in one hand, but I ignored that, staring instead at the pistol in his other hand.

37.

"Well, well, well, aren't we clever," Serge growled. "I thought you might pull something like this."

"How dare you point a gun at us," I said, trying my best to sound much braver than I felt.

"Knock it off. Just turn around and head back where you came from."

Just then Granger and Stevenson came around the corner of the tunnel, and for a moment we were all sandwiched together.

"Go back," Serge said. "I got 'em."

"It's those kids," Granger said, sounding totally shocked, as if he couldn't get it through his head that we were there.

"Yeah, it's the kids," Serge said, sounding put out. "Just go back. Nobody can go anywhere 'til you guys move."

"Mr. Granger," I said, "this is an outrage. This man has a gun pointed at us. This is my grandfather's property. You are helping commit a serious crime. You need to let us go immediately."

"A gun?" Granger spluttered. "We have no

need for firearms," he said, sounding flustered. "Put that thing away immediately."

For a second, hope bloomed in my chest that Granger knew we had him red-handed and would do what we told him. After all, I reasoned, he knew that he'd been caught, so now it was just a matter of how many laws he would be accused of breaking. Also, he was the boss, so the other two would do what he told them.

I couldn't have been more wrong.

"Put the gun away," Granger repeated as he and Stevenson, and then Finn and I backed into the treasure room, Serge coming last.

"Good job catching them," Granger said, sounding rattled and uncertain because Serge still hadn't put away the gun.

"He didn't catch anybody," I insisted. "We're going to the police."

Despite trying to sound sure of myself, we had a big problem because Serge was blocking the opening to the tunnel.

"How did you kids get in here?" Granger demanded.

I stepped a little bit in front of Finn. "We came through the other entrance."

Serge shot an ugly look at Granger. "Why'd we have to dig a bloody tunnel if we could have come down a ladder and walked in?"

"There are traps," Granger said.

"No, there aren't," I lied.

"Maybe they just didn't work after all this time, but they're there," Granger said. "Besides, we couldn't exactly have driven a truck onto Morrisey's beach and loaded it with treasure."

Serge grunted, seeming to mock Granger's answer.

"That's exactly right," I said. "You definitely could not have driven a truck onto the spit and loaded it up because that would have been stealing. If we go to the police now, it will simply be trespassing," I shot a glance at Serge, "and maybe threatening somebody with a gun."

I looked at Granger, hoping he'd order his big thug to get out of our way. "You need to let us go," I said when Granger wouldn't respond. "The longer you keep us, the worse it will look for you."

Granger licked his lips. He seemed nervous and unsure, like he was about to cave in. That was when Serge said, "Shut up, kid."

"Well," Granger began to say, "she is technically correct—"

"You shut up, too," Serge said.

"Don't you dare tell me—" Granger's voice died when Serge raised the gun and pointed it at his chest.

"Get over there by the kids," he said to Granger. "You, too, Stevenson."

"What . . . what are—"

"Move!" Serge shouted. He swung the gun to one side, away from all of us, and pulled the trigger. The gun exploded like a bomb going off. Splinters blew out of the wall and stung my skin. My ears rang, and my head bubbled

with near hysteria. What scared me nearly as much as the gun was the idea that this room was like a weapon. This whole place was built to kill people who tried to steal Black Jack Burton's treasure. Firing a gun like that was a death sentence.

For several seconds everyone froze, fearing what might happen next. Even Serge seemed to realize he'd done something really reckless, but almost as quickly, his ugly expression came back, and he waved his gun toward the now open door into the tunnel. "Get in there."

Granger's mouth opened and closed a few times. He looked like a goldfish gulping fish food. Stevenson was as quiet as a statue.

I cleared my throat. "You, sir, are making a terrible mistake."

"No, I'm not. I'm making myself very rich."

"We will turn you in. We'll just climb out and go straight to the police."

"We'll see about that."

He moved us into the tunnel and herded us toward the shaft. We all obeyed, having no choice given Serge's size and the gun in his hand. I tried to think of a way to get Serge to walk in front of us so he might fall into the pit with the sharpened stakes, but that became impossible when he made Finn and I turn on our flashlights and insisted we go first. We all leaped over the stakes, and when we got to the end of the tunnel and the shaft came into sight, Serge stopped us.

"Lie down on your backs," he commanded.

I tried to lie closest to the treasure room, still hoping that I could make a run for it but Serge kicked me and told me to move closer to the shaft. He made Granger lie down first with his head pointing toward the treasure and his feet toward the shaft, then Stevenson, then Finn, then me.

"Any of you move or try to get up, I'll shoot you. Trust me on that. I've shot people for less."

When we were all lying down, Serge walked to the end of the tunnel and shined his light at the rope and the ladder, snickering when he saw the broken rungs higher up. Then he shined the light down at the stinking pool of dark water.

"You go ahead and climb right out of here," he said with a laugh as he realized the emptiness of my threat. Then, as if underlining how trapped we would be, reached into his pocket, clicked open a knife, and a second later I heard a faint splash as something hit the water far below. When I raised my head, I could see what was left of the rope, dangling in the middle of the shaft. Grabbing it would take a desperate jump even for Laura Croft, one that would be impossible for any of us.

There was only one thing to do, and I was the only one who could do it. I jumped to my feet even as Serge started to turn. Instead of trying to run toward the treasure room and escape, I went in low, hitting his leg with my shoulder, trying to knock him off the side of the tunnel and into the water far below.

A blinding pain shot through me as I bounced back onto my butt. I might as well have tried to knock down an oak tree, and my head spun as I heard Serge laugh.

"You got guts, girl. Too bad you had to stick your nose where you had no business."

I looked up at him, ignoring the throbbing pain. "You are an evil man," I said. "You won't get away with this."

"*Oh really?*" he mocked, shaking his head. "I'm going to be a rich man, a *very* rich man, sweetheart. I'm gonna get away with this just fine."

"You don't even understand what I'm talking about," I said. "You're too greedy to even understand what I'm talking about," I said.

His expression hardened. "That big mouth of yours is about to get you tossed into that pit, so you better shut it."

I glared up at him, putting all my anger into my eyes. He snorted, stepped around me, walked down the tunnel toward the swinging door, and slammed it shut behind him as he went into the treasure room. We were left in total darkness.

A couple minutes later we heard the sounds of heavy, metallic thumps against the swinging door.

"What's he doing?" Stevenson asked.

"Gold," Granger said.

"What?"

"He's piling gold in front of the door so we won't be able to get out."

"He's leaving the gold down here?"

"He's sealing us in until he comes up with something better," Granger said.

We didn't have long to wait to find out what Serge was planning, because a short time later we heard the sound of pounding.

"What's he doing now?" Stevenson asked.

"Sounds like he's nailing the door shut," Granger said. Something that sounded like a sob escaped him. "We're trapped," he blubbered. "We'll never get out of here."

"We're trapped by your greed," I said. "You tried to sneak all this treasure out of here, instead of just splitting what you found with my grandfather. You could be rich and safe right now."

We were sitting in the dark, but I could swear I felt his eyes burning into me. He said nothing.

Silence fell. I was surrounded by heavy breathing, and periodically thumps and clanks came from the treasure room. I knew Serge had to be loading out the loot.

As angry as those noises made me, it was better than the silence we'd be left with when Serge left for good. Knowing we were trapped made me want to scream and pound the floor, but it would do no good. Panic was never good. Panic got people to make reckless mistakes. Like me trying to stick my nose into Poppy's business. Like me trying to fix things I didn't know anything about. And like getting Finn involved.

I thought about my mom and dad and all the terrible things they'd already had to deal with as they worried about Mom's cancer. When I disappeared, they would worry and very likely never, ever find my body. I thought about how Finn just wanted to play baseball and because of me, he was never going to put on a mitt or get on a diamond again.

Tears were rolling down my cheeks. I was silently crying when I heard it. An incredibly faint voice.

And it had called my name. I blinked and shook my head, thinking I must have been dreaming, but then I heard it again. And I also heard barking, and the barking sounded a lot closer than the voice.

"Plankton!" I shouted, realizing I had forgotten all about him. He had jumped out of my arms when I ran into Serge in the tunnel. Had he run all the way home? Was it possible he had brought help?

"Why are you yelling?" Granger demanded.

"Quiet," I told him. "I hear something."

I inched my fingers along the wooden floor until I felt it end. Then, I crept forward, taking great care not to go too far, and when I was close I lay on my back and put my head into the shaft so I could see daylight through the small hole Finn and I had cut in the wood much earlier.

"Down here!" I called.

A moment later I heard Plankton barking furiously, and then I saw his head as he peered down the shaft toward my voice.

"Stay back!" I shouted.

I probably didn't need to warn him because Plankton was smarter than most people, certainly smarter than I was because I was the one stuck down here.

Over the barks I heard my name again, the voice louder.

"Poppy!" I cried at the top of my lungs.

Plankton kept up his crazy barking, and my grandfather made his way closer to the hole, his voice getting clearer and clearer.

Finally, I heard, "Plankton, get away from there." Next came growls, and I imagined Poppy leashing Plankton and dragging him away from the hole. When Plankton started barking again, but more faintly, I knew Poppy must have tied him up. A second, the silhouette of a head appeared far above.

"Callie!" Poppy's voice came down to me loud and clear.

38.

"We're down here!"

"Is Finn with you?"

"Yes."

"Are either of you hurt?"

"No, we're in a tunnel, but we can't get out. The ladder we came down broke."

"How far down? I can't see you."

"About forty feet," Finn called. He had crept up and now lay beside me. He turned his flashlight on and shined it up.

"Stay there. I'll go get help."

"Wait!" I cried. "There's treasure down here."

"What?"

"There's treasure down here."

"Yeah, well that can wait—"

"No!" I shouted, cutting him off. "You don't understand. There's millions of dollars of treasure. Granger dug a tunnel from those houses across the river. He never wanted to buy the spit, he just wanted to make sure he was digging in the right direction."

"Callie, we can talk about this later."

"No, we can't! Granger's trapped down here with us, along with another man. There's a third man who tricked us and locked us in here. He's trying to carry the treasure out right now. You have to stop him."

Poppy made a hemming and hawing sound as if he was confused by what I was saying.

"Go, you have to stop him!"

"Will you be okay down there for a few minutes?"

"Yes."

There was silence.

"What's going on?" Granger demanded.

"My grandfather knows where we are! Help is coming, but he's also going to stop Bullet Head."

"His name is Serge."

"I know what his name is. He's a jerk."

"I don't disagree."

"So . . . is your grandfather going to the police?" Stevenson asked.

"Of course! You and Granger will be very sorry for what you have done, and Serge will be even sorrier. I will happily testify that he left us down here to die."

"I'm sure you will," Granger muttered.

I refused to rise to his bait and remained quiet, letting him stew in his guilt as we all waited to be rescued. As the initial excitement of our coming rescue settled and darkness surrounded us again, time seemed to slow. What was taking so long, I wondered? Had Poppy called the police? Was he explaining the situation? Was he getting the fire department to try and get us out the shaft?

The police were probably arresting Serge at that very moment, I decided. Maybe he had fought them. Maybe they'd had to chase him, and they were trying to figure out where the tunnel started. It was probably hidden under one of the houses Granger had built, and it was taking a while to find it. I tried to calm my nerves, and finally I heard a loud squealing noise.

Finn said, "Somebody's pulling the nails."

"What?" I asked, not understanding.

"They're pulling out the nails that Serge put in the door. We're getting out," he said.

Finn's excitement hit me like a shot "We're in here!" I shouted. "We're in here!"

As good as we felt, Granger wasn't sharing the mood. He let out a groan as the door started to crack open, and I knew he had to be thinking of how much trouble he was in. Stevenson must've had the same bad feeling because I thought I heard him sob.

I was about to cheer, but the door swung wide enough for me to see and my joy froze in my throat. I watched in horror as a single person staggered into the tunnel as if shoved. Framed in Serge's flashlight beam, I saw Poppy. Just before the door slammed and we were once again enclosed it total darkness, I saw blood on Poppy face.

I heard Poppy's hands hit the wall as he stumbled, then heard him collapse. Then the sound of hammering came again, and I knew fresh nails were being driven into the door to hold it shut.

Not caring who I elbowed or crawled over, I moved down the tunnel toward my grandfather. "Finn, turn on your flashlight," I said. Then I called out, "Poppy, Poppy, can you hear me?"

"Yes, dearie, I can hear you fine," he said, but he didn't sound fine.

"Are you hurt?"

"No, I'm okay. I was reckless. I should've called the police right away."

"You're not okay, Poppy. I can hear it in your voice. Don't move. There's a trap in the floor. I'm coming to you."

Finn held his light on the pit with the wooden stakes while I moved past it. When I got to Poppy, I tried to look at his head, but he pushed me gently away.

"He just hit me with something. I'm fine."

This wasn't the time to argue. "When we get out of here Serge is going to wish he'd never been born," I said. "Can you make it across the pit?"

"I think so."

Finn and Stevenson stood up and reached their arms out to grab Poppy as he stepped around the side of the pit. He nearly tumbled in and was only saved because they pulled him across.

As I followed Poppy across, Granger said, "We're never gonna get out of here, kid."

On hearing his boss say those words, Stevenson started to moan.

"You are a terrible leader, Mr. Granger," I said. "Nobody should follow you anywhere."

"Shut up, kid

"My name isn't kid, it's Callie."

"Whatever, just shut up."

"You're the one who better shut up," Poppy said. "I may be old, but I'll shut your yap if you talk to my granddaughter that way again."

"Finn," I said, ignoring Granger, "how are you doing?"

"I'm thinking."

That was actually some good news, because Finn was much smarter than he thought he was. "What have you got?"

"Okay," he said after a few seconds, "here's the deal. If we stay right here, we die."

"Oh," Granger broke in, "that's brilliant. So now you're going to tell us there's a secret door."

"It's not secret," Finn said. "And it's not really a door."

Granger clapped. "Perfect."

"Mr. Granger, you need to keep your self-pity to yourself," I said. "Go on, Finn.

"The kid doesn't know what he's talking about."

"His name is Finn, and yes, he does know."

"Granger," my grandfather said, "last warning. Shut your pie hole before I come over there and shut it for you."

"Stay in your place, old man. You're just gonna get hurt."

"No," Stevenson cut in. "You shut up, Granger, or Mr. Morrisey and I *will* shut you up. These kids are at least trying to think our way out of here. You're doing nothing to help. If we want to survive, we need their thinking."

"You're fired, Stevenson."

Stevenson let out a bitter laugh. "I already quit, you fool. I never should have listened to your ridiculous ideas in the first place." He laughed again. "*We were going to be soooo rich,*" he said in a mocking tone. "*We were going to dig up Black Jack Burton's treasure because you were soooo brilliant and such a great detective.*"

"I made you what you were, you ungrateful whelp. You were nothing without me."

"I was already something. I had a nice wife and two kids, and I wanted a better life for them. I was naïve enough to listen to your bull and buy into it. I wasn't thinking, but now I'm being smart. Shut your mouth and listen to these kids. They managed to get themselves down here. Maybe they can get us out. Go ahead, Finn."

"Thanks," Finn said.

"So what's your idea?" I asked.

"Well, if we're right and that door is a trap," he began, "we know it will probably bring the river spilling into the tunnel."

"What door?" Granger interrupted.

"Shut up," Stevenson told him.

"What's your point?" I asked Finn, not understanding where he was going.

"So, *if* the river did spill in here, what would happen?"

"We would drown," I said.

"Duh," Granger said under his breath.

"But what would *actually* happen?" When no one answered, Finn went on. "Water would rush down the tunnel and go where?"

"Into the shaft," I said.

"Exactly, and when it filled up the shaft and then the tunnel, what then?"

"The water would start going higher in the shaft?" I said.

"Yes," Finn said, "until it was level with the river outside. So, if we could make sure we were treading water on top of that flood, where would we be?"

"Going higher up the shaft," I said.

"I think it could work, Callie."

"It's brilliant, Finn."

"It's a ridiculous idea," Granger said. "The water will never get up to the level of ground up above because the river is lower."

"It doesn't have to," Finn said. "There's a ladder in the wall."

"A ladder that broke," Granger said.

"Yeah, it broke about eight rungs down," Finn said, "right where it was supposed to break. There's also the safety rope Callie and I put in. Serge cut it, but we'll be able to reach the rope and the ladder if the water rises."

"I'd rather starve than drown," Granger said. "With your idea, we're sure to drown."

"What about the rest of us?" I asked.

"Finn's idea makes sense to me," Poppy said.

"Me too," Stevenson said.

"You are out voted Mr. Granger," I said. I

swore I could hear him grinding his teeth, but he said nothing.

"Okay, Finn," Stevenson said after a few seconds. "How are we going to do this?

Finn laid out his plan.

39.

We were all scared, at least I think we all were because we hardly spoke a word as we got into position. We had talked it over for a long time, everyone but Granger sharing ideas and helping, but in the end Finn's original plan was pretty much exactly what we decided on.

We bunched up at the very end of the tunnel, holding tight to each other, each person's chest pressing into the back of the person directly ahead, each of us in the exact same pose. All except Finn, who went back down the tunnel to the other end, because other than me he was the only one who knew what we were looking for.

As the sound of Finn's fading footsteps became the only sound we could hear, Poppy muttered, "I just hope we're right. I'll never forgive myself if something happens to that boy."

"He knows what he's doing," I said. "No matter what happens, it's the only way."

"Okay," Finn called down to us a couple seconds later. "Everybody get ready."

"We're set," I yelled back.

We heard a tortured creaking sound, like a

drawer that had been closed for a very long time and was being forced open. Right after came a rumble, and then a splashing like water pouring out of a huge bucket. Then a sound like thunder.

"It's coming!" Finn shouted as he raced down the tunnel, his flashlight beam bouncing as he leapt the pit.

"Hurry!" I called out at the top of my lungs. Then his flashlight went dark and there was only blackness.

I didn't know whether he had heard me over the loud rush of water. It hit my legs in a flash, shooting an instant chill through my body, coming hard against my ankles, and then my calves and thighs, then my hips and chest.

I was last in the line. Granger was in front, then Stevenson, then Poppy ahead of me. The three men were big enough to brace their arms against the tunnel ceiling, and all of us had our legs spread wide to let the water flow through with as little resistance as possible. I gripped Poppy hard, hoping we wouldn't come to regret trusting Granger to be a team player. In the end, we hadn't had a choice. Together we had a chance. Apart we had none.

For several frightening seconds as the water pressure built and its level rose, I still felt nothing from Finn. Finally, as the water rose almost to my shoulders, he hit me. He was low, off his feet, getting swept with the flood of river water that was torrenting into the tunnel.

His hand raked at my knee, but I forced my legs to remain straight and stiff and apart as Finn's grip tightened, then his body slammed against my legs. I sensed all three of the men straining to keep us in place against the building pressure as Finn struggled to stand and spread his legs like the rest of us. Finally, coughing and hacking, he managed to stand and grab hold of me as the water pressed us together and forward.

The flow rushed past our bodies and roared as it fell over the edge into the shaft. We were struggling to stay in place as the water continued to rise, quickly reaching our shoulders, then our necks and heads. I held onto Poppy's back to keep my own head barely above the torrent. Behind me I could feel Finn doing the same thing. I took a deep breath as the gap narrowed between the wild tumult of water and the top of the tunnel. My lungs started to burn. It felt like we had been there for hours, but I knew that it had only been about a minute when the roaring water changed, the pressure seeming to lessen.

In front of me, I felt motion as the others let go, then I let go, and Finn let go of me, and we began to kick frantically out of the mouth of the tunnel and up.

It felt incredibly scary, swimming in total blackness, as the current buffeted me back and forth. I felt bodies knocking into me in the blackness, and several times, I got kicked or raked by another person's hand. I had no idea if it was Finn or one of the others, as we all struggled to get to the top.

The current was flowing up and down, backward and forward, all at once as the water sloshed into the pit. My lungs were on fire, and I was getting tossed around so much it became impossible to know which way was up. I was terrified I might be swimming deeper rather than upward, but then I remembered what Finn had said about the water pressure and that if I went deeper, I would feel it in my ears. Right away, I focused on my ears and realized the pressure in them was dropping. Knowing I was moving in the right direction, I redoubled my efforts to swim upward. A second later, my head broke the surface. I pulled air into my starving lungs and saw a small square of daylight overhead. It was still far away, but at the same time so welcome and so incredibly wonderful, throwing just enough illumination into the shaft for me to make out the shapes of the others all treading water.

"Everyone okay?" Finn called out.

"I'm good," said Poppy.

"Me, too," Stevenson replied.

"Me, three," I said.

Granger said nothing. I began to wonder if he had made it, but I saw him treading water in silence.

Our voices must have carried to the top of the shaft because the next thing I heard was a bark. When I looked up again, I saw a small head peering over the edge. "Plankton,"

I called up. "Stay! We're coming."

Plankton, must've chewed through his leash, seemed to understand me because he began to bark furiously, his front paws kicking loose sand down through the hole so that I had to turn my eyes away to keep them clear.

For a moment, I felt a stab of fresh panic when I looked for the ladder and saw the unbroken rungs still a little out of reach. Hope soon followed panic as I realized the water was still continuing to rise as the inrushing river pushed us higher up the shaft. It seemed like Finn's idea was working brilliantly.

Finally, the dangling safety rope Serge had cut came in to reach. I grabbed it, looking around for Poppy and Finn in case they needed to hold on to it. "Anybody need the rope?" I asked. "Poppy?"

"I do," Granger said.

"Other people get it before you," I said.

"Why?" he demanded. "I'm a human being, too."

"You're not *as* human as all the others here," I snapped.

Granger ignored me and started to swim toward the rope. That was when Stevenson swam in front of him and blocked his way. "You heard Callie," he said. "Mr. Morrisey and Finn get the rope, not you."

To my surprise Granger said nothing, just silently treaded water. Knowing Poppy had probably been hit pretty hard by Serge, I was relieved when he came over and grabbed hold of the rope. After a few more seconds, Finn reached for it, too. I let go and moved over to tread water near the ladder. Up above, Plankton kept up his frantic barking.

By now the water level had risen to the point where we were even with the rungs that had broken under Finn's weight. Fortunately, the river continued to inch us upward, and we finally floated up to the rungs that hadn't broken. Had they been booby-trapped like the others, I wondered? Would they break when we tried to climb out? It was impossible to know for sure. Earlier, we had all agreed that it made the most sense to take the fewest chances. Therefore, we would wait until the water seemed to reach its highest level, and then I would be the first to climb out. Since I was the lightest, me going first would put the least stress on the rungs.

Poppy finally said, "I think we've pretty much stopped rising. I think it's time to climb out, Callie."

I kicked over and started to reach for the rungs, but before I could get both hands on the ladder, an arm came out of nowhere and threw me backward and under water. In the next instant Granger was at the ladder, grabbing hold of the rungs and racing upward much faster than I would have expected him to be able to move.

Stevenson swam over and tried to grab Granger's leg, but it was too late. Granger kicked Stevenson's hand away and moved out of reach. We watched Granger scramble up, all of us with our hearts in our mouths, wondering if he would make it out or come plummeting down into the water.

As if by a miracle, Granger made it up and out the hole that we had cut in the wooden barrier. Plankton's barking got even louder, and then I heard an angry exclamation, and then a yelp of pain.

A lightning bolt of anger shot through me, knowing Plankton had probably tried to lick Granger's face as he climbed out and been rewarded with a kick. It made me even more determined to make sure that I settled things with him.

Then I heard a sound that made me feel a little bit better—Plankton's angry snarl and then another cry of pain, only this one human. Knowing Plankton had just taken a hunk out of the back of Granger's leg made me feel good, but at the same time I knew Granger was escaping.

"Okay," Finn said, breaking the stunned silence that had followed Granger's escape. "Keep our original order. Callie, you go up, then your grandfather, then Mr. Stevenson, and me."

"I'll go last," Stevenson said. "We wouldn't be here if it wasn't for you, Finn. Besides, I'm heavier than you."

"Okay," Finn said. "We've got the rope, so we can get you out even if the ladder breaks."

I went up the ladder next. Unlike Granger who went up like a speeding monkey, I went slowly, taking care to put as little stress on each rung as possible. I could feel the warm light and smell the fresh air, and I could hear Plankton as he eagerly barked for me to hurry to the top. He was pushing so much loose sand off the side of the barrier that I didn't dare look up.

When I finally hauled myself out, I nearly cried with relief, but didn't open my mouth because a small pink tongue was licking every square inch of my face.

I only gave Plankton a quick hug and pat, because three people were still down below, needing to be rescued. As part of Finn's plan, he and Stevenson tied the safety rope around Poppy's middle, and when my grandfather said he was ready to climb I helped pull him up the ladder. I wasn't really lifting him. If a rung broke, I knew that I wouldn't be able to hold him, but Poppy was still woozy from Granger hitting him on the head and my pulling helped Poppy lift himself.

Finally, he came through the hole and rolled onto his side, exhausted. I could see that Poppy head was still bleeding a little from where he'd been hit.

Plankton's joy at seeing Poppy was explosive. He jumped on Poppy and started to lick wildly. Plankton quickly narrowed his attention to the cut on Poppy's head, which he licked with the gentleness of a nurse caring for a patient. Unfortunately, Plankton's tongue was far from an antibiotic, but I guessed it was probably cleaner than the water in the shaft.

As Finn made his way out, Poppy was sitting up, and the two of us held the rope as Finn climbed. Finally, all three of us held the rope as Stevenson made his way up.

When Stevenson finally rolled free of the hole and began to untie the safety rope, I let out a huge sigh of relief. Thankfully Poppy's injury, while painful, didn't appear too serious. It seemed we were all okay, in spite of everything we'd gone through.

"We need to get after Granger," I said to Stevenson, thinking he'd be the most logical one to go while I stayed with Poppy, and Finn went to call the police. But then I noticed blood pooling under Stevenson's ankle. "You're hurt," I said.

He winced as he tried to move his injured ankle. "Something sharp hit my leg when all that water started pouring into the tunnel."

"Can you walk?"

He rolled onto his knees, slowly rose to his feet and took a slow, limping step. It was obvious that he would never catch Granger. Our cell phones were soaked. There was no way to call for help. Had we come so close, only to lose? I teetered on the edge of despair yet again. "We can't let Granger and Serge get away with stealing that money," I said. "It can save Mom's life."

Finn jumped up. "I'm going over to those houses. That's where the tunnel comes out."

"It's my mother. I'll go," I said.

"Not alone," Finn shot back.

"You two stay right here," Poppy said, trying to sound stern and in control.

I shook my head. "I'm not hurt, but you are. I can't just sit here and let Serge and Granger take the money that could save Mom. You wouldn't do that if you were me."

Poppy struggled to his feet, letting out a loud groan and swaying as he stood. I thought that he would lay down the law and try to make us stay. Instead, he sighed. "You two can follow Granger, but only if you promise to be extremely careful and stay together. Watch him, but stay at a safe distance. That other man is armed and dangerous, so whatever you do, *don't* get near them. You stay out of sight and don't take *any* chances, understand?

He paused, waiting for us to answer. When we were too slow, he repeated, "Understand?"

"Yes, sir," Finn and I both said.

We had permission to go, but I hesitated. "You sure you'll be okay?"

"Yes," Poppy said. "Stevenson and I will help each other get to a phone and summon help."

I looked at him and nodded, and then Finn and I turned away and went to find Granger.

40.

The sun was bright, but the air was cold. For the first time since we had gotten out of the shaft, I realized that I was shivering. Finn looked just as cold as I felt, but we both knew what we had to do if we were going to stop Granger or Serge from getting the loot.

Hurrying through the bushes back out to the river bank, we threw ourselves into the water. It felt cold, even colder than when we'd been in the shaft and tunnel. Thankfully, the river wasn't very wide, but I clambered up the opposite bank with my lips turning blue.

Being half frozen didn't matter in the slightest. The money that was going to save my mom's life was going to be stolen if Finn and I couldn't do something. I knew the police could probably catch Granger and Serge eventually, but if we couldn't stop them now, how could we later prove the loot had been stolen from Poppy?

I had watched enough TV to know we needed proof. Even if Granger and Serge went to jail for what they'd done to us in the tunnel, it might be their word against ours that all the loot wasn't some old property that Granger or Serge's family had owned.

I couldn't think about that. Not when we had to figure out a way to stop them. Shivering, Finn and I crept up the riverbank, staying low to be harder to spot. I didn't really think we had to worry about anyone looking for us because whichever of the two thieves had won, they would be more focused on loading up the treasure and getting away. Still, it made no sense to take unnecessary risks.

The perfect situation would be where both Granger and Serge had fought and knocked themselves out. Then we could just tie them up and wait for the police. In spite of how great that would be, I didn't think it was very likely because Serge had a gun.

As we crept through the thin barrier of bushes that separated Granger's unsold houses from the river, we found ourselves in the same place we had been the first time we crossed the river, behind the house with the big pile of dirt where a swimming pool was being dug. Unlike the last time we'd been there, a panel van sat parked near the shallow end of the pool. The van's rear doors were open. No one was in sight.

We stopped, and I tried to keep my teeth from chattering long enough to listen for sounds that would tell us what was happening. I heard nothing. Finn ran in a crouch toward the van, and I followed. We squatted beside it and looked down into the hole.

"That's got to be where the tunnel starts," said Finn, pointing toward the dark opening in what would be the pool's deep end.

"You think Serge and Granger are in there?"

"They have to be," Finn said.

"Then we have to go in, too," I said.

"We should stay right here. Why would we go in there?"

"That's where the treasure is."

Finn raised his eyebrows as if he wanted to tell me how little sense I was making. "We have no idea what's going on. One of them may be dead or knocked out by now."

"That's the whole point. I need to know what's happening with the treasure. You should wait here," I said as I started a fast sneak down the ramp.

Finn shook his head but followed right on my heels. "Going back into that tunnel is the worst thing we could do," he whispered.

"My mom needs that treasure."

He grabbed my arm, stopping me. "Then wait here. Someone will show. We'll memorize the van's license number and back off to someplace safe. That way we can figure out what's going on, and then we can tell the cops." I tried to jerk my arm free, but he was too strong. I let out a frustrated sigh. I stopped trying to move, and we listened for another few seconds. We heard nothing. "They might not even be in there," I whispered.

Unable to stand it any longer, I gave my arm a big jerk, pulled loose and crept to the bottom of the ramp where I squatted beside a very small front-end loader. Beside it, the dark opening disappeared in the ground.

I felt Finn's hand again, this time on my shoulder. "Don't go any farther."

I certainly didn't want to, but I had no choice. I shook off his hand and crept forward. If I was still cold, I no longer noticed because my heart was hammering so hard that I thought it might break my ribs. At the mouth of the hole, I held my breath and listened, hearing a faint sound. Finn was still beside me, both of us tense as we tried to understand what the noise meant.

"I think Serge and Grange are fighting," he whispered after listening to what sounded like distant grunts. "We should just wait here and see who wins."

What Finn was saying made total sense, anyone could see that. Only, I couldn't, not when the money that could pay for Mom's treatments was so close.

I took a deep breath and stepped into the tunnel. As soon as I was inside, the heavy, damp air and the narrow walls and ceiling brought back the feeling of being trapped just a short time earlier.

For a second, fear locked my knees, but the sounds that had been so faint outside the tunnel were a lot louder. I forced myself to move. The tunnel went straight, dropping at a steady slant. Unlike the pirate tunnel, this one had electric lights strung along the ceiling. They made it just bright enough to see.

Up ahead the shaft turned cutting off my view, but the noises of men fighting were louder. Finn grabbed my arm again. I knew he was right, that we should stop and go outside, but determination drove me forward. I couldn't stop when I was so close.

I pulled loose again and crept forward until I could peek around the corner.

The tunnel forked there, as if at some point Granger had started digging one way, then changed his mind—probably based on what Finn and I had shown him—and gone in a new direction. It looked like the fork had also been where Granger had hid and waited for Serge to bring out a load of treasure. Once Serge had gone past, he probably slipped behind and beaned him with the shovel.

That's what it looked like happened because Granger had somehow managed to get the gun. He was standing beside a tipped over wheelbarrow holding the gun in one hand and a shovel in the other. A bunch of gold bars lay on the dirt where they had spilled. Beside the wheelbarrow Serge was down on one knee, holding his head.

Granger was screaming. "Get up! Get up! Go get more treasure!"

Serge just stayed on his knees, holding his head. "It's too dangerous," he said. "The water's coming in too fast."

"I don't care about the water," Granger cried. "You're going to help me get that gold out of here!"

"It's too late," Serge said. "Just take what's here."

It looked like he was right because water was already pooling around Serge's knees and coming in quickly. The swinging wall had held back the river up to now, but it must have been leaking badly, which meant the treasure room was flooding fast.

Granger wasn't buying it. "Get up!" he shouted. "That's *my* treasure in there! I discovered it! Nobody else! Nobody else was smart enough! Nobody did the work! I did it all! Get up! Get up now before I shoot you."

Serge shook his head. "You're out of your mind, Granger."

"Out of my mind? Really?" Granger was shaking with rage and greed and excitement as he straightened his arm and aimed the pistol.

I was frozen, terrified he was going to shoot. Behind me I heard Finn suck in a sharp breath, but then I felt his hand on my shoulder, pushing me to one side of the tunnel. I looked back to see that Finn had the small gold head in his hand, the one he had put into his pocket when we first walked into the treasure room. As I watched he wound up and hurled it down the tunnel like a fastball. It hit the back of Granger's gun hand with loud smack.

Granger cried out as the gun flew from his hand. He stood in shock for a second, and that was all it took for Serge to come up off his knees. The two men started to fight again, both hurt, both trading wild blows. They slipped in the mud and went down as the water continued to rise and rush in.

"Run!" I yelled as Finn and I turned and began to race out of the tunnel. "Get out of there!" I shouted, not looking back.

The sounds of fighting continued as we raced up the tunnel's steep slope, both men seeming to ignore everything but their need for the gold. As we burst back out into open air, we kept going, all the way to the top of the ramp.

In the far distance, I could hear sirens and knew Poppy had been able to make a phone call and get help. My relief turned to horror as a loud gurgling echoed from the tunnel. It sounded like it came from a huge mouth or maybe a massive load of wet sand being dumped out onto the ground.

I turned to Finn. His eyes were wide with shock. "It caved in," he whispered.

We looked down at the opening as the sirens got closer, hoping to see Granger and Serge stagger out, but no one appeared. Seconds ticked by, then a minute. Water was spilling out the mouth of the tunnel now. The sirens were very close, and seconds later we heard the sound of slamming doors.

Three policemen ran around the side of the house. When they saw Finn and me, they asked, "Are you okay?"

We nodded. "But there are two people still in there." I pointed toward where the mouth of the tunnel had been. It was just a big wall of mud where water now gurgled out, starting to fill the bottom of the pit.

"Are they armed?"

"One was," Finn said. "But now I think they're trapped. I'm pretty sure the tunnel caved in."

"Tunnel?" the policeman asked, bewildered. He stayed with Finn and me as the other two officers moved cautiously down the ramp. What had been the opening to the tunnel was now just a barely visible outline at the bottom of the watery pit. "You say there are people in there?"

"Desmond Granger and another man," I said, my voice quavering.

The two policemen stood at the edge of the water and tried to peer inside what was left of the tunnel mouth. As they watched, the water rose a bit more and began to spill out of the tunnel and into the bottom of the pool-sized hole. The officers shook their heads, turned and came back to where Finn and I waited. "Let me understand this," one said. "The person who called us said something about an armed robbery and attempted murder."

"My grandfather called you," I said. "And that's accurate."

"You said someone down there is armed?"

"A man named Serge had a gun, and he and Desmond Granger were fighting," Finn cut in.

"How far does this . . . or did this tunnel go?"

"All the way under the river and onto my grandfather's property," I said.

"And how far into the tunnel were those men?"

I looked at Finn, who pointed, "Under the river."

The policeman thought about what that might mean. Then he shook his head. The three policemen stepped away from us, and after about a minute's conversation, they got on the radio and called for an ambulance.

41

Finn and I were still standing near the dirt
pile when Poppy arrived in the backseat of
another police car. The policeman who picked
him up had wrapped a gauze bandage around
his head and was trying to get Poppy to ride
to the hospital with the EMTs for an X-ray.
Poppy was refusing until he made sure Finn
and I were okay. Finn's grandfather showed up
a couple minutes after Poppy and frantically
inspected Finn for damage.

"I'm fine, Grampa," Finn said as Mr. Finnigan
checked him all over. "We're both fine."

Before Mr. Finnigan could drive us away, the
policeman who seemed to be in charge asked
if Finn and I felt well enough to answer some
questions before we went home. We said we
did, so he asked us to start at the beginning
and tell him what happened.

Poppy still hadn't left with the EMTs, so he
and Mr. Finnigan also listened as Finn and I
told the officers how Desmond Granger was
supposedly buying Buccaneer's Spit from Poppy;
how we had seen Granger on the beach when
his plastic bag blew into the ocean; how the

sea turtle ate it; how we had gotten that same plastic bag when we visited the turtle hospital; and how it had turned out to have a map inside.

The policemen and our two grandfathers were wide-eyed, but they told us to keep talking, so I did. "Finn and I thought the map showed something the Navy had left behind after World War II, and that Granger planned to use it to get around some environmental rules. Then when Granger told Poppy the deal was off—and because Poppy needed the money to pay for my mother's cancer treatments—Finn and I went to his office to offer him his map, hoping he would decide to buy the spit after all."

"Okay," the policeman nodded. "I get that. What happened next?"

"Before we gave back the map, we explored the spit ourselves and we found a strange wooden platform. We thought it was the thing Granger was looking for," Finn said.

"And you told this to Mr. Granger?"

"Yes, we even showed him where it was."

"Out of curiosity," the policeman asked, "how did you figure it all out?"

I turned to look at Finn. "Finn did it all by himself with some really smart detective work."

The policeman gave Finn a nod, clearly impressed. He looked back at me. "So, go on with your story, young lady."

I stole a glance at Finn's grandfather, who

was looking at Finn with a surprised expression. I felt good about that. "When we took Mr. Granger and the two men who worked for him to see what we had found, they acted very strangely, like they had some big secret. It made us determined to figure out exactly what it was."

The policeman nodded for me to keep talking.

I took a breath, knowing that we might get into big trouble with what I was about to say next. "So, we snuck out at night, cut a hole in the wood, and when we found this really strange shaft, we decided to wait until the next morning to explore it."

"And what happened when you did?"

I told them how I climbed down the ladder into the shaft, but how the rungs broke when Finn tried. "He fell into the water at the bottom, but eventually got out. Then we started to explore the tunnel that was down there to look for another way out, and we found what Granger was really looking for."

"What was it?" the policeman asked.

"Gold."

The policeman tried to bite down his smile, but he didn't quite make it happen. "Really?" he said.

"Yes, sir."

"What kind of gold, exactly?"

"Bars of gold."

"And you found it where, exactly?"

I hated lying to a policeman, but if I was ever going to tell a lie, it had to be for a really good reason. This was one of those reasons. Even if Stevenson tried to tell it differently, it was his word against ours. Finn and I just had to be sure we never, ever contradicted ourselves.

"We found the first of it right inside the mouth of the tunnel. It was pirate treasure, and there was even more of it in another room."

As I said this, the policeman's eyebrows went up in disbelief. "And you saw this as well?" he asked Finn.

Finn nodded his head, "Yes, sir."

"What made you think it was really gold?"

"Gold is heavy. These were, like, twenty-five pound bars," Finn said.

"When you see the shaft on my grandfather's spit, you'll understand how much trouble somebody took to hide it." I waited a few seconds. "We can show you if you like."

"Yes, I'll need it see it once we're done here," he said.

After we finished answering their questions, one ambulance took Poppy for X-rays, while the policemen and EMTs from the second ambulance tried to figure out if there was any way that Granger and Serge could have survived. Sand and dirt had totally filled up the old tunnel mouth, and when Finn and I explained how the river water had flooded the tunnel that went all the way from the shaft on Poppy's side of the river to Granger's tunnel, they finally gave up on finding anyone alive.

The last thing we did was take a group of the policemen over to see the shaft that Finn and I had discovered. When they shined a light down through the hole we had cut, they could see the broken ladder and then water below.

A couple of rescue divers went down into the shaft and tried to get into the tunnel. They came up after only a few minutes and told us that river mud from the cave-in now filled up almost the entire thing and they had been able to go only a few feet before turning back.

By that time Finn and I were barely able to keep our eyes open. I hadn't seen Stevenson since we escaped from the shaft and wasn't sure whether he had been taken to the hospital or down to the police station for more questioning. I didn't really care either way.

When Finn's grandfather took me home, Martha was waiting there, and she broke into a huge smile when she saw both me and Plankton get out of the car. She had made some cold soup, and she served that to me along with some yogurt and fruit and a loaf of crusty bread that she had baked. She gave Plankton a leftover steak bone.

I was still eating when a police car drove up in front of the house and Poppy got out. He was moving slowly, like he was quite sore. Martha fussed over him and asked if he wanted to get into bed, but he said no and came to sit with me at the table. Martha put a plate of food in front of him, but it took me several seconds to realize he wasn't chewing, just staring at me.

When I looked at him, his eyes were so full of wetness that I thought tears were about to spill out. "I'm so thankful that you're home safe," he said in a soft voice.

"Me, too," I said.

He gave me a sad smile and nodded, and then his eyes moved away from me to someplace above my head. Right away I knew he was thinking about Mom and how there wasn't going to be any money from the sale of the spit to pay for her cancer medicine.

"Poppy, there's something I didn't tell you earlier," I said.

"What's that?" he asked, still not looking at me.

"It's about the gold Desmond Granger was trying to get."

Poppy nodded. "I doubt anyone will ever get it now," he said in a voice so full of sadness it made me want to cry.

"They got some out."

He looked at me, not understanding.

"Maybe I should say Finn and I got some out."

Poppy's eyes were suddenly alive. "How much? Where is it?"

"That truck that was parked at the top of the ramp."

"What about it?"

"The gold was inside the back."

"What happened to it?"

"Finn and I moved it."

"The gold?"

I nodded.

With food in my belly, I should have been even more incredibly tired than I had been before I ate. Poppy should have been exhausted, too, but I think we both felt the same excitement at the idea that everything wasn't lost. We got into Poppy's car and drove back to the house where Granger had dug his tunnel. Granger's van had been towed away, but it took only a few minutes to dig the six hunks of metal out of the dirt pile near where the van had been parked, and load them into Poppy's trunk.

"Finn says they're worth about five hundred thousand dollars each," I said.

Poppy picked one of the hunks up and held it in his hands, raising and lowering it slightly as if trying to prove to himself that it was real gold and really heavy. "Oh, my God," he whispered to himself. "This will pay for your mom's treatments." This time when he looked at me, tears really did spill down his cheeks. "How did you put this here?"

"Finn and I noticed it in the van right after the cave-in. The police got here really quick, but we had time to toss these out of the van and kick some dirt over them."

"You didn't say anything to the police?"

"About the gold? No."

"Why?"

"We thought they might take it as evidence and you might not get it back."

Poppy looked at me for a few very long seconds, and he didn't even try to wipe away his tears. "You are a very sharp young lady," he said at last. "And Finn is a very sharp young man."

42.

Once we got back to the house, Poppy and I slept most of the day, but that night at dinner, we talked for a long time about the gold. He never told me it had been wrong to hide the gold we found in the panel van, and he never told me that I had been wrong to say nothing about it to the police. Even Poppy didn't know that the gold we found might not have been technically under his land and had perhaps been under the river. I don't think those things mattered to Poppy any more than they mattered to me because we both knew what was really important. Nothing was going to make either of us risk my mom's cancer treatment.

We talked about other things, as well, and after our talk, I went into Grandma's old closet and pulled out her overnight suitcase. Poppy said that he still hated to go into her closet because it made him remember things too sharply. It made me remember things, too, because the closet still smelled like her perfume, and the scent brought a wave of sadness and a reminder that something big was missing from our lives.

I stopped myself from dwelling on Grandma because Poppy and I had too many things to do. He was busy in his office, where he had been ever since dinner, making phone calls. His office door was open, and I could hear him talking, his voice happy, clear, and firm, so different from how he'd sounded when he'd been talking to Desmond Granger.

In order to finish my job, I grabbed a bunch of newspaper from the recycling bin, then wrapped the present I had for Finn. Afterward, I wrote him a long note, then put that and the present in the overnight bag. Then, with Plankton on his leash, Poppy and I jumped into the car and headed for the Finnigans' house. Poppy had called ahead to make sure Mr. and Mrs. Finnigan and Finn were still awake, so they came to the door as soon as we pulled in.

We went into the living room, and Finn's grandmother brought us all plates of some cake she had made, then she sat next to her husband.

Mr. Finnigan cleared his throat right away and said, "That was quite a terrifying adventure these two young people had. Finn has explained his role in the whole thing, how he persuaded Callie to sneak out with him and go down into that pit." He shook his head and turned his head to shoot a look at Finn. "We're terribly disappointed in his judgement but so relieved that the consequences weren't much worse."

It seemed like Mr. Finnigan intended to keep talking about Finn's poor judgment, but Poppy held up a hand. "I don't know whether you are aware, but I did something very foolish yesterday after my Jack Russell came home barking hysterically and led me to where Finn and Callie were trapped. They told me to get help, but like some foolish old man, I thought I could handle the situation myself, and I went into that development Desmond Granger built."

Mr. Finnigan nodded and cut in. "Finn explained that you also were exposed to great risk, and we are all terribly sorry. It was—"

"What I'm trying to explain," Poppy said, speaking over Mr. Finnigan, "is that my foolishness got me trapped along with these two kids. The people who captured us were dangerous and filled with greed. It was a dire situation, but it also gave me a chance to see your grandson in action firsthand." With this, Poppy shifted his eyes to Finn, who was sitting by himself in a chair looking like he expected harsh punishment.

"Your grandson showed remarkable courage and a cool head under extremely difficult circumstances. He also showed keen intelligence, and by figuring out the physics of how water would behave when it came crashing into the tunnel and then into shaft, he saved all of our lives. Not many people his age, or any age, could do such a thing."

Mr. Finnigan was no longer trying to interrupt. Instead, he glanced at his wife, and then they both turned to stare at Finn. They looked like they had just realized there was a stranger in their living room.

"My granddaughter also behaved in a manner that makes me extremely proud. And not to contradict Finn's story, I think that you both need to understand that what led these two kids to sneak out in the middle of the night was *not* some teenage prank. I'm sure you are aware that I was planning to sell Buccaneer's Spit to Granger, but you may not be aware that I was selling the spit because my daughter, Callie's mother, has a very rare cancer that is extremely expensive to treat. When Callie and Finn managed to get their hands on Granger's strange map and then found out that Granger was threatening to walk away from the purchase, they determined that discovering what the map led to might salvage my land sale."

Poppy paused, then looked at me and at Finn. "These kids weren't being foolish. They were being incredibly brave. And Finn was being a very loyal friend." He paused for several long seconds to let his words sink in. Finn was still looking down at the floor, but no longer like a person about to get punished. Now he just looked embarrassed.

"There is one more thing we need to talk about," Poppy said. "It appears that Finn's version of events has been colored by his attempt to paint Callie in a good light, so he may not have told you quite everything. So, I will tell you that in addition to everything else they accomplished, the kids found some gold that had been brought out of the tunnel before its collapse."

Finn looked up in surprise at my grandfather's admission because earlier we had both agreed that it was important that nothing at all was said about the gold. Judging from the shock on his grandparent's faces, Finn had kept his part of the bargain.

"Because my preliminary conversations with some people who are going to help turn the gold into cash have provided me with strong assurance that what these two young people found will be more than sufficient to pay for my daughter's treatment, Callie and I would like to propose something.

Poppy nodded at me, and I picked up Grandma's overnight bag. It was heavy and made a thump as I put it on the floor in front of me and unzipped it. I took the package out and started to unwrap the newspaper around it.

"Finn told Callie about his difficulties with reading," Poppy went on as I tried to make as little noise with the paper as possible. "As a retired educator, I am very aware of the assumptions made about the intelligence and efforts of a student with dyslexia. However, dyslexia *does not* mean that a student is lazy and it *is not* caused by a lack of intelligence, but rather by a difficulty decoding words and sounds. It often takes an approach tailored to the individual in order to overcome the problem, and depending on where a person lives, often this is best done through accommodating private schools that are very expensive."

Poppy paused while I finished unwrapping the

thing in the suitcase. "What we would like to propose is a reward," he went on when the twenty-five pound gold bar lay there all shiny and new looking because I had cleaned it up specially for Finn. "This is one of the gold bars stolen from my property. It should be enough to pay for Finn to go to the best school in his area. His improved academic skills combined with his already excellent baseball skills should be enough to guarantee him a number of scholarship offers when he is ready for college. Even if the scholarships don't work out, there should be enough money left over to defray most of his college costs, as well."

Poppy looked at me, and I knew it was my turn. "But," I said, emphasizing the word, "we only want to offer that reward if you guarantee that the money will be used as we intend it."

At first, Mr. Finnigan seemed taken aback by my condition, but he looked at his wife for a few seconds, then they both nodded to each other. He turned, looking at me, then Poppy. "What you are offering is extraordinarily generous, and I'm sure Finn's parents will agree to your terms. However, you aren't under any obligation to do this."

"I know," said Poppy.

"But for Finn's sake we accept."

43.

The next morning after breakfast, Poppy told me that he had called Mom and Dad the night before and filled them in on everything that had happened. He said that they wanted to talk to me as soon as I was ready to speak to them.

Instead of getting on the phone right away, I took Plankton for a long walk around the neighborhood, trying to sort out my feelings. Part of me was angry because I'd been lied to and sent to Poppy's while Mom went through her first treatments. Another part of me felt like I didn't have any right to be angry because Mom was so sick. Yet a different part of me felt like a little kid inside, one who would start bawling the second she heard her mother's voice.

When I got back to the house, my hands were shaking as I sat down at Poppy's desk and called home. Mom answered on the first ring, as if she'd been waiting for my call.

"Callie," she said, and I could hear tears in her voice.

"Hi, Mom," I said, stifling a sob.

"I'm so sorry we didn't tell you the truth about what's going on."

"That's okay," I said, even though it really wasn't. I didn't know what else to say.

"We just didn't want to upset you."

"I know, but I thought you were getting a divorce."

"I'm so sorry. Your father and I just didn't know how to handle this. We apologize if we did it badly."

"I guess . . ." I trailed, still not knowing what I was supposed to say. "There really wasn't a good way." That felt like the only real truth I knew.

"And now your grandfather has told us about what you did. We're so relieved that you are okay, and we're so proud of you for your courage and . . . and everything."

"You've saved your mother's life," my father said, sounding as if he had his ear right next to the phone. "You're *our* hero."

"I wasn't trying to be a hero," I said. "And I didn't do it alone."

"We understand. Both of us want to meet Finn and thank him personally," Mom said. "He sounds like quite a fine young man."

"He is." I felt the heat rise in my cheeks as I said it.

We talked for a long time after that. I asked questions about Mom's cancer and about the treatments she would now be getting. She told me they would take four months, and while she might feel horrible after taking the drugs, the prognosis was promising.

When it was their turn to talk, Mom and

Dad asked me questions about how Finn and I had discovered Black Jack Burton's treasure, and I told them everything.

They seemed shocked at what Finn and I had done, and when we finally ended the call, I felt strange, like something between us had shifted. I was still their daughter, and they were still my parents, but somehow I felt as if I had become different in their eyes. And maybe they were different in my eyes, too. It felt a little like I'd gained something, but also lost something, and I'd have to decide how I felt about that. Maybe that was what growing up was like, I thought.

I spent the rest of the morning reading and thinking, and somewhere along the way I realized that my spring vacation was half over. I couldn't believe all of the incredible experiences that I'd had in just one short week, and even though I hated to be bored, I sure hoped the next week would be calmer than the first one.

With only one more week to spend with Poppy, I realized that I didn't feel the same way about being here that I had just a few days before. I had come down here feeling like I was losing something I cared about deeply because I thought my parents were shoving me away so that they could get a divorce. I wouldn't have guessed my mother was sick and they were trying to protect me from seeing the worst of it. Now, a week later I had learned that my parents still loved each other and that there was real hope for my mom. I had also learned that time changes things and Finn was no longer the obnoxious, baseball obsessed kid I'd first met, but a brave, wonderful, smart, and fun boy who had taught me a lot about nature and a lot about friendship, and, oh yeah, who had saved my life. I was starting to realize that I was going to miss a whole lot more about South Carolina than Poppy when I had to go home.

After lunch with Poppy, I leashed Plankton and headed for Buccaneer's Spit. As I got close, I spotted a truck parked at the entrance to the gouged-out road that Granger's men had made. My first reaction was red-hot anger. I wanted to shout at the two men who were working there and tell them they had to quit *right now.* But as I took a deep breath and got ready to yell, I noticed what they were doing, and I smiled.

I walked up to them, looking at the holes they were digging and the plants they were putting in them. "Excuse me," I said.

One of the men stopped digging and turned to look at me. "What can I do for you, young lady?" he asked with an easy grin.

"Did **Mr**. Morrisey hire you to plant these bushes?"

"**Mr**. Morrisey?" the man asked. Then he shook his head. "Mr. and Mrs. Finnigan hired us," he said. "They told us it was a thank you present." He pointed at what they were planting. "We're supposed to narrow things up so it doesn't look like a road anymore."

"That's a great idea," I said. "Thank you."

"Who might you be?" the man asked. "One of the friends?"

"Yes, sir," I said.

The man hooked his thumb toward a place farther down the path toward the beach. "The Finnigans are down there now if you want to see them."

"Thanks!"

Plankton and I picked up our pace and hurried down the rutted sand to where I spotted Mr. Finnigan giving Finn instructions on how deep to dig a hole where they would plant another new bush.

"Hi!" I said as I approached.

Mr. Finnigan and Finn turned and smiled when they saw me. Across the path, Mrs. Finnigan straightened up from where she had been patting dirt and sand around the roots of yet another bush.

"Thank you for doing this," I said. "Does Poppy know?"

Mr. Finnigan shook his head. "We wanted to surprise him."

"He'll be so happy," I said, excited thinking about Poppy's reaction.

Mr. Finnigan reached out and tousled Finn's hair. "So are we."

Finn's grandparents told us that they would finish up the planting and for Finn to take a break. He asked if I wanted to take a walk down the spit to our usual place. When we got to the beach, we looked around for migratory birds, and seeing none, I let Plankton off leash. He went running along the seafoam left by the incoming waves, splashing and barking with joy.

"You know," I said, "I never thought I'd say it, but I'm going to miss this place a lot."

Finn cut me a sideways look. "You didn't want to come down for spring vacation?"

I shook my head. "I wanted to see Poppy, but otherwise, no. My parents weren't coming with me. Everything was strange at home, and it just didn't seem right to be coming here."

"To be honest, I didn't want to come, either. I wanted to stay home and get a jump on baseball season." Finn laughed. "And then when I found out I had to have dinner with the stuck-up girl from New York that I'd met a few years earlier, I almost pretended I was too sick to go."

"Stuck-up girl? Me?"

He nodded, smiling.

"And you were the little boy who never took off his baseball glove. And you made me try to catch your pitches that one day."

"Ahhh, yes. I hoped you'd forgotten that."

"How could I? You never got a single throw even close to me. How did you ever think you could be a pitcher?"

"Wanting something bad enough is the first step to actually figuring out how to do it."

I looked over at him, and I could see he was serious. "The way your grandfather talks, I thought you were a natural."

"Far from it." He fell silent for a moment, then added, "But as much as I really didn't want to come down this year, I'm really glad I did."

"I'm glad you did, too," I said.

"So you haven't been as bored as you thought you'd be?"

"Between all the crazy adventures we've had?" I laughed. "I never imagined so much could happen in just one week. I haven't had a second to be bored."

"Yeah. Where else could you see your dog almost get eaten by porpoises, and then get trapped in a pirate cave?"

I bumped my shoulder into Finn's chest. "Yeah, with a kid who doesn't realize how smart he is, yet he's the only one who can figure out how to get us out of there alive."

Finn looked down at the ground the way he often did when he was thinking, and then after a second his arm came up across my back. I hadn't expected it, and I felt myself tense, but the weight and warmth and his hand cupping my shoulder felt so good that I relaxed. Neither of us said anything. We just walked in peaceful silence, and then my arm rose almost without me telling it to and went around his waist.

We stayed like that all the way to the end of the spit, where Plankton sat waiting for us beside the log where I'd been sitting the day I first saw Finn. I still wasn't talking, but my heart was hammering, almost as loud as when we'd been in the pirate tunnel, only now for very different reasons.

"Remember the Red Knots we saw that first day?" Finn asked when we came to a stop.

"How could I forget? A strange boy told me that I almost let Plankton kill them."

"That boy doesn't always choose his words very well."

"But he was right."

"Yeah," Finn agreed.

"Why did you bring up the Red Knots?"

"Well," Finn said, drawing the word out slowly. "Cause they've come such a long way to get here, but they've still got a long way to go and a lot of things to do and a lot of choices to make." He paused. "Kind of like the two of us."

He fell silent and just stood with his arm around my shoulders, and me leaning into him with my arm around his waist, and I was pretty sure we were both thinking the same things. Here I was, walking with my arm around a boy who just a few years earlier had been a chubby, baseball-crazy goofball, who I never imagined I'd want to spend any time with. It made me wonder how many other curve balls life was going to throw at me. Probably a lot.

When I thought back over everything we'd done in the past week I felt lightheaded with joy because my parents weren't getting divorced, and Mom was going to get her treatments, and Poppy wasn't going to have to sell Buccaneer's Spit. But an even bigger part of my lightheadedness came from feeling Finn so close to me. The only other time I'd had a boy this close, it had been Tommy Bluestein, and I had just wanted to get away. This time was different, and I wanted Finn right where he was.

I was thinking how much things had changed in so many unexpected ways, and so quickly. One minute I'd been sad and resentful that my parents were pushing me away. Then when I found out about Poppy selling the spit and Mom's cancer, my whole world had seemed even more hopeless, full of terrible risks and bad outcomes. Somehow, with the help of a boy I didn't think I ever wanted anything to do with, we had found a way to face huge difficulties, conquer danger, and we had learned a lot about each other and ourselves in the process.

Now, instead of yearning to get back to New York, I was feeling sad and empty at the thought of having only one more week with Finn. Spring vacations were the only times either one of us came to visit family in South Carolina, which meant it was probably going to be a whole year before I saw him again. A week suddenly didn't seem like nearly enough.

That was when something happened that stopped my breath almost as much as when the porpoises had nearly eaten Plankton. Like he was reading my mind and feeling the same things I was, Finn stopped walking and turned toward me. "Maybe like the Red Knots come back every year, we will, too. We'll both be living our lives and doing different things and making lots of decisions, but . . . I don't know."

"You don't know what?" I prodded.

He gave an uncomfortable shrug. "Maybe we can come back together and be the way we are now."

"I'd like that, too," I said.

With that, he put both hands on my shoulders, slowly lowered his face to mine and kissed me. For half a second or so, I stood there in shock, but then I relaxed and let him keep on kissing me. At some point, both of my arms went around him, as well, and when we broke apart, we hugged for a long moment, and with my head against his chest, I could hear the strong beating of his heart. Also, Finn actually smelled good.

I felt peaceful and keyed up all at the same time, also very happy. It was totally different from that gross kiss with Tommy Bluestein, and even though I didn't have much to compare him to, I thought Finn was a pretty good kisser.

After a time, I raised my head from his chest, then turned and looked out at the spit, at the soaring gulls, crashing pelicans, and few yards offshore a loggerhead turtle that surfaced for a moment then went back under. It reminded me that in another month or so the turtles would be coming ashore, digging nests and laying eggs. Farther down the beach a flock of small birds were racing up and back with the tideline, and I thought they might be Red Knots, resting up before continuing their trip north.

Buccaneer's Spit was a delicate place, as fragile and complicated as any human life and just as beautiful. It was also just as much worth saving. Poppy had been put in a terrible position, having to choose between his daughter and the spit, and even though he'd been ready to make the only choice he could, I had seen how much it tore him apart.

In that moment, I realized that Finn and I really were like the Red Knots, both of us on unique journeys that would take us far from each other and from this place. We would grow and change as we faced our unique problems and challenges, and whether we came together down the road as friends or as something more, only time would tell. I knew what I hoped would happen, but no matter what the outcome, our time together and all the challenges we had faced and the things we had learned about ourselves were incredible.

As we continued to hug, my thoughts bounced back and forth between our miraculous escape from Black Jack Burton's pit, saving the spit, getting the gold that would pay for Mom's cancer treatments, and Finn having the money to go to a school where he could get the right help and accommodations for his dyslexia. I was also thinking about the ache that I would feel a few days in the future when I would leave Finn and go back to New York. Even so, I had to admit that some problems were a whole lot better to have than others.

Buccaneer's Spit is not a real place, however the book was inspired by a real spit of land near my home in Charleston, South Carolina. Like Buccaneer's Spit, Captain Sam's Spit is a fragile, pristine, and beautiful place where porpoises can often be seen stranding mullet, where birds like red knots stop to rest and refuel on their amazing 9,000-mile migrations, and where other birds like pelicans, herons, and egrets roost, build nests, and raise young. It is a spit where sea turtles come ashore to lay their eggs in the sand and where people can come to witness the yearly miracles of nature.

Also, like Buccaneer's Spit, this other spit has been threatened by developers who want to cut down much of the maritime forest, level the dunes, build homes, and bulldoze roads. Environmentalists, nature experts like the Audubon Society, and others believe the spit is too delicate to sustain such aggressive development. The Coastal Conservation League of South Carolina has led the way in defending Captain Sam's Spit and maintaining its beauty and fecundity for future generations.

And yes, the sea turtle hospital is a real place. In the South Carolina Aquarium, veterinary specialists really do perform endoscopies on sea turtles, which often mistake plastic bags and other refuse as food. Reducing our use of plastic and recycling whenever we do use it is a great way to help protect nature.

Another idea would be to contact organizations in your area similar to the Coastal Conservation League or the South Carolina Aquarium and ask about opportunities to volunteer or provide other support. Whether participating in a family volunteer work day, joining a 5K run or walk-a-thon, or organizing some kind of event at your school to raise awareness, you could get involved, have fun, do a lot of good, and learn a lot in the process.

Environmental organizations in praise of *Buccaneer's Spit!*

"J. E. Thompson has done it again! Set in the beauty of coastal South Carolina that Thompson calls home, **Buccaneer's Spit** is a page turner that sweeps the reader along in a tale full of mystery, danger, and adventure, all the while offering a great deal of information about coastal landscapes and waterways and the issues currently facing the health of our environment. Protagonist Callie and her friend Finn are determined and brave, and they will certainly inspire the next generation of conservationists to help protect special places like Buccaneer's Spit—remote, beautiful, and essential places where dolphins strand feed, sea turtles lay their eggs, and migratory birds stop over on their transcontinental journeys. We need these places now; we need them forever."

—Laura Cantral, executive director, Coastal Conservation League

"It truly takes an army to protect and conserve South Carolina's sea turtles. It's our Sea Turtle Care Center™ team working tirelessly to rehabilitate and release sick and injured sea turtles, yes;

but it's also the dedicated volunteers, the turtle patrol teams, the rescuers, and the indefatigable staff at the South Carolina Department of Natural Resources who make it all possible.

"Lastly, and perhaps most integral, it's the children. They visit the Sea Turtle Care Center, experience a connection to sea turtles, and are inspired to make a better world for them. These children grow up to become sea turtle biologists, veterinarians, volunteers, conservationists, and lifelong protectors of sea turtles. These children, like Callie in *Buccaneer's Spit,* are the reason we can hope for a brighter future for sea turtles, for wildlife, and for the world."

—Kevin Mills, president and CEO,
South Carolina Aquarium

"Early on in J. E. Thompson's *Buccaneer's Spit,* sixth-grader Callie notes, 'When my plane landed in Charleston the beauty improved my mood right away.' I felt the same way as I made my way through this book! The story follows Callie as she leaves her Brooklyn home, and parents hiding a secret, to spend the spring with her grandfather in South Carolina. What follows is a delightful mystery, as twelve-year-old Callie explores the natural wonders of the Lowcountry and learns about the importance of environmental conservation while trying to thwart a treasure-stealing plot. *Buccaneer's Spit* has the potential to inspire the next generation of conservation leaders who can make lasting impacts on protecting and restoring lands and waters for birds and people."

—Justin E. Stokes, executive director,
Audubon South Carolina